Mirror IMAGE

DOROTHY COLLINS

Author of *Today the Waiting*

ISBN: 978-1-4834-9746-4 (sc)
ISBN: 978-1-4834-9745-7 (e)

Library of Congress Control Number: 2019901606

Lulu Publishing Services rev. date: 03/12/2019

In Memory of my late daughter Bonnie
Who inspired me to publish the novels I have written.
And
Thank you to Terry Unger in appreciation of her encouragement.

chapter ONE

Trina picked up the phone to hear a pleasant female voice inquiring if she was Trina Grant. When she replied yes, the woman's soft voice conveyed the message. "You have won a trip for one to Australia and one thousand dollars in cash.

Her first thought was *Is this for real or a joke?* During her ecstatic, "WOW!" Her mind running amuck the receiver was plunked down.

The phone pealed again. "Mrs. Grant, please don't hang up until I give you all the details. You won the door prize yesterday during the Literacy Seminar to promote literacy. Congratulations, we will be sending your holiday package by mail. Mrs. Grant have a good trip." The line was disconnected. Trina's elated thanks went unheard.

She vaguely remembered a reference of a prize, which wasn't the lure for her to the seminar. She just wanted to give others the gift of the written word.

Wasn't that odd? Trips were usually for two. If a couple had won would the husband and wife fight over who went alone or who paid the difference? Being a divorcee, she would only need one ticket.

Trina excitedly wanted to share the news. Should she telephone Briana, her daughter or her friend Amanda first? The pictures from Amanda's Australia trip five years ago popped into her head. Would her friend really want to go? They had enjoyed several previous trips together.

She did a bit of a jig, then felt a bit foolish, plunking down on a chair. Dreamily gazing out the window, oblivious to the beauty of the sun filtering through the trees. Her tortoiseshell cat, Neptune leaped into her lap for some loving attention. She automatically patted a contended purring cat, in her musings of faraway Australia.

The images of the colorful waterfront of the Sydney Harbor along with Fraser Island filtered through her mind. Fraser Island with its natural uncivilized beauty. Her video favorites of Amanda's trip, she had viewed with her.

The ringing of the phone brought Trina back to her surroundings. She answered the telephone to discover Amanda's voice. At last, she could share her good news. "Amanda, I just won a trip for one to Australia," Trina hesitated. She was giving second thoughts to inviting her along for some unknown reason.

Strangely she felt, this particular trip was to be for her alone. Her usual nature was requiring others in her life. Could this trip possibly be her destiny? For reasons unknown 'destiny' was there, invading her mind.

Amanda reluctant to end the call continued talking, hoping for an invitation.

But that inner feeling in Trina was saying *not this time.* A personal invitation wasn't part of Trina's plan. Her guilt inducing her to finish off the call by saying, "I haven't let Briana know yet." This was the first time she hadn't expressed her true feelings to her friend.

While Trina continued to sit there, the ringing of the phone pierced into her thoughts, automatically lifting the receiver.

Briana immediately expounded into her latest conquest in the business world, that was giving her accolades from her boss and fellow workers. Not intending to burst her daughter's bubble too soon. She patiently waited till Briana drew to a close.

Trina's excitement of her good fortune was suppressed inside.

At last her daughter paused for a breath.

She praised her daughter's accomplishments then inserted her own good news. "Briana, I won a trip for one to Australia."

"Oh Mom, that is great," Briana exclaimed. "Will you ask Amanda to go with you?"

Cautiously Trina replied, "not this time. I need to go alone." She quickly added. "The trip is only for one.

Briana's concerned voice rapidly came back with. "Need? Alone? But Mom you have always enjoyed yourself on past trips with Amanda."

Trina could understand Briana's concern at her sudden preference for solitude. But that really wasn't necessary. She just desired some seclusion to ponder her future, because she wanted more out of life maybe a different path. Her thinking was going in that direction lately.

"Briana, I am quite capable of doing things on my own you know," said Trina firmly.

"I know Mother, but I worry about your sudden remoteness. You always wanted to be with others," she said with real concern in her voice.

She knew Briana was being apprehensive about her wish for solitude of late, by the formal 'Mother'.

"I promise you I'm not regressing or about to go off the deep end anytime soon, Briana. I just feel my life is stagnating, and I need a change."

At last, Briana seemed to believe her, or just gave up. "All Right, Mom," she said. "I'll come to visit you soon."

Trina's mind was racing off before the receiver was back in place. When was the best time to go? Christmas was for Briana and the children, that can't be missed. New Year's Eve was the big party at the Castle Inn, out on the highway near town. She usually attended annually with her friends, David, Amanda and Ted.

Her thoughts were wending towards March or April as possibilities. She was now torn between the month of March with fewer commitments, and its winter doldrums or April that Amanda had said was a good time weather wise. Neptune interrupted her train of thought with her furry body rubbing against her legs. The cat meowing loudly letting her know, it was dinnertime. Entering the kitchen, Trina glanced over at the clock, noting the lengthy passage of time during her meditations since the surprise phone call.

When Neptune's food finally graced her mat, the cat proceeded to eat with a meow of thanks which held a note of disdain. She was never a patient cat.

Trina was not into gourmet food when she was alone and settled for heating some leftover stew to drizzle over reheated mashed potatoes. The task of laying the table being a mundane job, Trina's wandering mind was filtering through her closet, for clothing possibilities for the trip.

The microwave pinged, mingled with the pealing of the phone. It was Amanda. More on the direct approach, she stated, "I am willing to arrange to be available to join you on the trip to Australia." Being blunter this time.

Unhappy at hurting her best friend's feelings as she expressed, "I need to do this alone." Her independence was important to her at the moment. She managed to finish the phone call in an upbeat manner, by inviting Amanda to the Castle Inn for Sunday Brunch. The tab which she intended to pick up, in hopes to remove some of her guilt.

The evening passed and Trina's mind was made up for April, to be the best time. The thought popped into her head, was this to be her destiny or a new direction in her life? There is that thought again, 'Destiny'.

—

The next day, following her usual ritual of rising and doing a tango with Neptune wanting her breakfast, Trina prepared the breakfast coffee. The ringing phone invaded the room. In her most cheerful voice Trina said, "Good Morning." Fully expecting to hear Amanda's voice with a further attempt at cajoling her into an invitation to the trip.

"Oh! Hi Briana." Which she barely got out before her daughter started her tirade.

"Mother, you will not go to Australia alone," Briana stated firmly. "Last night while Ken was attempting to talk me into accepting your independence, and your adventure, I recalled a book I once read."

"So?" Trina queried.

"Well, it was about a woman who wanted to mark her 60th birthday by driving around the outer circle road of Australia. The book, a true story outlines the dangerous and challenging task it became," Briana rushed on.

"Mother, it summarizes the nasty side of Australia. The heat, the bushflies, the sandstorms, the flash floods, and the not so nice people, she ran into along the way. Really Mother, I don't think you should contemplate this alone. If I get the book from the library will you read it, before you book your trip?"

Oh dear, that all telling word 'Mother' was back to haunt her. "I will read it but I am sure it won't influence me in my decision," said Trina firmly.

At noon, Briana arrived with the book in her hot little hands. Her grip said it all.

Trina took the book and glanced through it, trying to keep her ire in check at Briana's interference with her pleasure in planning her Australian journey. At the same time, tried to keep an open mind to her daughter's concerns.

"Well, Briana, you certainly made good time getting the book to me. You must have taken an extra early lunch today," Trina commented facetiously.

"Please read the book before you do anything more towards booking your trip. I spoke to Amanda and she is only too willing to go with you."

Trina was trying to keep her cool at this latter comment, by glancing at the image of the jewel-studded turban the author wore during her travels.

"All right, I will read the book. I know just by the drawings, I am going to like this woman."

She led the way towards the kitchen through the ornate hallway. Briana followed her determinedly.

"Relax Briana, I'll put together an easy lunch." Trina endeavored to calm her down, as she seemed to be really worried about her decision.

The kitchen was large but had a cozy atmosphere with light oak cabinets giving a warm feeling along with the regal looking deep maroon countertops and dusty rose walls.

"Tuna sandwiches and French Vanilla Yogurt, is that okay?"

Right on cue, Neptune stepped into the kitchen with hopes of tidbits. "I swear that cat has built in radar." Glancing at her daughter chuckling.

Her daughter was a slim girl, who had her grandmother's long thick brown hair. Trina was always envious of Briana's casual acceptance of her beauty. Her clothes were stylish, gracing her figure perfectly. She had a natural flair for clothes and make-up. Briana did not take after her.

Trina was a nice looking but was a little more solid in stature like her father and had wavy blonde hair. Her height at least made her appear slimmer. She was more the outdoorsy type, in her casual attire.

Briana removed her jacket and draped it over the chair. Sitting down at the glass top rattan table, looking towards her mother she said, "Tuna and Yogurt is fine."

Neptune sauntered over to the daughter for some attention. She picked the cat up automatically to give her some love pats, accompanied by the cat's loud satisfied purrs.

Trina asked about the children. "How are Scott and Kathie?"

"They're fine." The abbreviated answer let Trina know, there was no way she would deter her daughter. She placed the food on the vivid patterned place mats on the table in the bay window area.

Briana, so wrapped up in her focus, impatiently awaiting her mother to alight, didn't notice her surroundings.

She sat across from her daughter, and gazed at her determined expression. "I wish you would understand why I feel this urge do this alone. Usually trips are for two but this trip is only for one. I consider this an omen. I intend to treat it that way."

"Mom just read the book, please." Briana expounded more reasons against her going alone. She stood up having finished her lunch and her comments. "Well I had better get back to work in a hurry. My lunch time ran longer than I am allowed." She made a hasty exit, calling out that she would phone her tomorrow.

—

Keeping her promise to her daughter, Trina picked up the book on the way to the bedroom that night. As usual, Neptune bounded down the hall before her.

If only Briana understood that she needed to be her own person. Self-reliance was something she had strived for since her husband, Devlin and she had divorced. Their marriage was definitely missing that necessary element required to continue. For the first few years, the loneliness was almost devastating even though they had agreed amicably to part, without the usual nastiness involved in divorces.

Still you can't live with someone for over twenty years and not have some regrets. Sometimes, she saw him in a store or passing by in his car, and her heart would skip a beat. Devlin was still a handsome man. At those moments, she felt sad that they had not tried hard enough to mend the gap. But it was too late now, because he had a permanent lady friend according to Briana.

Trina chided herself, enough with the regrets that is past history.

Besides I am kind of proud, that at last I am rather enjoying my freedom enough to look for new horizons. Oh well. I will read the book Briana has given me.

She adjusted the covers and picked up the book. She glanced at some of the pictures, then flipping back to the beginning. She settled down to some serious reading.

She liked the way this writer put her feelings in print and was also able to laugh at herself from her caricature drawings depicted throughout the book.

She wiggled her shoulders seeping amongst the pillows. For Briana's sake she was going to keep an open mind, at least until she read the book.

Coming to the chapter *Nightmare*, she figured this was the part that Briana was concerned about. Dual trucks with numerous thugs aboard were harassing this poor woman. She was so scared she wrote a letter to her children. Hoping if anything serious happened to her, someone would find the letter and pass it on to her family.

Trina believed this could not possibly happen to her, after all she was going on this trip with the Australian Tour Company, which would include a driver, tour guide and other passengers on the coach. She would never really be by herself. Within reason, she would stay with the others at all times.

She was more determined than ever that this trip was to be her way... alone!

chapter TWO

Next morning as Neptune and Trina had their breakfast; she wanted to finish the book. After all, she did promise Briana she would read it all staying awake really late. Today happened to be a leisure breakfast, due to the fact that she had a free morning from her busy schedule of volunteer activities. She later intended going shopping at the food mart. Two cups of coffee later, although she had been trying to stick with one, she finished the book.

All in all, it was a fascinating account of a trip by a Canadian woman in the Australian Outback. She certainly was brave to attempt this trip alone. Especially when it incurred miles and miles of dry creek beds and land covered with dry salt-brush and mallee growth. Where spare water and petrol became a valuable commodity against the parched desert. Filling stations a rarity and always included in one's trunk were spare tires and car parts the book portrayed.

After reading the book, she now understood Briana's concerns rather than overreacting. The part about writing the letter to the children was heartrending. She was sure the author was glad the letter was nonessential in the end. Despite the unsavory conditions the author's trip was a success.

Trina thought Briana needed to be reassured that the dueling trucks scene wouldn't be part of her particular trip, as the Outback was not on the agenda.

The best time for phoning would be later after shopping. After rising from the table, she cleared away her used dishes. It was time to get showered and dressed.

She put on her teal blue pantsuit, as she always felt the pantsuit flattered her figure. Her hair was not cooperating the way she wanted at first, but with a brush and some persistence she was ready for her day.

She loved to walk to the nearby stores but today she had heavy items on her shopping list, which would require the use of her car. After parking her blazing red Mazda car in a space near the store, she decided to take back the book Briana had borrowed from the library first.

The village was picturesque and easily accessible. She liked the quiet small-town atmosphere with its sidewalk cafes and quaint shops lining the streets. Only disturbed occasional by the high-pitched sound of the fire siren, that set the local dogs to howling.

Heading down the lane, she emerged amongst the little shops that graced the town's main street. The Christmas decorated windows caught her gratifying gaze. A few passing villagers exchanged greetings. She noticed Amanda's car parked near the library. Oh dear, she forgot Amanda wouldn't be working today.

She looked up at the clock atop the Town Hall, knowing full well that Amanda would no doubt delay her shopping plans.

She entered the grassy courtyard enhanced with its flowing fountain and scattered benches. She liked the ambiance of the Town Hall where the library was perched in one corner along with a quaint Coffee Café, accessible while absorbing some of the library's literature.

The clock began chiming the hour with its clarion bells.

Amanda spotted her as soon as she came through the library door. She nailed Trina before she could put the book in the return slot. Amanda's manner was more forthright this time, making it a definite demand to go.

Trina steered her out of the silent library before answering. They had been friends for many years. They always got along well and spent quite a bit of their free time together. How could she delicately explain without hurting her friend's feelings? She hoped to gently dissuade her. *Why am I being so adamant about going alone?*

She finally said, "Amanda I can't explain the urge to go alone. I guess it is a case of finding myself somehow. So, bear with me on this, as I don't want to lose you as a friend."

"Okay but remember if you change your mind, I will make myself available."

"I will keep that in mind." Going their separate ways, a friendship saved.

She packed her multiple shopping bags in the trunk in an orderly fashion. She needed to get home to call Briana. When she turned the key in the lock of her house, she could hear the phone ringing. Being a person who hates to miss a call, she threw open the door. Her keys and purse landed on the hall table, as she leaped for the phone.

"Mom, where have you been? I have been calling and calling," Briana said with a concerned voice. It flashed into Trina's mind briefly that Briana had been worried about her being alone lately.

"Well dear, I went to do some shopping and I stopped in at the library where I met Amanda. She tried again to persuade me to accept her company on this upcoming trip. She is being most persistent."

"You know I would feel better, Mom, if Amanda did go along. Why not let her?"

"I can't explain it, Briana but I just feel it is important that I make this trip by myself. Why can't you accept that?"

Briana trying to reach her mother from another direction asked, "did you read the book?"

"Yes, I did. The author's type of writing style appealed to me with its vivid detail and humor. If anything, the book made me more positive to do this trip alone." She paused for effect. "Wish me well and accept that you have tried your best to dissuade me. Just be happy for me instead. I just know this is the right thing for me to do."

"All right Mom, I accept that there is no changing your mind, and therefore go with my blessing. The children wish you well too. They couldn't understand why I was objecting, and neither could Ken."

"Thank you and I know this is going to be a trip of a lifetime. Remember always, Briana, I love you and the children. I would never do anything foolish to jeopardize my return to all of you," said Trina breathing a little easier.

"Well I have to go now. Scott and Kathie want to go to the movies to see Walt Disney's *Lion King*. Don't forget to return the book to the library when you finish it." Trina often wondered who was the mother, Briana or her?

"I already did, that was why I called in at the library today. Say 'Hi' to Scott and Kathie for me and tell them to enjoy the movie. I hear it is excellent and worth seeing."

As Trina replaced the phone receiver in an abstract way, her mind was playing over Briana and Amanda's wants. But the final die was cast, Australia here I come.

———

Amid the many seasonal activities, Trina had taken some time to obtain apparel for Australia in a boutique that catered to southern vacationing winter travelers. The trip was finally in place and scheduled for April 4th to 26th. She had booked for an additional five days in Sydney at the beginning of the trip and an extra three days in Darwin at the end of the Gold Coast Tour she had won.

Trina was looking forward to seeing the Sydney of Amanda's video. This is what she needed, a new purpose in life. Something exhilarating to look forward to. Her steps were livelier on her way to the kitchen. Neptune needless to say bypassed her, cat laments sounded loud and clear.

"Neptune, I just know you are going to love it at Briana's in April while I am away. Scott and Kathie will make such a fuss over you." Trina proceeded to get a special Christmas morning breakfast for them both.

She was anticipating Christmas dinner, as Briana's culinary expertise always complimented her family dinners. Afterward, the ritual of opening the presents one at a time, so each could view what the others were getting. She agreed with this particular tradition of Briana's.

Trina came home that night with an armful of presents. Briana was always so generous in her gift giving. As she got ready for bed, she was thinking how enjoyable the day had been with her family. Feeling lucky she had someone to share this occasion with each year.

The holiday season continued with Amanda inviting Trina over along with Ted and David for a Christmas brunch on Boxing Day. When David and Trina both arrived, Ted was already there with Amanda. The brunch was laughter filled conversation, being such good friends for quite a while. Amanda was big on gifts too. Each year Trina tried to dissuade her. She felt donations to a worthy cause was more beneficial, rather than Christmas traditions of gift giving. Amanda made a donation now in Trina's name but still gave her a gift.

———

New Year's Eve finally came. Trina was putting the finishing touches to her makeup for the Castle Inn party, she was attending with David. This had become a yearly event for Amanda, Ted, David and her for the past three years.

She hoped David wasn't late. He was prone to be tardy. She grabbed her wrap from the bed, starting down the hallway. Her heels clicked on the ceramic tiles in the foyer, just as the doorbell sounded.

"David, how are you?" Trina asked as he reached forward and gave her a peck on the cheek. He glanced up and there was some mistletoe suspended from the light, thanks to Briana. He pulled her into his arms. He wasn't going to past up this golden opportunity, without taking full advantage. Pulling her body against his lean frame, he kissed her deeply. When he released her, he stepped back to look at her warmly.

She was wearing a slim sheath skirt of green silk with a softly draped chiffon top of the same color. It gave her eyes a green hue.

"You look great Trina, really great and very festive." Smiling with a sparkle in his eyes as he was feeling great himself after that stolen kiss.

"You look quite dashing yourself. Do you want a drink before we go?"

"I think not, as we will be having champagne later and I am driving. We had better get going as I told Ted, we would be picking them up at 8:15."

As they walked towards his car, she noted that the moon was quite bright and the stars were numerous twinkles in the clear night sky. It was chilly but not freezing as she settled her wrap closely around her.

David opened the door of his Grand Marquis with a flourish and she slid gracefully into the passenger seat, carefully arranging her silk skirt.

As David passed in front of the car with a buoyant gait, she observed that he was a nice-looking mature man with a swarthy complexion and brown wavy hair. A tall immaculate man with broad shoulders. Sliding into his seat, he playfully leaned over and nuzzled her cheek. "You do smell so enticing tonight. What do they call that alluring perfume?"

"The perfume is what Briana gave me for Christmas. The name of it is Temptation," she said trying to sound tantalizing in keeping with the perfume's name.

He chuckled. "It surely is well named."

The car slinked through the moonlit streets with a purr to its motor. The distance soon disappeared as Amanda's place came into view. Ted and Amanda came out the door on their arrival. They were laughing as though something really funny was tickling them.

"What's so funny? Come on share it, David and I would like a good laugh too," said Trina jokingly, as they entered the car.

Ted laughingly said, "Amanda took great joy in hearing I got a ski pass for Mt. Washington for a Christmas present from Jared. My son knows full well I don't ski, and it just happens to be Jared's favorite skiing slopes, knowing I would probably just end up offering it back to him."

Amanda was still laughing. "The perfect gift for a man who has everything and would generously give it away to someone who would really appreciate it."

"Smart boy, always thinking ahead that's Jared." Ted laughed.

David and Trina joined in the laughter.

"Ted, you could always go and watch Jared ski. Think of the fresh air and scenery from Mt. Washington, and the companionship with your son. That way you would be sharing your gift," David said helpfully.

"Burr... no thanks, I'll forgo the privilege and just sit in front of the warm fire, and read a good book instead. Jared gave me a book by *Clive Cussler* too, knowing full well that I'd appreciate that a lot more," Ted replied with a laughing lilt to his voice. He really appreciated his son and his kind of humor.

"Besides, I think the gift your son gave you Amanda is equally funny," Ted added.

"What did your son give you, Amanda?" David inquired.

"Tim gave me tickets to one of the Canucks hockey games in Vancouver," Amanda admitted.

Ted laughingly said, "and she doesn't even like hockey."

Trina laughed too. "Amanda that is doubly funny because you don't even like going to Vancouver anymore and he probably knows it."

"Maybe that was his main purpose to get me over to visit, as Iris and my son George have the seats beside us as well, thanks to Tim. Ted would you like to go with me? Tim gave me two tickets, which I do intend to use."

"I thought you would never ask," said Ted. "I am dying to go and I'll even take you to dinner before the game."

"Good it's a date," replied Amanda as she settled against Ted giving his arm a hug.

When they arrived at the Castle Inn, it was lit up with fairy lights that glittered. It was quite a sight to see making the Castle seem more enchanting. A millionaire had originally built the castle for his wife. When she passed away; he turned it into a hotel. The castle contained a large ballroom, because this millionaire's first love was to dance.

In the tradition of the past centuries, there was an era costumed Greeter at the door. The Greeter took each couple's name as they arrived and then announced them as they entered the ballroom in a loud voice. Their host wanting to share memories of a time when he and his wife had experienced the same grandeur while attending a ball in England, during their early years together. A little fanciful though for Qualicum.

The stairs leading down into the ballroom were as majestic as the grandeur of the ballrooms of the past. The tiered chandeliers were an array of sparkling prisms, to add to the glitter of the gaily-decorated ballroom. Trina and David followed Amanda and Ted graciously down the stairs, luxuriating in the richness of the red velvet carpeting. Trina felt like a debutante at her coming out ball.

They were met at the bottom of the stairway by the Maître d who showed them to their table on the left side of the dance floor.

"David, how did you get such wonderful seats?" Trina asked in awe.

"Trina, the question isn't 'how' the question is 'who do you know' that is what makes the difference," David said proudly.

Turning to him, Amanda patted his arm. "I think you did well David and you should be commended." Then turning to Trina. "Don't you feel like a princess this evening, Trina?"

"Debutante was what popped into my head, Amanda." She gave a chuckle.

"Would you like to dance, Trina?" David offered his hand gallantly. They both were suited in height and made a striking couple, stepping onto the dance floor. She was smiling dreamily, gliding around to the orchestra's rendition of the Strauss Waltz.

As the evening progressed, they swayed to the music and shared the champagne and hors d'oeuvres. At last the countdown for midnight would soon begin. The emcee was announcing. "Everyone on to the dance floor. After the New Year has been rung in and Auld Lang Syne has been sung, everyone be sure to hold your places. We have a special prize, a trip to Nassau for some lucky couple."

Quickly the dance floor filled with jubilant dancing couples. Excitement was abounding with the expectation of ringing in the New Year, aided also by the possibility of being on that one particular spot. The bubbling laughter and excitement was causing an adrenaline high, as they all danced gaily around the floor. The lights flickered twice, and the orchestra raised the drum roll as the cymbals clanged, a loud "Happy New Year" was heard. The New Year had arrived with a roar.

Couples kissing and hugging each other, along with close dancing neighbors, while the band faded into Auld Lang Syne. Everyone held crossed hands with those close to them and their voices trilled. An expectation of excitement for the New Year, rang through the crowded ballroom.

As the music faded, the emcee was yelling above the din.

"Hold your places everyone, you may be on that all-important lucky spot for the prize of a week in Nassau." The noise of the ballroom disappeared.

Everyone froze in place, looking with great expectation towards the emcee; awaiting the next few words that would indicate who the lucky winner would be. "Without jostling each other too much, look to the floor and see if you can find the star."

Amid the laughter, couples jostled each other bumping and knocking into the close-knit bodies, maneuvering to look down. Amanda pointed at the star half under Trina's dancing slipper. Ted grabbed David and Trina's wrists and shot them up in the air. "We have a winner. It is this fine couple here which are my best friends," Ted yelled proudly.

David sauntered toward the stage, clasping Trina's hand. The jovial crowd made an ample path. Couples congratulated them as they passed with many saying, "Happy New Year."

Another fanfare from the band as their names were announced. They accepted their prize with huge smiles and thanks.

When they reached their table after wending their way through the dancers swaying to the melodious music. Ted looked up. "Congratulations, when are you two lucky ones going to Nassau?"

David gazed questioningly at Trina who was about to refuse, and feeling guilty in the bargain. She confessed, "I can't go, my trip to Australia is on the horizon. David, I do hope you will understand?"

He tried not to look too disappointed. To cover he jokingly said, "how much am I bid for these two tickets, the destination Nassau?"

Ted looked at Amanda saying, "Nine hundred as I know for a fact that they are worth a lot more."

"Sold to the highest bidder," chanted David like an auctioneer.

Amanda glowed. "Does that mean you are inviting me?"

Ted quickly replied, "I guess I could invite Jared."

Then at Amanda's crestfallen face Ted responded sexily, "Yes, of course I mean to invite you, my love. You are the only one I would want to take."

Amanda brightened quickly then shot up and threw herself at Ted, kissing and hugging him exuberantly.

It appeared that Amanda and Ted's relationship had progressed further than Trina had imagined. David and she looked on with warm smiles.

"You take the money Trina, as you were standing on the star. I want you to enjoy your trip to Australia and I will enjoy the telling when you get back."

"Thank you, David." She turned into his arms kissing him on the lips.

His arms tightened and he kissed her more fully ending it with the observation. "Now that kiss was worth every cent."

Trina blushed deeply. He danced her back amongst the throng of dancers to the sound of the orchestra's 'Good Night, Irene'. They were clinging together while he was crooning in her ear, "Good Night, Trina."

This surprised her greatly. David until this evening was not the kind to be openly affectionate towards her, always just portraying them as good friends. He was certainly acting differently tonight. It would seem the excitement of the evening added to the enchantment of the castle atmosphere was making a fairy tale ending.

chapter
THREE

Finally, the day of the big trip had arrived and Trina was flying out of Qualicum Airport at 1:20 pm.

Pack! Pack! Pack! This had been running through her mind for over a week now. Checklists made and packing items on the bed in the spare bedroom. Have I missed anything?

Would the suitcases actually reach their destination? You say goodbye to your luggage at check-in at the airport of origin. Regardless of how many changes of planes one takes, they assure you that your luggage will greet you at your destination. She had seen the carts of abandoned luggage sitting on the runway until the first plane arrives nearby. No wonder her mother's luggage went to Bermuda when it was supposed to go to Brandon, Manitoba. Trina remembered her mother once telling her that.

Her mother loved to travel. Trina didn't recall ever being concerned about her travelling alone. Briana didn't need to worry about this trip either.

Trina glanced at her watch as she finished her packing. Time was flying by, as she grabbed her clothes and headed for the bathroom. David would soon arrive.

Her friends had arranged for a Bon Voyage lunch along the way to the airport. Then they would wave her off to that far away destination.

She sauntered out the door. She headed towards the front hall. Along the way she had picked up her packed suitcase, dragging it behind her with her travel bag in hand. Opening the door, she looked at her watch to check the time.

Just then David arrived. He entered and walked to Trina. He had a sad look on his expressive face. "I want to say my goodbye now in private."

He reached over and drew Trina into his arms and kissed her soundly. She was a little uncomfortable about this, as David's manner towards her had become almost possessive since that night at the Castle Inn.

"Have a great time and come back to me," he said wistfully.

She pulled herself away gently and said evasively trying to ignore the 'me' and the sadness in his request. "David, you know I have every intention of coming back." He bent down and gallantly picked up her luggage leaving Trina to lock up while her luggage was placed in the open trunk. She greeted Amanda and Ted who were sitting in the back seat.

During the Bon Voyage luncheon, David was very attentive. Trina was excited about the trip but sad to leave her friends behind knowing she would miss them. David's arm was making caressing contact with her arm during the meal. She wondered if it was by accident or by design. She was relieved when Amanda and Ted were regaling them with tales of their hockey game trip to the mainland the month before. "Amanda imbibed too much wine, became the life of the party at one of the area nightclubs after the game," Ted laughingly said. "It was hilarious, and now she is denying all."

At last they were off to the airport. Amongst the many wishes to have a great time, Trina walked out to the lone plane waiting on the tarmac for her and her fellow passengers to board. She turned once more and waved.

—

Maybe Briana was right. Could anything else possibly go wrong, as her plans quickly sidetracked. The flight from Vancouver was delayed due to mechanical problems for an hour. Then the overbooked flight from Honolulu to Australia by ten passengers made Trina one of the first ones bumped off the plane. How could this happen? She knew she had booked well in advance. After waiting until a later flight, she finally arrived in Sydney. She was relieved to locate her luggage after the unexpected change.

Arriving in the courtesy van provided by the hotel, she found her hotel reservations had been given away as a no-show. Now she had no place to stay as everything was booked up solid, she was told. She had noticed on the way in a banner depicting **1994 World Chess Tournament**. She was stranded till Monday. What more can happen, trying hard not to be deflated?

Trina asked to speak to the manager. What he could do for her she didn't know, but it seemed like the logical thing to do under the circumstances. They do it all the time in the movies, upgrading them into the honeymoon suite.

The manager was a debonair man with an immaculate manner and a very polished appearance, with absolutely no sympathy for Trina's dilemma. With somewhat of a haughty manner, he directed her to a nearby hotel dismissing her as unimportant. This was not at all like the movies that she had viewed.

She thanked him very sweetly, not bowing to his level of haughtiness and gathered her luggage to proceed to the desk and insisted that there should be no charges on her credit card for something she had no control over. Determinately she stood there until she was assured that this had not happened. Then she promptly removed herself from the hotel with great dignity.

She did not let her shoulders slump until she was well away from the hotel and the doorman. Fortunately, there was a taxi at the curbside so she climbed in while the driver put her things in the boot.

"Please take me to the Hotel Samatra," Trina said with hope evident in her voice.

"You will be pleased with that hotel," the driver said promptly. "The hotel has a family atmosphere that caters to the comfort of their guest. Not at all like the stodgy hotel you just left."

Looking in the rear-view mirror he said, "No offence but I get the impression you're not wealthy, the way you were shown the door at the Hotel Windsor. If you were well off, they would have taken care of you regardless. I think you will enjoy this new hotel much better," said the driver congenially.

She was looking around at the famous city that she was here to enjoy for the next four days. The taxi soon pulled up in front of a Victorian building with an entrance that was inviting. She had reached the Hotel Samatra.

A cheerful young lady greeted her enthusiastically at the reception desk. Darcy acknowledged a vacancy was available in their quaintest room, for the five nights required for her stay in Sydney. "Is the dining room still open?" Trina inquired. Her rumbling stomach acknowledged all the disruptions in her travels that day and a missed dinner. It was now after nine.

"Actually, the dining room is just closing but I will contact the kitchen and ask them to provide something for you. It will be ready when you come back down from your room. The dining room is just through that doorway there." She indicated with a wave of her arm for direction.

"Thank you, Darcy." There was a young man reaching for her luggage ready to show her to her room.

Darcy handed her several tour brochures. "You might enjoy some tours during your stay." With a courteous smile she went on, "I hope you have a pleasant visit while in Sydney.

This was so different from her reception at the other hotel as Trina returned her smile. The taxi driver was right, this was a better option.

Samuel, as his nametag indicated, took her luggage and proceeded to the elevator with a smile and a wish for her to follow.

"Samuel, how many rooms are there in this hotel?" asked Trina noting that there were four floors on the indicator above the elevator.

"There are six rooms on each floor and two suites on the top floor with a semi-suite. The semi-suite is where you will be staying. Myself, I think it is the best room here, overlooking the harbor and the Opera House in the distance."

He placed her bags in an alcove near the bathroom. He adjusted the air conditioning and indicated some of the room's many features.

Trina was looking around with interest. She was very impressed with the quaintness of the semi-suite. It was larger than most hotel rooms and was decorated in a Victorian Colonial style motif. A cluster of two chairs and a sofa were in the middle with a massive bed off to the side. There was a small table and chairs in the rounded window area that overlooked the fabulous view of the harbor which Sydney was noted for around the world.

The display of twinkling lights on the distant Opera House made the folding scallops of the cement shell-roof appear audacious, as she glanced out in that direction. Trina turned away from the window to notice Samuel was waiting for her to become aware of him, as he wanted to ask if he could be of more service to her.

"May I suggest that you do not delay too long, your dinner will be waiting for you downstairs," he said pleasantly.

"Thank you, Samuel," she said as she gave him a tip, which he hastily refused. He explained, "there is no tipping allowed in Australia."

Trina quickly dispensed with her jacket to her pantsuit and freshened up. She proceeded down to the dining room with such a good feeling after all the eventful delays of the day. The room was overlooking the well-groomed garden at the back of the hotel. There was a terrace with tables and chairs for the guests during the day.

A young man greeted her. "Good Evening Mrs. Grant, your dinner is ready for serving. Right this way." He graciously sat her at a window table for two, overlooking the softly lit terrace. A young lad approached carrying buns and water to the table.

Trina didn't know what to expect for dinner, as Darcy had only said that something would be provided. She must have let the dining room know her name she presumed. Such a difference between this friendly hotel and the one she had encountered earlier.

The plate that was placed before her was Veal Medallions over rice covered by a wine sauce and an unusual array of vegetables. She asked for a red wine to compliment the meal. Her plate was so tastefully decorated that she was hesitant to disturb it. She dipped her fork in to taste the appetizing dinner.

She glanced around the room. The atmosphere of the room was charming. The round tables were nicely covered in lacy linen and azure blue napkins draped in wine glasses. She thought round tables looked cozier somehow. She noticed there were two couples just leaving and a gentleman sitting two tables over from where she was seated. He appeared to be lingering over his after-dinner coffee with leisure.

Trina continued daintily eating, as she nonchalantly looked around only to encounter a set of staring blue eyes. His appraisal was not a casual glance but an intense stare. The color seemed to drain from his face. Was that just her imagination? She dropped her eyes quickly to her plate hoping to discourage the man.

She continued eating with a casual air hoping the man's interest had gone elsewhere. The dinner was delicious and a tribute to the chef for his artful presentation and taste. After she thanked the staff for providing her late repast, she departed towards the door. In passing in his general direction, she glanced causally towards the lone gentleman. Only to encounter again that relentless stare fastened on her.

She sauntered out the door, as though she hadn't noticed anything untoward. Taking the elevator quickly to her room, before the man could accost her. Because of the piercing stare, she wondered what interest the man could possibly have in her.

The next morning arriving for breakfast, she noted that the dining room was quite full. Hopeful she looked at the young maître d, which was the same man from the previous night, for confirmation that there was still seating.

"Good Morning, Mrs. Grant, right this way."

As he held Trina's chair for her to be seated, she couldn't help but ask, "you don't have a twin, do you? I did see you working here last night."

"This is a family owned hotel and I am a nephew of the owners. I work all three meals with breaks in between for four days then have three days off. I don't mind the long hours, as the time off does allow me to surf my favorite beach. There the waves break higher, making extra good surfing."

Trina ordered breakfast of fruit and a cranberry muffin with Earl Grey tea. While awaiting her breakfast to arrive, her eyes skimmed over the other guest with a natural curiosity only to jolt back to the same gentleman from her dinner last night. Those eyes were fastened penetratingly on her again. **Why?**

She decided this time to give him a half smile before dropping her eyes. He didn't respond with a smile, but continued to stare with more intensity than she felt was necessary. She was certainly not looking for a pickup anyway. These stares were very disquieting to her.

She concentrated her gaze on the grandeur of the lovely garden beyond the window. The floral arrangement was a profusion of colors and variety. Despite her concentration on the garden scene, Trina could still sense that stare giving her eerie and uncomfortable feelings. She finished her tasty breakfast quickly. She just wanted to disappear from the dining room. This was beyond any experience she had ever known.

She went up to her room to collect her camera and map. Her intention was for a day of exploring the Circular Quay of Sydney Harbor. She wanted to put that man and his bizarre behavior behind her. She once again thought, she had never experienced this before in all her travels.

She was definitely going to discount 'The Eyes' as she had dubbed him, as not the hotel's fault in any way. She just wanted to think the move she had made to the Hotel Samatra was somehow meant to be. She certainly liked the semi-suite and the welcoming atmosphere of the hotel. The willingness of the staff to make her stay very pleasant with a nestling sensation.

She wandered through Sydney remembering the places Amanda had told her about. She felt carefree and flamboyant in her steps, which was a good feeling after her disappointing arrival in Sydney at the Hotel Windsor. At last her footsteps were drawn to the famous Sydney waterfront with its many tiny stalls and mime actors.

They were fascinating in the skillful art of mime. Trina felt she could watch them for hours, as they entertained the wanderers on the Circular Quay.

She understood now as she glanced around, why Sydney is noted for its famous waterfront. The thick traffic was a continuous change of various sized yachts, billowing spinnakers from the sailboats, container ships, luxury liners and the sleek lines of the steel grey Australian warships slipping in and out of the harbor.

Looking out from the quay, she could see the famous bridge, which was a century old landmark of the British Colony. She peered closely at the dark single span structure known as 'The Coathanger'.

She remembered the story as told by a guide in the Australian video, the bridge traffic came to a complete stand still when the actor, Paul Hogan (of *Crocodile Dundee* fame) was recognized, while he was painting the bridge. Apparently, he had won a talent contest the night before on TV, bringing him to the attention of the Sydney populace.

She swiveled to her right, taking in the ever-famous Opera House with the free-flowing spinnaker like design. The curvature that seemed to portray a reflection of the Australian free spirit.

As she turned her steps back towards the rest of the waterfront, she screamed with shock to the accompaniment of laughter from the crowd watching the mime actor.

The mime had fallen at her feet. She stopped like a frozen mime herself. She guessed that the mime actor wasn't about to be ignored. He certainly had her attention now. He arose with a fluid motion and resumed his statue like posture not moving a muscle, nerve nor eye movement, which they are so expert at. She gave him an extra big smile and a chuckle, which he did not acknowledge in any way, but continued in his mime stance.

Strolling onward, she perused the armada of boats in the clear cloudless sunny day. Seeing the yachts, she wondered how far they had cruised and where their next destination would be, traversing into eternity maybe.

She continued along the wharf until she came to two large sightseeing boats. Would it be fun by herself? As she questioned the possibility, she noted it was advertising the trip as a luncheon cruise. She realized the time had quickly gone and she was hungry. It would be so nice to have good scenery to compliment her meal. She approached the booth to pay her fare and then stepped onboard, to the inviting sound of a guitar trio playing romantic music.

A young man gave Trina a wink. "Your table awaits you."

She smiled her thanks and sank into the wooden chair he held for her, that he expertly maneuvered in such a way, so she felt like a princess being paid homage to. The cruise boat, Matilda II had pulled out of its docking space, heading out into the harbor.

She glanced down as a young man placed a basket with rolls and a bowl with aromatic soup in front of her. Dipping her spoon, she observed the taste flavorful enough to come from a chef of great renown.

The scenery slid by to the sound of the harbor history monolog interfaced with guitar music. It was done in such a way that you could enjoy both. Viewing the sites with added interest because of their vintage, like Fort Denison and the steep bluffs of Sydney where it funneled out to the cobalt blue Pacific Ocean.

The barbequed steak was palette enticing. As she enjoyed her meal, she observed the shoreline of stately architectural masterpieces of the clustered hillside homes, along with unusual rock formations surrounding the basin. What a perfect day. Trina was indeed glad she had decided to take the luncheon cruise. The Coathanger bridge sprang into view with the imposing Opera House off to their right. The sun was reflecting off of the curving modern splendor of that building's assemblage. A perfect blend of old and new.

It seemed all too soon that the launch arrived back at dockside. The young cocky sailors were biding us adieu as they gallantly helped the passengers to alight from the launch. With a slight wobble to her step after the swaying vessel, she traipsed back along the wharf with its varied activities drawing her interest.

She drank in as much as possible of the surrounding city as well, before she strolled back towards her hotel. She intended to enquire about tours for the next two days that she had seen in the brochures. Perhaps Darcy could suggest the best ones for her short stay.

Arriving at the hotel, she made the arrangements for a couple of tours, she was sure she would be happy doing.

Back in her room, Trina admired the suite's pleasant décor of antique furnishings. She was quite relaxed, while admiring the view. Reviewing all she observed on her travels that day. Whiling away the time before dinner with a cold iced tea she had purchased during her roaming.

chapter
FOUR

"Good Evening, Mrs. Grant."

"Good Evening, Wiley. How did your day go?" Trina had inquired as to his name at breakfast.

"No mishaps it flowed quite nicely and how was your day?" Wiley asked in return.

"I loved your Sydney Harbor and all it had to offer. It kept me busy most of the day. I had a scenic lunch on the Matilda II cruise." She followed him to a table at the center of the room. She observed that all the window tables were occupied. People seemed to like window tables best or was it the staff that thought those tables more cheerful.

A young girl approached her with a menu. She introduced herself as Janet and reamed off the specials for the evening. She had Janet describe in detail the special seafood entree. She decided on the special, acknowledging her taste for seafood. "Could I please have white wine to enjoy with my meal?" Trina requested.

Dare I cast my eyes around the room. She just had to find out if *he* was here. Nonchalantly without appearing obvious from where she was sitting, she picked up her wine glass lifting her head to sip. She glanced over the rim to casually scan the room. Her eyes encountered the interested eyes locked in her direction. 'The Eyes' was here. As she placed her wine down on the table, she was thinking. Why the constant attention? What was he seeing?

She considered herself a nice looking blonde but recognized she was not considered beautiful. She preferred the natural look, so she never wore much in the way of make-up. She liked clothes but never dressed extravagantly.

She looked again. This time she held his gaze longer but he still didn't smile but he did look kind of amazed or puzzled with a hint of sadness. Did he enjoy staring contests? She didn't think so by the astounded look on his face. She was not going to let this man spoil her time at this enchanting hotel or her enjoyment of Australia.

Janet was back with her dinner, making a few comments about the tourist aspect of Sydney. Having been born in Sydney, she was familiar with the influx of tourists each year. Her pleasant manner helped Trina to ignore 'The Eyes'.

She tasted the cuisine adorning the decorative plate. Once again, the dinner was exceptional. She expressed her pleasure to Wiley's gratification as she was leaving. She made her way out of the dining room with a salutation that she would see him in the morning.

Trina was too keyed up to just stay in her room. She decided to go for a ride on the Sky Train. Alone at night probably wasn't wise but she didn't think she would run into any difficulties. She wanted to observe from the elevated train, this glamorous city with its brilliant lights and color.

The overhead rail ride sped along with the swiftness of a hunting tiger through the lite night. Eventually suspending her over the water at Darlington Harbor. Then on to the wharf area where her departure was amongst the glitter of lively little shops and restaurants nestled there. Waterside dancing drew her attention. She decided to stop for a drink and watch the dancers.

The close-knit tables were filled to capacity. Trina observed a nice young smiling couple was encouraging her to their table. They introduced themselves as the Wendell's. Soon conversation flowed naturally between them. It was not long before some nice gentlemen had taken her to the dance floor with her consent. She was having a good time.

The evening had disappeared. "I think I should be going now, it is getting late. Thank you for sharing your table with me."

"Why don't you stay a little longer?" The Wendell's were smiling encouragingly.

"No, I should get back to my hotel. Good night. I enjoyed meeting you."

"We enjoyed your company too. Good night."

At last, she retraced her steps back to the Sky Train for the return journey to the hotel, gazing like a typical tourist at the city of lights unfolding below them.

All too soon it was her station. She meandered back through the streets towards her hotel. As she passed through the busy Hyde Park with its wide paved walkway, she became aware of the mantle of trees forming an arch of greenery in a steeple like effect, with glittering fairy lights. She felt like she was in a cathedral and was slightly awe inspired.

She entered the hotel feeling pleasure from the wonderful evening.

—

The stay in her delightful hotel and the scrumptious meals served to her, along with the obliging staff made Trina thankful for being directed here by chance.

She gazed around the dining room the next morning but there was no eye encounter. *He* wasn't there. She was relieved but curious why did he seem to be disturbed by her or was he the disturber. I will never know why this man seemed to perceive me in such a way.

The rest of her stay was taken up with her tour excursions she had applied for and a trip to the Opera House for a closer look. The days were easily filled with her meanderings.

At last the day arrived when Trina was to connect with the Gold Coast Tour Group.

She would be leaving Sydney behind, that had made her feel so welcome despite 'The Eyes'. She felt that she would like to return there again someday.

The bus driver introduced himself as Marc with a wide smile in greeting.

Elizabeth, the tour guide greeted the group congregated beside the coach. They were all handed information sheets and a red kangaroo pin with their names embossed on them. Many seemed interesting, as she skimmed her glance over the passengers.

Trina sat towards the back of the bus seeing as she was unaccompanied.

The first picture stop was Lennox Head, where they all got out milling around looking for that perfect shot. After everyone piled back into the bus (like herds of sheep trickled through Trina's mind) until the next photo stop, the number one enjoyment of tours.

"This New South Wales area was known for its penal colony when prisoners arrived from England, a century ago," Elizabeth imparted.

When the coach stopped in the next town, the old quaint churches and the beautiful gardens drew Trina for their splendor. She leisurely roamed the street drinking in its ambiance.

The coach was awaiting the groups return. Amongst the group, there were several passengers from Germany, quite a few Canadians, some Australians with some representatives of other countries. Trina was yet to make any direct overtures towards any particular passenger, while enjoying the ever-changing companions for meals. Meanwhile, she wandered around alone enjoying the delightful scenery.

Back on the bus Elizabeth announced, "Port MacQuarrie would be the first night's stay. Enjoy your stay and be sure to take in some of the local area."

Later in her room, Trina was thinking over her day. Perhaps she was carrying her independence too far. Maybe she should be making some effort to strike up a friendship with her fellow passengers. Did the others think her a standoffish snob?

The next day, the Big Banana Plantation was one of the major stops. Trina along with the others were taken on a tour of the groves with the trees showing blue plastic bags instead of yellow bananas. Apparently, this is how the bananas are protected and ripened, they were told. They were all given a couple of bananas as souvenirs.

Many sights to see and several camera shots later and she still made no contact with any particular person. She just kept enjoying the sights in a sort of third person situation of tagging along with a sociable couple.

The coach negotiated its path through Coolangatta, which is the gateway to the Gold Coast.

Elizabeth announced, "in Surfers Paradise, Hotel ANA is the accommodation for the night."

In glancing around, it struck her that Surfers Paradise seemed to be Australia's 'Waikiki' with lots of high-rise hotels on the beach.

As they piled off the bus, Trina had a fleeting glance of a man staring in her direction for a few moments, before he ducked into a waiting car near the hotel entrance. She was pretty sure it was 'The Eyes' but she had doubts. Yet the feeling was of a bold stare. Was Briana right after all? Was she in some unseen murkiness here? Was travelling alone a mistake?

To fend off the eerie feeling, she was drawn to the endless beach. Trina started out walking to relieve her unsettled mind and her cramped legs from the confining lengthy bus trip. Despite her joy at the expanse of beach before her, her mind was troubled by *his* appearance, if in fact it was him. She had thought that 'Mr. Eyes' was left behind her in Sydney.

Her thoughts turned to the fact she had won a ticket to Australia for one. She had been thinking along the lines of this being her destiny, with her looking for a new direction in life. But what did she find? Not destiny but a pair of blue eyes that stared. *Was it for evil purposes?* Why was she still seeing him on her travels? He didn't appear to be a traveler viewing the gold coast. Who was he? What was his interest in her?

———

Day Three started with a confrontation with Trina's touring companions. Her morning stroll along the beach had unknowingly taken her past the hotel on her return. Unaware of bypassing her hotel, her steady pace was taking her further away. No Hotel ANA. Where was it? Then she thought that maybe she hadn't been walking fast enough so she speeded up, but still no Hotel ANA. The disaster was building with every step she took. Her hotel was now far behind.

Then the horror stepped in. The hotels were very similar. Here was this row upon row of high-rise hotels and an endless beach. Was the hotel ahead or behind her? As she looked around none of them were depicting the name ANA.

Trina stopped, looking down, her watch had to be wrong. At this exact moment the bus would be loading and departing the hotel. She hadn't a clue where she was, other than being on this never-ending beach. She concluded finally, she had to get off the beach. Direction was needed if she was to find the hotel or maybe a taxi.

The different men planting gardens or polishing cars were as clueless as she was, as to the Hotel ANA's whereabouts. 'I'm sorry I have no idea', was the usual answer. What did they mean they had no idea? Didn't they open their eyes to their surroundings? This was not what she wanted to hear. Where is a taxi when you need one? Surely, they would know where her lost hotel was.

She was hustling back now towards the direction of origin. The morning seemed to be embraced in a bitter heat and the sweat was pouring down her face and back or maybe a panic attack was in full bloom.

Finally, a knowledgeable man babying his flowers, informed Trina she was a block away. In anticipation her feet were doing triple time and her lost hotel appeared in huge letters **ANA**.

Things still looked bleak, the driveway was empty and she was 20 minutes late. No bus only a concierge ensconced in the entrance. Trina's heart fell.

Her mind flipped to the information rules **'If you miss the bus loading, no waiting. That person was on his or her own to reconnoiter their own transportation to that night's stop.'** She had visions of a taximeter spinning merrily to $600.00, as it crawled towards her ultimate destination.

The normal routine was, to set the luggage out before breakfast. Her luggage would be making the trip at least, she thought with a sinking feeling.

Her anxiety and sweaty red face triggered the concierge to realize this was the missing passenger from the tour bus. He quickly approached her. "Relax, go to your room for your things. The bus is only circling the hotel area looking for you but will be returning before heading north."

This gave her such a feeling of relief, her heart that had almost stopped started beating again.

"Thank you." She loped towards the hotel to retrieve her carryon with the hopes to descend before the coach reappeared.

The driver and the tour guide were standing there with smiles, with her sudden appearance. The coach was parked along the driveway. Marc touched her arm reassuringly, giving a chuckle at her agitation. His amusement was supposed to reassure her, she guessed. Elizabeth was saying reassuring things too. They did a group hug before Elizabeth inserted her 'but'.

"But the rest of the passengers are not happy with you and some were downright indignant."

Trina approached the coach with as much dignity as she could muster, blushing she cautiously stepped onto the coach. Everyone gave Trina a hard time with remarks, some cajoling others not cajoling, and some down-right annoyed about her wandering off.

How did she make friends under these conditions?

However, Marc tried to booster her feelings during the day, with his ready humor.

They stopped in Brisbane for more passengers. The newcomers were an older couple with a teenage daughter and a young honeymoon couple. The latter only had eyes for each other and would no doubt miss most of the scenery along the way.

The teenager was a slim girl with a long face beneath short black hair. Her unhappy face indicated that she did not want to be here. The parents were smiling, and trying to make the best of their daughter's attitude. It seemed obvious that they were forced to include her in their trip. Perhaps not wanting to leave her at home alone.

The trip continued with Trina entering the bus first, stop after stop for the duration of the day. She spread smiles upon various passengers at different times throughout the day's travels, trying to smooth things over with her travel mates. Her morning tardiness had certainly not endeared her to them. Will these tour companions ever forgive or forget?

The day included an excursion to the BIG Pineapple Plantation the sign depicted. They have a thing about "big" in Australia, the Big Banana and the Big Pineapple just like Texas.

They toured the area on a miniature railroad with a commentary of the plantation and its tropical fruit orchards of pineapples. While encased in the small miniscule train car, Emma, a lady in her late 40's, seemed to respond to her attempts for friendliness. Later they laughed outrageously, juice trickling down their chins trying to consume the juicy pineapple at the sampling area. They both bought plastic containers of the sweet fruit.

Her travel partner was established as Emma sat down beside her on the return to the bus. "That was fun wasn't it?" Emma smiled in her direction.

"Yes, even though I wiped my chin, it still feels sticky."

Another photo stop at Coffs Harbor where she learned that Emma was quite the camera buff. Her camera being 'state of the art' with multi lenses, unlike Trina's simple mid-range automatic focus type. At every possible opportunity Emma was snapping pictures with great enthusiasm.

Trina felt obligated to take the occasional picture rather than just enjoying the view. There was quite a contrast between the two women, where cameras were concerned.

Today, they made an earlier finish because they were going to be staying on Fraser Island. The expectation was high. A catamaran, Kingfisher II was waiting at the Herve Bay wharf for them to board.

As the boat approached the island, Emma and Trina noticed that the island was primitive with no evidence of civilization.

"We have seen no houses, no small boats, or docks jutting out into the water. It only has the appearance of being an untouched thick jungle with rainforest density." Trina eyes were scanning the island.

"Do you think there really is life here?" Emma queried. "Perhaps natives will pop out of the dense foliage any minute."

The Kingfisher II sailed around the bottom of the island and lo and behold in a bay, a dock was protruding out into the water with two shack-like buildings on shore and the jungle pervading behind. The shacks were not big enough to house their entire group, other huts must be tucked away somewhere in amongst the dense forest.

The big reef like rocks jutting from the water made docking a challenge. Trina held her breathe while the captain who had probably made this trip many times, skillfully maneuvered the boat until it cozily nestled the dock with a slight bump. She felt they should have clapped or cheered, but the excited group only wanted to experience the unforeseen ahead of them instead.

There was evidently life on this island somewhere, as several young men appeared on the dock.

There was a road or more aptly termed a track of sorts wandering into the forest. Emma and Trina looked at each other, then gamely headed for the track, which they had been told to follow.

"Follow! Follow the Yellow Brick Road," Trina said jovially. "Our destination must be just ahead."

Emma eyed Trina, they shared a giggle. "I'm game if you are." Emma waved her hand forward invitingly.

They both tramped up the track, invading the dense forest until they eventually burst into a clearing. Pods of joined shacks like units in groups of four were off to the right.

Ahead, they approached a larger building fairly modern in stature but quite rustic in design, which had to be the main lodge. They had arrived at the Kingfisher Bay Resort which was built in keeping with the natural surroundings. She stood gazing around with expectation, Trina felt this was her place.

"Trina, I have a good feeling about this island, don't you?" said Emma positively.

"I agree. This resort was just the right design for this sort of island. I think it would be wrong to have anything modern here amongst this jungle of trees." She was in accord with Emma.

The main lodge array, was shiny wood floors, rustic walls and rafters. The furnishings and hangings were of native decor. The group was milling around waiting for Elizabeth to provide them with their keys. Emma and Trina had asked Elizabeth if possible, to put them close to each other. They seemed to be forming a durable relationship, Trina hoped.

Elizabeth mentioned while issuing the keys. "There are only two resorts on the island and a couple of very small stores up island. The two shacks near the dock only open for buying souvenirs and snacks, after a boat load of passengers arrives. Weekend mainlanders come for fun, drawn by the extra rugged trails traversed only in special 4WD vehicles."

Keys in hand, they wandered out towards the outer huts, for sleep lodgings. The walkways were wood because it was boggy underneath and the units were formed around a fascinating lagoon in the center court. Were there unwelcome predators here, ran through Trina's head craning her neck to see, but did not voice.

Some units were small and some looked larger.

After unlocking the door, Trina peered into the room commenting, "they are larger than they appear. Do you want to meet in half an hour?"

"Yes, I will call for you then." Her place was two units past Trina's.

As she went to close the wood door, she heard a greeting from Rod and Malina, the neighbors in the unit next to her. She knew them both as she had eaten dinner with them one evening, at the beginning of the tour. "We have really enjoyed our trip thus far. What do you think of this island?"

"My first impression of this jungle island is, I know I will feel comfortable here." Trina was feeling forgiveness was starting to happen.

As she entered her room, the feeling of comfort warmly embraced her as she scanned the room and its decor. Her gaze was captured by the lagoon, which was adding to the ambiance. This island was calling to her in a most rewarding way.

chapter
FIVE

It seemed like less than fifteen minutes when a knock came on the door. Trina was so enraptured with the setting adjacent to the lagoon, that the time had sped by. She opened the door for Emma and invited her inside. "I'm sorry I am not quite ready yet."

"Trina, I arranged to sit with Ron, Sandra, Max and Elaine for dinner. I hope you don't mind?" asked Emma while Trina was putting the finishing touches to her makeup.

"Sure, that is fine with me. I don't think I have met them."

"Ron and Sandra are a young Canadian couple on holiday here, from the Shanghai Canadian Embassy. Elaine and Max are Australians from Adelaide. I have been quizzing them about their country. They have been enjoyable dinner companions." Then Emma changed the subject worriedly.

"Trina, about this morning, I know you are feeling embarrassed and a bit disturbed about the talk and comments of tardiness. But just let it go and put on a smiling face. Okay?" Emma suggested, "I just wanted this out of the way, so we could enjoy our evening, and you can feel more relaxed with the others."

"Thank you, Emma, for your understanding of the situation. I really felt terrible. I certainly didn't do it on purpose. In fact, I thought the bus had gone without me. I felt quite heartbroken and disappointed at missing it. When I couldn't find the hotel, I was getting so panicky and hot that I thought I would expire. Especially when I kept asking local people for directions and no one seemed to know or even heard of the Hotel ANA.

Do you know how that felt? I thought I was doomed to walk that beach forever."

"Marc and Elizabeth were both super," Trina continued, "and they made me feel welcome back on the bus, much to my amazement. I will just have to prove myself to the others, as tardiness is not usually a fault of mine."

"No more lateness and they will forgive you. Are you ready now? The two couples I mentioned are supposed to meet us in the lobby."

"Yes, I am." Trina picking up her room key and purse from the dresser. Then they exited the room.

As Emma and Trina gazed around the lobby looking for the others, Trina spied a man with eyes focused on her near the office to the right of the reception desk. "Oh no!" Trina gasped. **'The Eyes'** were looking at her again. It was *him*. *How did he get here? Is he following me?* Trina felt he was going to speak to her. What should she do? Leave, no certainly not, she had to find out once and for all what his interest in her was. The stare was not so intense now, it seemed like he was just gazing at her. The opportunity was lost with the approach of another man greeting him as 'Mr. Hunter.' After shaking hands both men retreated into the office.

She didn't want to let on to Emma the sinking feeling that was affecting her. But she must have noticed Trina's startled look and her gasp, because she asked. "Are you feeling all right?"

Trina replied, "yes." Explaining her reaction to 'The Eyes' since Sydney.

Emma listened with rapt interest. She now understood the strange look that had appeared on Trina's face. Emma suggested, "ask the receptionist who he is, then maybe you will feel better about the situation."

"I'll be right back. You look for the others while I go and inquire." Trina wandered towards the reception desk wondering about the best way to ask for information from the smiling girl. She edged up to the desk tentatively.

"May I ask if you happen to know who that man is that just went into the office beside you?" Trina had decided on the direct approach.

"There were two men actually that went in that office. Which man are you enquiring about, Mr. Hunter or Mr. Jackson?"

"I believe the man that had just entered the lobby addressed him as Mr. Hunter," said Trina determinedly.

"Mr. Hunter is the owner of the Kingfisher Bay Resort and several others here on the Gold Coast or I should say his family owns them. Although I am not sure, I believe that this one Mr. Hunter owns by himself."

Trina nodded, as she thanked the girl and turned to smile at Emma who was standing watching her. She must have had a relieved look because Emma smiled broadly back at her.

Then Emma turned away as Ron, Sandra, Elaine and Max greeted her warmly. Emma made the formal introductions upon Trina's reaching the group. Trina recalled having spoken with them on some past occasion. She may have glanced at their nametags but not retained their names.

Ron said, "I reserved a table for six while Sandra, my wife was getting ready." He teased Sandra about her lengthy preparations for the evening. She blushed prettily.

They all proceeded towards their table in the dining room. They settled into their seats and were served a glass of wine. Toasting each other for a continued good trip. Then they sauntered up to the buffet line.

Emma positioned herself behind Trina in the line for the buffet, taking the opportunity to quiz her about 'The Eyes'.

"I have no idea why he keeps staring at me but at least I don't feel he is being sinister or stalking me anymore."

Emma wanted to know her reasoning. "What did you find out?"

"He happens to own this resort and his family owns several hotels on the Gold Coast along with him. So that explains why he keeps appearing at the hotels we stay in. And here I have been thinking he was stalking me for devious reasons. How ridiculous of me," said Trina chiding herself.

"The receptionist acknowledged him as Mr. Hunter but that is all I found out so far." She chose some salad and shrimp positioning it on her plate along with some mushrooms and tiny tomatoes. Slowly moving along, she choose a vinaigrette dressing for her garden salad. She also put some seafood sauce on her plate for the shrimp, deciding to come back later for the hot portion of her dinner.

But Emma wasn't ready to let go of their conversation just yet.

"Trina, that's a relief. I'm sure he has an interesting reason also. I agree it might not be sinister especially if he owns this resort and has reason to be here." Emma kept making her culinary decisions for her plate. "Do you want me to approach him?"

Trina's face held a look of horror. "No! No! Just let's drop it. Are you ready to go back to the table yet?" As they turned away Trina said feebly, "it may be just coincidence and my overactive imagination."

She made a hasty retreat into her seat at the end of the table. Thankful she could drop this line of questioning, and Emma's distasteful suggestion. She waited to pick up her fork until the others had settled in their seats.

Ron was chiding Emma about her rather full plate to which she promptly replied. "It was too hard to make choices everything looked so good."

The dinner conversation was lively and the interchange was as if they had known each other a long time. The buffet meal had caused a lot of laughter, juggling positions each time someone wanted to go to the buffet, as their table backed onto a wall.

Suddenly a waiter appeared at Trina's side with a bottle of wine in an ice bucket.

Removing the bottle, he held it so she could peruse the label. "Miss, is this to your liking?"

"I didn't order wine," Trina said hastily looking up at the waiter. "There must be some mistake. We were only supposed to get one glass of chardonnay with our dinner. It has already been served when we arrived at the table."

"I am aware of that," replied the waiter, opening the bottle with a flourish. "This is complements of Mr. Hunter the owner of the Kingfisher Bay Resort."

The waiter paused, waiting for Trina to taste the wine before he poured for the others

Emma and Trina traded looks, as she lifted her glass to take a sip. "Thank you that is fine."

Ron and Max were joking, indicating they could certainly imbibe more wine. Trina knew that she was going to be up for more teasing once the waiter was finished pouring. She glanced at Emma and her knowing look confirmed she agreed with her.

Sandra inquired, "come on Trina, fill us in here. Why would Mr. Hunter be sending you a bottle of wine?"

"Yeah?" asked Elaine.

Blushing Trina replied, "I don't know Mr. Hunter."

"Come on," said Ron slyly, "a man doesn't send a bottle of wine to a lady without a good reason."

Max raised his glass. "A toast to Trina and her secret admirer. Here! Here!"

Emma piped up after she drank the toast. "Mr. Hunter is known to Trina as 'The Eyes'. He has been staring at her on several occasions in Sydney and other times on this tour including this evening. I wanted to ask him why for her, but she is trying to downplay the situation. Aren't you, Trina?" Emma inquired.

"I am not going to engage him in any conversation and neither are you Emma. I probably will never see him again." Trina tried to sound positive.

Max gave her a sly look. "Any man who sends a lady a bottle of wine intends to see that lady again. Trust me," his voice was very firm on that point.

"Yes," Sandra put in "after all you could at least thank him for the wine."

"That would certainly give you an opening," Elaine chimed in.

The conversation continued in a teasing manner, when they congregated in the lounge after dinner.

There were sly looks from Emma towards Trina.

She would have to impress on Emma once again, when they retired to their lodgings, that she definitely wanted this to go away with no further investigation.

Eventually they all said good night. They strolled back to their own huts.

As soon as they left the others Trina said, "Emma, you are not and I repeat, you are not to speak to Mr. Hunter about me. Is that understood?"

"Ah! But now I know he does want to get to know you. Especially now that he has acknowledged you. The bottle of wine arriving at the table tonight was quite a grand gesture, don't you think?" Emma said coyly.

"No Emma, I would like to think that Mr. Hunter is just saying no hard feelings for his stares but he is going to forget about me."

When they reached Trina's door, Emma asked if she could borrow her nail file if Trina had one, as she had broken her nail and it was bothering her.

"Sure, come in and I will find it for you."

Emma walked in ahead of her. She stopped dead when Trina flipped on the light. She bumped into her as Emma gave a little gasp. "Trina, there is a pink rose and a chocolate on your pillow with a card." Emma started towards the bed. "Quick look, what does it say?"

Trina walked over to her turned down bed, picking up the pink rose and the card that the chambermaid must have put there. The message Trina held was in bold masculine writing.

"Well?" Emma was curious as to this mysterious card.

"It just says *'**Sweet dreams**'* and is signed, ***L Hunter.**"*

Emma was bouncing around in excitement. "I told you he was interested in you. I just knew it. Aren't you excited?"

Trina should have been delighted, when instead she was deeply puzzled. "But why? There is nothing exceptional about me? I am reasonably good looking, but certainly I am not classified as beautiful. I am approaching my senior years. I will be sixty-two soon and Mr. Hunter looks in the range of fifty. Why?"

"Trina, you look fifty. If you hadn't told me, I would never have placed your age anywhere near sixty. In fact, you should not consider that an issue in this case."

"But Emma, the fact is I am sixty-one and I am not going to make a fool of myself over a younger man. Besides these little mementos may have nothing to do with wanting to know me on a romantic level, but just an apology for staring."

Emma started assessing the man. "This man is attractive with a worldly look and appearance, you certainly have to agree. Mr. Hunter has devastating eyes and his dark thick wavy hair enhances the blue of his eyes. He dresses well and wears suits with quality written all over them. He fills out his suits to perfection and with your classic body and blonde hair, you would go well together." Emma was looking at Trina critically but in a complementary way as her words were indicating.

"Okay, I will sleep on it, Emma. Will that satisfy you?" Trina's voice was still hesitant but she was dreamily looking at the pink rose, which she held to her nose to breathe in the flowers delicate scent.

"Good Night, Emma." Trina was gently steering her to the door.

"You forgot the nail file," Emma responded part way out the door.

Trina reached for her cosmetic bag, unzipping it quickly to grasp the sought-after nail file. Placing it in Emma's outstretched hand, Trina said once again. "Good Night, Emma. Do you want to come by at seven for a walk before breakfast?" Trying to placate Emma for the way she was literally throwing her out of the room.

"Okay, good night. Sweet dreams!!" Emma said coyly.

Trina wandered around the room sort of dreamy like with the pink rose waving under her nose, inhaling the scent and looking at the bold writing on the card. It was wrong for her to say those things to Emma, because in fact her heart was responding in a romantic way. She definitely could feel it was fluttering and her tummy had butterflies flitting around gaily.

Was he interested in me in this same manner or was his interest of another nature? Just for tonight, let it be in a romantic way. Every woman no matter her age loved a romantic interlude, she mused. Her gaze roamed to the moon's reflection dancing on the lagoon's rippling water.

Shaking her head, Trina prepared for bed. When she slipped under the covers, she placed the rose beside her pillow along with the card. Then she savored the rich chocolate letting it melt in her mouth. Now she would have to get up and brush her teeth again. But did she really want to spoil the taste in that way? No, she wanted to savor the moment.

Mr. Hunter was quite attractive and his deep blue eyes were compelling. Definitely in a nice way Trina thought, not a sinister way, as she had previously felt or believed. Although he had still stared, his eyes seemed softer when she saw him this evening at the lodge.

She turned over, placed her hand on the card and dreamily went off to sleep.

———

Emma and Trina's early morning walk was curtailed, as the cultivated area around the resort was just the track to the loading dock and a bit going around the back of the resort. Otherwise there was plenty of dense forest in every direction. They kept repeating their path, cleaved out of the forest, just to continue exercising somehow.

Emma had been prodding Trina for a decision about Mr. Hunter since they had started walking.

She put her off by talking about the way the resort blended so well into the island setting, which seemed untouched by civilization. This was her way of delaying the subject. She had not decided yet.

But there was no way that Emma would be put off for too long. She was being persistent for an answer. Although she did agree that the beauty of Fraser Island was inviting, in order to placate Trina in the hopes of obtaining her decision.

With exasperation Emma gripped Trina's arm and dragged her to a halt. "You are not putting me off any longer. Forget the island and its beauty for a minute. No more delaying tactics. You just need to thank him for the wine. See where things might lead from there. He surely will explain his interest in you. Then you will know. After all, his gestures last night were very promising, you have to admit."

"Okay, okay already!" exclaimed Trina nervously. "When we go into the lodge for breakfast, I will inquire if he is around. You have finally convinced me. I get the feeling that if I don't, you will. Now let's continue our walk. I really do need the exercise, even if we appear to be going back and forth quickly with this short distance this island allows."

On their final return trip, Emma's footsteps picked up to double the pace. The resort was coming into view once again and she was definitely eager to see this through with Mr. Hunter.

Trina steps slowed down, falling behind.

At the entrance to the lodge, others of their group waylaid them; greetings were abounding about the expectations of their day and comments on the island's primitive nature. Emma was talking very quickly trying to get the G'days (as the Aussie say) over with while edging Trina inside.

There was a pleasant smiling young man at the reception desk this morning, which Emma was thrusting her towards. You could tell immediately with his expansive smile, he was waiting to please any guests who needed assistance. Emma thought he was just the one to help them. She pushed Trina forward again.

"Good morning," Trina said as Emma was still guiding her closer. "Could you tell me if Mr. Hunter is around this morning?" Her eyes strayed to the closed door of the office where he had disappeared yesterday.

"I am sorry, Mr. Hunter left early this morning on the Kingfisher II. Can I help you?"

The thought struck Trina immediately that when they had walked to the dock that the boat had been missing.

Noting Trina's silence, he continued. "He won't be back until tomorrow night. Is there possibly something I could help you with?" the young man asked with a pleasing look on his face. His manner indicated, he certainly knew he could help them.

"No thank you. It isn't anything important," Trina replied quickly scooting in the general direction of the dining room. The two couples they ate with last night would be waiting, for Trina and Emma to join them for breakfast.

Emma grabbed her arm and drew Trina to a halt. "Not important? Just a chance officially to meet **the** man of your **dreams**. Trina, you did dream about him didn't you, Miss Rose & Chocolate Receiver." She addressed her.

"Oh Emma, you are such a persistent romantic for something that may never come to anything personal. His mementoes, as you have called them, may be just a way of thanking me for being a guest for five days at the Hotel Samatra, that his family might own."

Trina certainly wanted to ease out of this situation. Deep down she was slightly disappointed and relieved at the same time. At least his overtures here seemed friendlier. Not like the sinister gaze of 'The Eyes' in the first encounters, which Emma had changed to 'Mr. Blue Eyes'. Emma was trying to put a romantic connotation on their relationship and 'Mr. Blue Eyes' sounded much more in keeping with her romantic notions.

chapter
SIX

As the remnants of the early breakfast were cleared away, the tour group congregated near the so-called road. They were ushered into vehicles that were half 4WD and half tank, a track instead of wheels at the back. The cab was enclosed with enough space to accommodate a dozen or so people in each. There were three vehicles in all.

The bushman, who appeared to be their tour guide on the trip, was a true Aussie by his appearance and manner. He explained, "the trek through the virgin rainforest is not your usual smooth surface, but a trail that requires all-terrain vehicles." He warned, "we will sometimes have difficulty getting around and over hilly grades even with this tank carrier. The trail in many places is undermined by watery bogs. Enclosed in this sturdy all-terrain vehicle will keep you safe."

He proceeded through the encompassing rainforest in its natural uninhabited form. Nature in its raw state, giving the group a feeling of discovering the unknown.

At this point he informed them, "Too many of the islands are so modernized, losing their unrefined splendor. Fraser Island is being pressured to make the change also but so far it has been successfully avoided."

Trina thought that would be a shame.

Continuing his motoring he stated, "Fraser Island is known as the largest sand island with a profusion of tropical plants, vines and trees and many lakes to add to your experience."

Emma was in her glory recording frame after frame of all the greenery in its magnificence.

The tank carrier suddenly gave a lurch and slid sideways. There were squeals and frantic grabbing for hand holds and each other. It came to a stop and seemed to be teetering. Apparently, it had slid onto a rock which had stopped it. The bushman tried rocking it to no avail. Then he backed up but that just sent the front end up in the air. At the gasps of fright, he stopped. The other drivers quickly came to their rescue.

The bushman said. "These vehicles are too heavy to lift so they are going to push us off the rock hopefully. I warned you that this could possibly happen. Don't worry you are safe inside this vehicle." "Ready," he yelled to the other bushmen. He tried backing up again and at the same time the bushmen were pushing the vehicle. With a grinding noise the carrier slipped off the rock onto firm ground.

Cheers of joy were issued by the passengers. The two bushmen smiled deeply in appreciation. With a sigh of relief by some the trip continued.

They stopped for smoke-o (tea break) mid-morning. "You are in for a real treat," said the Aussie bushman. "I put Damper on to cook earlier before your ride started. This is a real bushman's fare, Billy Tea and Damper."

"'Billy' relates to the metal container that I am setting to boil in the fire's hot coals. and the Billy cups, I will be serving it to you in." Then he tossed in a palm of tea leaves. "While we wait for this to brew into tea, I will explain the process."

He continued in great detail. "Damper is the Australian Bushman's bread. The basic recipe is 1-cup flour plus a generous pinch of salt and a scant 1/4-cup of water. Too much and it tastes like old boots." He grinned as if in memory. "You dig a foot-deep hole near the fire and then add two full shovels of the hot coals and ash. Using a camp oven (big pot) or sometimes metal foil, to contain the damper mixture and it is lowered into the hole and covered with earth. During cooking the dough increases to double its size."

"There is a definite art to it," he said "if the coals are too hot the outside burns and the inside is raw, while if undercooked by not hot enough coals, you'll get a flat rubbery mass."

All the while the bushman was telling them this, he was cutting up pieces of damper bread in chunks and setting out butter and homemade jam as compliment to their Billy Tea which he was pouring. They found it was delicious with the butter melting into the hot bread.

While Trina was partaking of this damper, and the knowledge ingested with it. Emma was out with her camera taking her fill of an Iguana suspended on the trunk of a Satinay tree not far from the campfire. It was being observed by many as a camera shoot. The Iguana had stayed there, seeming to enjoy the activity.

———

The bushman shared, "Fraser Island, takes its name from Eliza Fraser shipwrecked in 1836 having been saved by the Aboriginals," while continuing in their up and down lumpy trail journey.

The highlight of that morning was a swim in Lake McKenna. It was a sight to behold, as they burst from the never-ending forest suddenly to perceive this spectacular blue lake glistening in the sun, making it extra dramatic. The large lake abounded by sandy shores and the odd piece of interesting driftwood.

After a frolic in the water that refreshed them from the hot noon day sun, they piled back in the vehicles to be transported to their lunch stop, which happened to be at the only other resort on the island. It was known as Happy Valley Resort. The group all agreed they liked the ambiance of their own resort better. The lunch was good and lots of food was provided in generous Aussie style.

Afterward, they continued on their outing. This time, they piled into a bus as the Happy Valley Resort was near the ocean up the island from their own resort. The bus took a short trek to the beach. Then the beach became a roadway known as 70-mile Beach. Miles and miles of wide beach, which the large bus navigated along speedily. When they finally stopped and departed the bus, they discovered airplane rides were available from the beach, to oversee Fraser Island. Some of their gang took advantage of this opportunity to view the island from the air.

Trina and Emma took in the Cathedrals instead, consisting of pinnacles of ancient sands which wind and erosion have sculptured into majestic cliffs. The spire like formations became camera ecstasy to Emma.

Several buses were travelling on the beach from the two island resorts that had spewed their guests out to the beach for the day. The lead bus, Trina and Emma had been riding on provided the amusement for the scorching afternoon. It had a flat tire. Typically, 12 men from their bus passengers were doing the role of foreman,' the driver didn't need. This caused much laughter and innuendoes from the other bus drivers, as they stopped rather than passing.

While this comedy performance was being enacted and the heckling continued, Emma and Trina had lots of time to wander the beach.

There was tiny marine life burrowing into the wet sand as the receding tide left them behind. As these creatures burrowed just beneath the surface, they were pushing out little balls of sand behind them.

There were rivulets of water coming through the sand also on the beach that made fascinating patterns with the black and sand mixture. This stirred Trina to take pictures, as she was very impressed by the unusual designs found in these water sculptures. This entire island appealed to Trina's love of nature with the feeling of wanting to stay forever.

Emma of course was in seventh heaven with her powerful lens focusing and capturing the surroundings. While exploring the beach, they came across a shipwreck half submerged in the sand. Showing evidence, it was from ancient times. The name Maheno barely visible on its protruding side. The skeleton ship was slowly deteriorating with the years it had been reclining there. Emma snapped merrily away at this tremendous discovery. "I want the viewer's imagination to leap to the conclusion that the ancient sea serpent of wood, perhaps may have belonged to a plundering pirate." she told Trina.

While Emma had been thinking of pirates and plundering, she had been thinking of 'Mr. Blue Eyes.' *Would she ever see him again? What was compelling him to notice her?* The gifts from him seemed to indicate this was non-threatening. Trina needed to turn off this path of thinking. She shrugged her shoulders hoping to shed her concerns of 'Mr. Blue Eyes'. She would probably never see him again.

Briana was quite wrong, a woman alone in Australia is quite safe even on a primitive island.

Her thinking switched to the fact that she wasn't seeking the ire of the other passengers again by being late back on the bus.

"Emma, come on." Trina pleaded. "Emma, I think we should go back now. In our explorations, we wandered a long way from the others. Despite unwanted help the bus driver received, he must be finished changing the tire by now and rounding up the passengers."

She started back up the long beach, pacing quickly. Looking up the beach, Trina could see men frantically waving in their direction. "Emma, let's go, we have to get back as the men are waving at us to come." They both quickly retraced their steps in double time, hoping to discourage any nastiness of their fellow passengers.

The afternoon was fading, although the sun was still blazing, when they stopped at Elie Creek. The bus driver instructed them that if they walked to the top of the hill, where the stream cascaded over the fairly steep incline, the current would float them to the beach where the creek flowed into the Pacific Ocean.

"Emma, I don't want to do that. The very thought of riding on the bus in wet clothes is not appealing to me."

Emma of course clicking away hoping to get that all-important perfect picture replied, "me neither."

Many of the more daring passengers were game to try this playful pastime. They were having tremendous fun by the sounds of their laughter, as they sailed by Emma and Trina.

Trina did snap a couple of pictures, as it was such a pretty spot. She commented, "I'll need to keep in touch with you to obtain copies of your wonderful pictures."

Emma didn't respond snapping pictures merrily. Too soon according to the bathers, they were ushered back onto the bus, as their tour was coming to an end for the day.

They met with their Aussie bushmen to transport them back to the Kingfisher Bay Resort in their all-terrain vehicles. The dank forest enveloped them once again. After they completed their jungle ride back to their resort, everyone was tired.

The group of six arranged the time to meet later for dinner.

Emma and Trina headed for their lodgings and a much-needed shower. Emma excitedly said. "I got some excellent photographs today." Then pausing to say. "I will meet you at six." Parting at Trina's door.

"Okay."

Trina's glance immediately was drawn to the coverlet gracing the double bed with hope. Disappointment rapidly hit her, no message. Mr. Hunter was truly gone. She secretly had wanted further acknowledgement from him.

She had her shower, letting the water spray soothingly over her, trying to wash away her disappointment, along with her fatigue. Refreshed, she returned to the bedroom to get attired for the evening ahead.

Emma's greeting when she arrived at the door, included an enquiry if there were any more surprises. In a sprightly voice Trina responded, "no, why would there be, he has left the island remember." She quickly dropped the subject by grasping her purse from the table and picking up the key.

The others were awaiting their arrival in the lobby, with a comment by Max and Ron, about her ability to provide extra wine for their indulgence.

Laughing, Trina tried to be nonchalant but jovial in her reply. "You want to be indulged every night." She was glad for this enjoyable relationship with these new friends, looking forward to its continuation throughout the trip. Her faux pas forgotten. After much ribbing and laughter, they sauntered in for their mealtime.

Marc and Elizabeth stopped at their table to chat. As the two had not been with them during the day. They asked about their trip. The group expressed their fun with their bushman guide and his all-terrain vehicle, as well as the beach bus's fiasco in some joyous detail.

"Our day was quiet compared to that." Marc replied to an inquiry.

———

In the morning, the group quickly boarded the Kingfisher II with some sadness at leaving Fraser Island for their destination of Herve Bay, to continue their north bound journey.

Trina knew that she would miss this tropic paradise.

She had been thankful, when the six met for breakfast that there were no further comments about her lost lover, as they had the previous evening at dinner with joyous tones of laughter.

The excursion this day took them through the fertile Burnett River region. It was a long dreary day. The travels for the day ended at the Tropic of Capricorn, at the entrance of the metropolis of Rockhampton the 'Beef Capital of Australia'.

Marc and Elizabeth jointly agreed to pose for pictures, for each passenger's memorabilia album. The Tropic of Capricorn sign was the backdrop.

The honeymoon couple asked Trina to take their picture too, she complied. Deeply enthralled with each other, the young couple did not drift into a friendship with others of the group so far.

Back on the bus, they headed for their night's stay.

Emma and Trina reviewed the day, lazily lounging on chairs on Trina's balcony. They mourned for the miles and miles of dead trees.

"Why would anyone want to wind wire tightly around the base of the trees to kill them?" Emma said to Trina angrily. "I would like to get a hold of that brainy nincompoop that came up with that devastating idea. To think anyone would believe eradicating trees would make the land more fertile. Didn't he realize trees provide shade for the cattle and nutrients for the soil. What a tragedy, the idiot."

"Yes, Emma it was a crying shame, to see all those dead trees for such a wrongful reason. Even Elizabeth tried to get our minds off those bleak statues by having us play bowling on the bus."

"We as the Knobby Knees, of the right side of the bus won, against the left side Butterballs victoriously," Emma said crowingly.

Trina said jokingly, "I am afraid I made a fool of myself, when my knees made a cracking sound, much to the total merriment of everyone on the opposing team. Heckling me for being too doddery to bend down for my shot."

"Trina you showed them. You got a strike to the dismay of the jeerers."

"Well let's go to meet the others. I feel like a drink before dinner tonight." Trina arose. They went into the room to pick up their purses.

As they walked out into the hallway, they smiled at their neighbors a Canadian couple. They were exiting their room across the hall. They gave the Clark's a friendly greeting. All were expressing joys of the trip during the elevator's descent.

Over drinks with our usual group, Trina was able to wind down from the day's outing. Sandra and Ron were cutting up Max for his efforts at the bowling contest that afternoon saying he was responsible for the Butterball's loss.

Max quickly chided his wife. "Elaine, you certainly helped with the loss too but I love you anyways." Giving her a big hug and a playful kiss to change the topic.

Ron wasn't going to let Max off that easy. "But Max, you were bragging about your bowling expertise, while others were taking their turns. But come your turn you blew it, big time."

"Yeah, but I did it with such style, didn't I?" Max replied.

"A score beats style anytime," said Sandra chidingly.

Emma got in on the banter. "Max, I did so appreciate your very graceful performance, so much so that our Knobby Knees won."

Max at last did look sheepishly at Ron, Sandra and Elaine.

Jumping up Max said, "it's time for dinner, isn't it?" Heading for the dining room and letting the others follow his lead.

Dinner was enticing along with the playful mockery that seemed to surround all their mealtimes now.

After dinner, they wandered into the lounge to toast the journey past and to the unknown ahead. After which they departed to their rooms to sleep so they would awaken refreshed for the next day's journey.

SEVEN

Marc was in his usual jovial humor the next morning. He took the opportunity to tease Trina about being on time for a change. She playfully patted his cheek like she was hitting him and they both laughed.

She tried to ease past two ladies that were arguing over location of their seats for the day. Some people just could not figure out this seat rotation of moving two seats towards the back of the bus if you sit on the left side and two seats towards the front on the right side. Surely, they should have figured it out by now as they had all been doing this for a week, but I guess not.

Elizabeth gave her usual early morning commentary, so we would know the day's events. Marc was getting the bus under way, Elizabeth's voice wavered as her body swayed to and fro, as the huge coach swung over the curb and out into traffic.

"Today's adventure will take us to 'The Sugar Capital' Mackay. The picturesque town with many palm trees and quaint buildings residing along the Pioneer River. A camera buff's dream place, which will also be our morning tea break." After many miles had passed the bus swung into Mackay.

After a quick gulp of tea, Emma was out the door with her trusty camera. Luckily, Trina had decided to sit with Ron and Sandra also today knowing Emma would abandon her. They did finish early enough to take in some of the town's ambiance. It was well worth the glimpse. Trina's eyes perceived an interesting building on the corner with a plaque dating back to 1830. After they stood in admiration for a bit, they continued to wander. Their path eventually led them back to the coach and onto their next venture.

After driving for a considerable time and seeing no towns only flatland and a few dwellings, there appeared on the horizon a town called Airlie Beach. The town had emerged as if out of nowhere in a land forgotten. Elizabeth said, "Airlie Beach is the main accommodation area opposite Whitsunday Islands. We will be stopping for lunch here."

The lunch stop sustenance for Trina was quiche, salad and iced tea from the fairly extensive menu. Mainly, it was the iced tea her parched mouth was yearning for. There had been a lot of light-hearted shouting and high jinxes in the team sports on the coach, alleviating the miles of miles of sameness during the morning drive.

It was early afternoon when the coach approached Shute Harbor where they transferred to their Catamaran ride on the boat Hamilton 2000. The boat negotiated through the calm waters of the Whitsunday Passage with its islands erupting from the sea. Hamilton Island was a large island in the middle of the passage. It was to be their destination for a couple of days.

This most flamboyant resort island, was quite different from Fraser Island. Hamilton Island was undeniably inhabited, with the spectacle of extravagant high-rise tower hotels directly in front of them as they approached the wharf. An array of restaurants and shops were visible off to our left. Executive type homes were splayed on the hillside.

While giving out the keys to their rooms, along with meal tickets for breakfast only, Elizabeth stated. "The breakfast tickets are usable in several complex hotels. The rest of the meals are to be in restaurants of your own choice from the many available as you witnessed from the wharf, along with the hotel restaurants. We will have our tour of the island tomorrow. Otherwise you are on your own for the two days you are here." They all were parading expectantly to their rooms. Many were looking around with curiosity.

Emma and Trina were occupying the same room at this hotel arranged by Marc at their request. He was such an accommodating young guy.

The Hamilton Beach Resort Hotel had a thirteenth floor, where they were domiciled in Room 1313. They acknowledged to each other thankfully, neither of them was superstitions. Both glancing around the room which was very posh like the hotel reception area.

They took in the panoramic view of water and more water before them.

When they looked straight down from their balcony, they could see three pools of various shapes and sizes as part of the expansive hotel grounds. Trina mentioned, "isn't that odd those multiple pools are also displayed at the other hotel nearby as well."

Emma pointed with a breath of awe. "Look outward to the wonderful beach area in the bay and beyond." Trina lifted her eyes to see the expanse of blue water of the Whitsunday Passage continuing to Dent Island in the distance.

After enjoying the view, they refreshed themselves. They were anxious to be out to observe their surroundings. Their escape from the room's confinement was made hurriedly.

Leaving the hotel grounds behind, they wandered around the other hotels to share their glamour and decadence. The Hyatt prominently displayed brochures that promoted the most elaborate wedding packages. This internationally famous event on Hamilton Island mostly catered to Japanese weddings but was available to anyone.

The bell boy noted their interest saying. "It is cheaper to fly here from Japan with their entire guests because weddings in their own country were unaffordable. The wedding package included Bridal Suite, wedding dress, bridesmaid dresses and tuxedos. Along with the flowers, a decorated limousine and a chapel complete with minister if required. A posh reception and photographer, completed the package."

"Another part of the Japanese wedding ritual was for the bride and groom to provide each guest with a gift. Then after the wedding was over, the guests in return provided a gift for the bride and groom. Naturally the shops flourished with these types of gifts making the ritual beneficial to the island's economy." He gave them a smile as he finished.

Thanking him with added smiles of gratitude, they stepped out the Hyatt Hotel. Immediately seeing a decorated limo, indicating a wedding was due to take place. The lovely bridesmaids appeared, only to linger on the hotel steps awaiting the bride. Trina loitered around in hopes of seeing the bride in her finery but she did not emerge.

Emma was still sauntering and Trina scurried to catch up.

They walked over to the quaint church, infusing the air with music. The wedding guests were entering. Trina, sentimental about weddings, had the yearning to enter.

Not Emma. None of that marriage nonsense for her was her comment as she continued walking. She was anxious to get away from there.

As Trina was turning away, she glimpsed the familiar figure of a man, then the dark interior swallowed him with the limousine's arrival. Her heart gave a flutter. She felt sure that it had been 'Mr. Blue Eyes,' as she loved to call him rather than the more formal Mr. Hunter. Maybe it was the combination of the heart-rending music or the wedding that caused her heart to react but deep down she knew it had been **him.**

She did linger to witness the bride alight from the limousine. She wore a traditional Japanese dress with threads of gold scrolled on an ivory background in an intricate pattern, with tiny seed pearls glistening in the sunlight. The five bridesmaids were wearing traditional western bridesmaid's dresses the hotel provided, as they congregated before the door. The combination of the dresses in shades of light and dark green made the bride's traditional dress more significant.

Emma was calling her trying to draw her away. Trina expressed her wish for a photo of the bride.

"I am not having anything to do with that falderal," Emma was muttering as she turned away.

Trina started after her, maybe she had had a bad experience in marriage. Emma had not shared much about her private life with her as of yet.

Leaving the scene of the nuptials behind her sauntering to join up with Emma. Soon she was deep in thought. *Was it really him or did I only want to believe it was him? Or was it the romantic setting of the charming church and the nostalgic music drifting on the evening air.*

Emma wasn't giving Trina much chance to dwell on her thoughts. She was plaintively requesting, "let's hit an eatery, it is seven o'clock."

Trina did recognize her hunger once she got past the fluttering of her heart.

The two then headed to the wharf area where most of the restaurants were located. Emma was always hungry when she wasn't merrily snapping pictures. Trina realized this during their lengthy trip together.

Emma apparently loved pizza finding a place nestled ahead. The menu included quite a variety. They shared a Thai chicken pizza and draft beer. Quick meals were Emma's motto.

She couldn't abide being away from her camera, the extension of her arm. Emma was an unstoppable force with the need to capture her surroundings. This was all too much for Trina, whose little camera sporadically claimed an imprint or two. Emma was all angles, depths and shutter speed while Trina pushed a lone button with no positive expectations.

They finally arrived back at the hotel to be greeted by a flashing light on the phone indicating a message. Emma dived for the phone in her usual perpetual motion manner. Perhaps that is why she enjoyed her photo taking so much, enabling her to keep moving.

She was calling the front desk. "It is for you Trina." Handing over the phone.

Trina told the lady's voice to read the message. "Mrs. Grant, the message reads, 'I am at the wedding reception at the Hyatt. I want to meet with you, if possible. Please call the Hyatt and have me paged. My name is Logan Hunter. Will explain when we meet. Hope to see you. I have to leave at ten to catch a plane.'"

Trina glanced quickly at her watch, dropping the phone back on its cradle. The dial showed the hands were at 10:13.

Emma watched her face, which went from happy to despair. "What's the matter?"

"Mr. Hunter wants to meet with me but he left the hotel at ten to catch a plane."

"Quick, phone the hotel desk and get her to phone the airport and have him paged there. They will know the phone number."

Trina quickly called the reception desk and they put her call through to the local airport, but the plane for Cairns had already taken off at 10:15 the voice said. She sadly cradled the receiver.

"He is gone, isn't he?" Emma asked knowing full well the answer. Trina looked so sad nodding her head yes.

"Tell me what his message said."

"Oh Emma," Trina said her voice breaking, "he wanted to meet with me to explain everything. I have missed him again. He was at the wedding, we saw earlier at the church. I was supposed to have him paged at the wedding reception at the Hyatt. But he had to catch a plane at ten." Dropping to the bed despondently. "His full name is Logan Hunter. Oh Emma, I missed him."

"Trina, I am so sorry. It's my fault I kept you out so late. I did want to see everything in one night," Emma said wretchedly.

"No, it is all right."

"It is not all right, I just didn't want to miss anything but we do have all day tomorrow and I should have taken that into consideration. I'm sorry."

"At least now I know his name, and I can stop calling him, Mr. Blue Eyes. But I am wondering what he wants to explain to me. What could possibly be important about me to him? In the beginning his look was not the least bit friendly but definitely ominous when I was in Sydney. I was quite disturbed at the time by his penetrating stare."

Trina slumped back onto the bed letting her disappointment totally consume her. So close to an answer but now she would never know what the mystery was about.

—

Trina's next day started with a resolve, to not let her disappointment over-shadow her enjoyment of the island and all it offered.

Destiny was just not letting the 'meeting' occur so she had to put it behind her. With her decision made and her chin firmly up, they headed to the Dolphin Room at the Holiday Inn for breakfast. The dining room was quite unique, it held a glass floor to ceiling wall aquarium at the far end. While they ate, there were a couple of dolphins frolicking, to their enjoyment. The room was well named.

After breakfast, they met with the rest of the group for an island tour. The tour guide's comments were. "The island is privately owned, 75% is preserved as a National Park. The other 25% included resort hotels, private executive homes, shopping area with restaurants. There is also an international airport and two ports. One port with a 200-boat marina for yachts and sailboats. The other port was where the Hamilton 2000 and it's like were docked."

Passing some elaborate executive homes Trina asked. "Emma, what would it be like to live here year-round? Does the view make their lives richer? Or does it become mundane after a while, this island living."

"For me it would," Emma replied easily.

The bus ventured to the hillside lookout for the expanding view of the hotel complex and to the yacht marina below. The two women stood side by side looking down. They noted the millions of dollars tied up by a few bonding ropes swaying in the gentle wavy moorage in one direction and the luxurious hotels in the other.

Neither taking in the technology or the shiny bells and whistles of the yachts or the prosperity of the hotels. Their minds going in entirely different directions. Trina thinking of faraway places to sail. Emma's picking the best angle while adjusting her focus of the lens.

Later after going to the Koala Park, the morning ended. They headed back to their hotel for some free time or a siesta. The tour guide mentioned. "Be careful as the temperature is soaring. Most activities on the island come to a standstill between 11:30 and 2:30 p.m. because of the excessive heat."

When they descended from the bus, Emma looked up to see the balcony railing of her hotel covered by big white birds. Naturally Emma was heading that way quickly yelling over her shoulder. "Come on Trina, we need to go to our room right away."

Trina ignored her, trying to finish up some arrangements for dinner. Twelve of them were planning to dine together at the Dynasty Chinese Restaurant at the wharf for their last night on the island.

Emma was long gone when goodbyes were said but she caught up with her at the elevator. "What is your hurry?"

"A picture of a lifetime if we hurry."

"What picture?"

"You will see when we get to our room. I think a bunch of cockatoos landed on our balcony and I want to get up there." Emma was franticly watching the three elevator indicators slowly moving upward. "Surely one should be coming down soon," Emma said impatiently.

"You could have gone up without me you know."

"I tried to but I just missed the last elevator by seconds." Emma was shifting from foot to foot, as though that would help bring the ascending elevator back sooner.

Trina watched her with interest this girl was in her usual perpetual motion. She got tired watching the continuous movement of her lithe body.

At last, the elevator pinged and threw back its doors. Several people spewed out while Emma was trying to tactfully slink in to press the button for their floor.

"Hurry! Hurry!" she was saying as the elevator took its own sweet time climbing and climbing. She raced out of the elevator as the doors slid back and loped to the door of their room. She was pushing the door open as Trina got there.

When they looked out onto the balcony, there were ten huge white birds and numerous smaller green parrots parading on the railing. They both took pictures from inside the room but that wasn't close enough for Emma. She stealthily crepted outside, waving quietly at Trina to join her.

The parrots took flight but the cockatoos kept preening for the camera and even seemed to be clowning around and kissing for their benefit. Emma ended up feeding them from her hand, as the cockatoos hung around seemly expecting payment for their posing services. Afterwards, flapping their wings they took off.

Experiencing the hottest weather since starting the trip, the two headed inside to their air-conditioned room. Lunch was a snack of fruit, which they had collected along the way, as neither were really hungry. Even Emma's body movement was curtailed to keep cool.

Trina suggested, "Emma instead of using the pools, let's swim in the water at the beach, we can see from our balcony."

"Okay but only after the heat isn't so intense. No way am I leaving this air-conditioned room at the moment."

When they eventually left the hotel, they ended up cooling off water wadding while watching the stranded sea urchins near the shore. Seashells littered the beach abundantly. Trina was picking up some of the more interesting ones for her seashell collection from her worldwide travels.

Dinner that night at the Dynasty Chinese Restaurant was a lot of fun. All seemed in a jovial mood with lots of joking and laughter.

They sat at low lacquered tables on colorful cushions in Chinese tradition of the restaurant that was quite affluent in its decor. The tasty dinner of varied Chinese dishes, seemed to be a nice way to end the day on this lavish island. They dubbed it 'the Rich and the Ridiculous' laughingly agreed by all.

chapter

EIGHT

O ur group of merry wanderers with great expectation, boarded the Hamilton 2000. No one seemed to regret leaving Hamilton Island and its opulence. That was a remarkable difference, from how they felt leaving Fraser Island with its natural beauty.

The catamaran cruised back to Shute Harbor. The tour coach was waiting with an open door, inside a smiling Marc. He had a special good morning for Trina as they larked around, stemming back to her beach fiasco.

Elizabeth's monolog this morning informed them. "We will be stopping in Townsville tonight. The coach is heading back into Airlie Beach again so you can take advantage of the shopping at a terrific Craft shop located in a small mall there." Trina purchased a Koala furry pillow for Kathie and a spicy scented potpourri container with an unusual design for Briana.

Later in the afternoon, they stopped at a Gem Place that was Trina's best find of the trip. They entered a spacey unadorned warehouse that contained many rows of tables and display cases. Opals and Emeralds were in abundance as well as other gems. She was in her element here, loving gems the way she did, looking around with enjoyment.

Trina excitedly acquired a brilliant emerald green crystal bell for her bell collection. She found it hard to bypass the rings but she held herself firmly in control, rings were her secret passion. Emma did a lot of looking but did not buy anything. Not Trina, she also purchased a delicate crystal vase for Amanda.

Emma quickly dragged her out of there before she bought anything else. Emma never seemed to buy souvenirs nor did she talk about family. Trina let her have her privacy by not inquiring, just accepted her friendship that made the trip more enjoyable.

———

The highlight in Townsville, third largest city in Queensland, was its magnificent view from the top of Castle Hill. Our big coach had trouble negotiating the steep narrow windy road. Many held their breaths at times, until they reached the top.

While waiting for the camera buffs to return Elizabeth told Trina. "We were supposed to have stayed the night on Magnetic Island. But temporary staff problems at the resort, made it necessary to accommodate the group in Townsville Travelodge instead. I am not going to tell the others, as this might cause more problems. I have been dealing with a small minority of passengers, that seems to show continual dissatisfaction of some sort with all of their accommodations thus far."

"I won't mention it to anyone." Trina gave her a smile of understanding.

Elizabeth thanked her.

The next day, they observed the Townsville Travelodge was shaped like a salt box with the spout open, viewed from their ferry ride to Magnetic Island. Trina's impression of the island was mainly outcroppings of granite and beautiful sandy bays.

The tour guide said, "the island's Koala Park has a breeding program for the preservation and protection of the Koalas and Kangaroos. In most parts of Australia, Australians were allowed to kill them especially the kangaroos. They can be quite destructive, especially when travelling in bands in the Outback."

Some of the members of their group took the opportunity to cuddle the Koalas, posing for pictures with them. It was difficult to get Sandra away as she fell in love with them. Wallabies and Wombats were in a nearby caged area, they viewed in passing.

Emma was more taken with the Mynah bird that called out, "You Bloody Bastard" in very clear diction, to anyone passing his cage. Ron took the opportunity to say. "Max does that bird know you?" Max reacted by laughing.

They slowly ferried back via the Passage route to Mission Beach where their coach met them. The group then headed off to their next hotel stay at Castaway Beach Resort. Thankful to be there after their long day on the water, the group of six arranged to meet for drinks before dinner.

———

Early next morning, Emma and Trina decided to stroll the beach while they waited for their cruise launch to Dunk Island to arrive. Naturally when they started out Trina took some ribbing from her fellow passengers not to be late, not letting her forget her earlier faux pas. Marc and Elizabeth however just said with large smiles on their faces, "just enjoy." Seeing the launch coming they scurried back, boarding with the rest of the tour group.

Elizabeth gave her usual commentary. "Dunk Island is famous for its rainforest, dense jungle, prolific bird life, many butterflies, and fine beaches. There is a swimming pool for your enjoyment or a trail up Mount Kootaloo. Lunch is picnic style."

The group of six traded anecdotes of humor over lunch while some others took advantage of the swimming pool.

"Who is game for a climb?" Ron got up from the picnic table waiting for a response.

"I guess we are doing some climbing next." Trina rose with the others.

The six trooped up the mountain trail, which was clearly marked, to the highest peak of Mount Kootaloo. Along the way they met two German girls, Karen and Hilda from their tour group. They asked if we would join them. Finally reaching the top, Ron and Max were playfully grumbling about height sickness and over-playing stumbling exhaustion. The German girls didn't know what to make of the two men but joined in the laughter anyways.

The view was well worth the climb which looked out over the airport and beyond to the water, on the opposite side of the island from where they had lunch. Ron jokingly tried to supposedly free hand glide. Sandra grabbed him in a panic as he neared the edge. The trip down went smoothly, as Sandra was not letting go of her husband. Ron was more docile as he must have realized, he had scared his wife with his attempted make-belief gliding. Even though his intention was only to be funny with his usual humor.

The idling launch was waiting to take them to a group of islands called the Family Islands. Some of the rock formations took on the appearance of warships sitting in the water.

After a full day of sailing and too many islands, as it seemed after a while for the group, the ferry finally dropped them back at dockside. Arriving back at the resort, the usual six didn't even bother going to their rooms but headed for the lounge. Everyone agreed too many places and too much sun boggles the mind, but unwinding over drinks was pleasant and relaxing after a tiring day.

———

The next day had us trekking into a rainforest forming the Atherton Tablelands. After all the islands and water this was a welcome sight. Trina was thinking that she must have a primitive heart, as rainforests were more to her liking. She roamed happily through the magnificence of the different greens of the plant life, the floral and the fauna. The sun's rays hitting the mossy trees was soothing to her.

They could hear the sound of water as they broke from the dense forest widening into Millaa Millaa Falls in its splendor. Odd that it was a double name.

It was at this point that Emma arranged a group photo of all twenty-eight Canadians from various parts of Canada. Emma had them all laughing so hard with her antics that they all had happy faces when the picture was finally captured. Trina wanted a copy of this picture for sure.

Not to be outdone the Germans asked Emma to do the same for them giving her some addresses to forward the developed picture.

Their lunch stop was to be at the famed Woodleigh Cattle Station owned and run by the Williams Family since 1877. It covered an area of 41,000 acres of space for the 2000 head of cattle. The hospitality of the family and station hands made for gracious hosts. After much information during a tour they were invited for a BBQ. A delicious BBQ steak dinner was served in the gardens around the station house.

One of the very young station hands made a teasing fuss over the lone teenage girl that had boarded in Brisbane. Her parents were happy she was getting some attention. It had been a difficult trip for the girl being the only young person on board, other than the enraptured newlyweds. Everyone watched with amusement at the shy looks she kept passing him, with a giggle at his antics.

Our coach trip continued with a cruise on Lake Barrine. The boat Captain entertained them by feeding the crested hawks in flight as the birds approached the boat. To the groups delight, the hawks put on quite an impressive show never missing a tossed piece of raw meat as they dipped and swooped around them. Finishing off their afternoon's entertainment.

Exiting the coach, they all went to their rooms to get ready for the evening ahead. Trina was looking forward to the night's festivities, a traditional Kup-Mari Feast.

She laid down on the bed while Emma took a shower. She soon dozed off. A familiar man appeared in the distance but she couldn't seem to get close to him no matter how she tried. She felt so disheartened at the illusion so near but still distant as she opened her eyes to Emma's comment. "The showers all yours."

Trina rapidly jumped up from the bed to hide the telltale tears that she felt on her cheeks. Even in her dreams she had no success of solving the mystery.

—

The Kup-Mari Feast was held at the Kewarra Beach Resort in Cairns. The watchers were entertained with amazing feats of the Suriul Titul war dancers' tribal acts to enhance the mystique, pleasurable evening. The younger costumed natives in the group served the native feast while the entrancing dancers performed.

Trina appreciated the way, the huge bonfires cast their light over the shimmering glowing bodies as they undulated to the ever-increasing rhythm of the thundering drums, with speed and intricacy. She was so entranced she did not realize that Emma had left her seat until a hand reached for hers.

She turned to see Logan grinning at her. Trina froze with shock, her eyes widened. He retained a firm grip on her hand as though he was afraid, she would try to escape. Finally, **he** was here with her and all he said was; "Hello."

Gulping shyly Trina replied the same, "hello."

"Will you come with me Trina, we can't talk properly here?" Logan asked invitingly. She looked up at Emma who was standing behind Logan, madly shaking her head 'yes'. Then Trina looked back at Logan. She still was in a state of shock and unsure. Ron and Max were shaking their heads encouragingly 'yes' too, as Trina still hesitated.

She arose with his help. Logan put his hand in the small of her back to gently guide her between the crowded tables. It seemed that he was heading for the resort entrance. They had finally met and all she wanted to do was run and keep running mostly from fright.

The final reckoning was upon them. Trina wasn't sure she could handle the reason for the cloak and danger situation, that had evolved between them since she had first encountered his stare. Memories of Sydney were rushing through her mind. Dread gripped her. But his manner on Fraser Island had been pleasant and endearing.

How can she be wanting and fearful of him at the same time?

Logan was talking in a soothing voice and the pressure on her back was light and non-threatening. Trina realized she hadn't heard anything he had been saying other than catching the words, "resolved tonight."

He led the way to a quiet area near the lobby with a comfortable sofa and lounge chairs, set around for intimate conversation. Needing to delay things Trina asked about the center table, which was obviously made from a tree trunk. He said although he knew her ploy. "It was made from a Kauri tree that is indigenous to New Zealand."

He must have arranged ahead for drinks to appear on their arrival. No sooner had Trina sat down when a girl in native attire appeared with drinks. She placed a flower in Trina's hair. Trina thanked her, knowing that he had probably arranged for the flower too. The charming girl smiled at Logan then she bowed to them both, slowly backing away.

This distraction helped to put Trina at ease. Her drink was in a pineapple with a colorful paper umbrella, and a spear of cherries sprawling out the top. This brought a smile to her lips as she lifted her eyes at last to greet his. Patiently waiting, Logan knew she had been avoiding eye contact with him until now.

"Trina, please don't be fearful of me. I mean you no harm." He gently picked up her hand, holding it lightly to reassure her.

"I only wanted to explain why I was so shocked when I first saw you in the dining room in Sydney, and why I could only stare. You must have wondered surely. You are the mirror image of my late wife, Linda. At first when I looked up, I thought you were Linda sitting there. I was taken aback by the situation. I could only look at you with a horrified stare. It took me a minute or so to come to my senses, realizing that it wasn't Linda. It had sunk in that was impossible. Linda had been deceased for quite a while."

"When I saw you after that I could only stare because I was intrigued with the remarkable resemblance to my wife. When I left Sydney for my usual trip to Fraser Island, I did so with some trepidation of meeting you there. I had found out from Darcy you intended to join the Gold Coast Tour and my resort on Fraser Island would be one of the tours planned stays."

"Did I really remind you of your wife?"

"Yes, you do remarkably." He continued soothingly, "I saw you in Surfers Paradise briefly, and then I knew I just had to make contact with you."

"Unfortunately, when I saw you at the Kingfisher Bay Resort, I was tied up with business, so I couldn't make your acquaintance. I sent you the wine and a message to your room. Fully intending to follow up the next day, but I was called away on family business before I could do so."

She was quietly sipping her pineapple drink. It was the only way she could remove her hand from his, feeling overwhelmed by him. Taking another sip, she waited for the completion of his story.

"I tried again on Hamilton Island as you know, but again regrettably due to commitments it wasn't meant to happen there either. Now after seeing you sitting here tonight, I am sure I have made the right decision, to make physical contact with you."

"Firstly, to reassure you that I meant you no harm. Secondly, because the more I thought about you, I knew I had to meet you. Despite the likeness to my late wife, Linda." Logan paused looking at her pleadingly.

What does someone say in a situation like this? Do I want to be a stand in for an unrequited love? Where would it lead anyway? Trina hesitated before she answered letting these thoughts flow through her mind.

"Well," she finally said, "I tried to think of all kinds of scenarios, but never visualized that it would be my resemblance to someone else. I just don't know what to say."

"Trina, I have a daughter that lives here in Cairns and I would like you to meet her. Would you at least do that for me?"

"Won't that be upsetting for her? I am sure, if the situation was reversed; I would be disturbed to meet someone, whose likeness to my late mother was so prominent."

"Actually, Linda died three years ago and I have been chatting to Sally, my daughter over the past couple of weeks about you. I feel she is prepared to meet you. I want all of us to become friends," Logan stated wistfully.

"Please Trina consider this, as Sally really wants to meet you. To see for herself the likeness, which I might add is quite uncanny."

Hesitantly, Trina replied, "maybe it can be arranged. I go to the Great Barrier Reef by catamaran tomorrow. We should be back to the Tradewinds Hotel where we are staying in Cairns by four or shortly after. Unless you would prefer to meet me at the dock at three," Trina said tensely.

"Wonderful, I will pick you up at the dock. The timing is perfect, that will give Sally time to have Danny up from his nap ready to greet you." Trina nodded her consent apprehensively.

"Now drink up and I will take you back to your party, so you can enjoy the balance of the festivities. You mustn't miss the fire-eaters. I know you will enjoy them." Logan hoping to relax her continued, "that will give you a little time to digest all that I have told you before we meet tomorrow."

Standing up he held out his hand to her and she looked up at him. His deep blue eyes were looking at her kindly, and his expression was friendly. Placing her hand in his, he helped raise her from the sofa. Their eyes met and held, as though they had reached a special understanding.

They arrived back at the bonfire area only to find out that the dancing was over and everyone was heading amassed for the coach departures to their hotels.

Logan squeezed her hand gently. She stepped away from him, feeling a loss as their hands parted. Turning he walked away, letting Trina mingle with the assembled tour group entering the coach.

She did appreciate that Logan left quickly. She didn't want to be singled out right now for special attention. She felt she couldn't handle enquiries into her disappearance from the feast just yet.

When she approached the coach, Emma grabbed her hugging her closely.

"I was so worried I had done the wrong thing by encouraging you to go with him, but I also knew it was really the right thing to do," Emma whispered.

"Emma, I needed to meet with him, to find out the reason for the stares. I need a little time to reflect on all that Logan said. To believe in the wonder of the unusual circumstance. I promise to tell you everything, when we are back in our room for the night."

She entered the coach. Marc winked at her and gave her a deep knowing smile. Apparently, Logan must have approached him before spiriting her away from the festivities. Seems Logan was indeed a caring man.

She strode down the aisle to her seat. To the cheerful teasing remarks of those who had seen her led away. Trina just laughed good naturally.

She also noticed thankfully that Ron and Max were already in their seats at the back of the bus. However, she did not escape, as they both started teasing her as soon as they alighted from the coach at the hotel. These two men had become steadfast cohorts in their shared humor and she was their target at the moment. She knew they were really not meaning any harm, but she was sensitive at the moment to their remarks. Just smiling at their teasing.

Emma was chomping at the bit to get to their room. She was not going to settle down for the night without the complete lowdown on the situation.

"Who would have thought it would be your likeness or mirror image of his late wife," Emma said after Trina had explained the night's clarification. "It seems so farfetched, compared to all the possible scenarios I was expecting. How do you feel about it, now that you have been told?" asked Emma curiously.

"I just don't know. Just sort of odd to be compared to his deceased wife. I understand his feelings, and the unbelievable circumstances leading up to our eventual meeting. The truth is, over the past two weeks, I have secretly hoped for more of a romantic attraction scenario." Trina continued, "but maybe just a little niggling of sadness. So, I don't know what to think now or how it will end. Now after that observation, Good Night, Emma."

"Good Night, Trina. Sweet Dreams! I know that is where this is heading by the way he looked at you tonight," Emma said lasciviously.

chapter
NINE

E mma bounced out of bed excited at the prospect of seeing the famed Great Barrier Reef. Known to her as 'camera heaven' Trina surmised.

She was not that excited. The night had been mostly sleepless in her reruns of her talk with Logan and apprehensive at meeting Sally today.

She opened her eyes reluctantly. Logan was a real person to her now. Was she going to be able to carry this meeting off with his daughter? Fearing the unusual likeness to her deceased mother might upset Sally.

Emma's cheerfulness made her put these thoughts aside for now, dressing for the day of sea wonders. She tried to join Emma in her cheerfulness. Her very enthusiasm for picture taking overshadowed her personal life. Trina really liked her but couldn't help wondering why she was not more forthcoming about herself.

Emma could hardly eat her breakfast. She wanted to be on her way to check her camera equipment.

Trina couldn't eat either, but certainly not from excitement but an inner dread. She should be excited to see Logan again. But she actually had mixed feelings where he was concerned. But the wanting to see him overrode her thoughts on futility. It was the visit with Sally that was clouding the day.

They went from the resort by coach directly to the dock. The Reef Cat vessel took them to Norman Reef, located on the true Outer Barrier Reef.

The ship tied up to a platform on pylons, so they could file out, scurrying in all directions to view all their eyes could take in. Trina stood watching the Reef Cat pull away to continue its daily run of mail to the scattering of islands. It would not be back until after lunch the crew had said. The large platform was stationary but the waves off the boat gave the illusion of riding the waves.

Trina looked around to see what she would do first. She caught a glimpse of Emma disappearing below.

Sandra came over to ask, "do you want to join Ron and me on a ride in the underwater submarine? Max and Elaine will be joining us."

"Yes, I would like to do that."

The submarine took them away from the platform and closer to the actual reef. A recorded voice intoned, 'that it was millions of years old and over 500 meters thick. It was formed from marine polyps, when they die leaving behind hard skeletons accumulating to form the reef. New polyps grow on their dead predecessors. They require sunlight to grow that was penetrating the water.'

The submarine hung in the water giving the feeling of being suspended in time. She observed the reef was a mass of living creatures many quite delicate, wafting in the current. Schools of tiny colorful fish jutted this way then that, ever so quickly. She noted the bigger fish moved more slowly and seemed to ignore the antics of the tiny fish and the submarine's viewing faces. She vaguely heard the others rhapsodizing over the Yellow Face Angel Fish, Sea Anemones and Sea Urchins.

She felt the quiet solitude pass over her in this multicolored underwater world, relaxing her from her inner turmoil. She had heard that water could be calming, deeming now it to be true.

After the submarine docked in its underwater nest, Ron led the way through a hatch into the bowels of the platform. "Someone said you can observe the scuba divers cavorting with sea creatures from the panoramic undersea window which is just ahead." They gathered around the window with interest. Emma wasn't there to their surprise.

Max put in. "Anybody hungry? I am."

"Your always hungry but I agree this time," Elaine said. "I heard when we arrived, there is a substantial array of buffet cuisine upstairs." They all traipsed upstairs to partake of the meal.

"The BBQ faire was delicious," Ron imparted as he rubbed his tummy.

"You didn't eat much Trina," observed Sandra.

"It was good. I didn't want to make a pig of myself," she replied excusing herself from the table with a smile.

Trina headed to the upper level which held lounge chairs for people to bask in the sun. After sitting down, her mind leaped to Logan. She knew she wanted to see him. Encouraged by her romantic implication, she had developed in her mind after Fraser Island. Regardless of what would eventually transpire.

The sun's heat finally penetrated her musings as she saw the Reef Cat coming in the distance.

She looked around for Emma that hadn't appeared since they had arrived on the platform. She finally showed up with the Reef Cat's arrival. Her fixation with her camera was becoming a bit annoying to her new friends.

———

Luckily, Logan was there when the Reef Cat docked. The rest were going onto Marine Land to observe more mammals of the sea and swim with the dolphins. Trina didn't really want to go as she had been looking forward to seeing him.

Logan and Trina had to take some good-natured ribbing before they were able to escape. Not to be out done by their cheerful comments, he playfully placed his arm around Trina and drew her close against his muscular body. At the same time, Logan announced, "I promise to return her safely to the hotel before the night is over." That only brought more teasing comments from Ron and Max.

Trina and Logan waved them off before they ventured towards his car, a grey Mercedes. He opened the door for her and she nervously tried to seat herself gracefully. She watched him with interested eyes, as he went around the front of the car. His smiling expression was a comfort but her insides were still a flutter. She was still not entirely happy about the reason for this upcoming visit. Entering the car, he reached over and squeezed her clenched hands. "It will be okay. Don't worry." The powerful motor leaped into life. Logan slowly entered the busy thoroughfare.

He talked about various subjects, after he had inquired about her excursion to the reef. She couldn't recall much of the conversation but she was sure Logan had coaxed some dialogue out of her.

All too soon, they seemed to arrive at their destination. Parking the car before a rambling ranch style house, in warm colors of green and white. Its flowering shrubs and green expanse of lawn made an attractive setting.

The door flew open and a little body sped to the edge of the veranda. Logan quickly advanced to catch a leaping giggling boy in his arms. The mother was framed in the doorway her half smile, showing her concern. Was it for the leaping child or the meeting that was to take place?

Logan was holding the boy over his head, to his laughing. "Hi Grampa."

He turned to Trina with the cheerful boy snuggling into his arms. "This young scallywag is Danny and this fair lady is Trina Grant."

"Grampa I am not a thallyag. I am a little boy." Without a new breath he continued. "Hi Trina."

"Hi Danny. It's nice to meet you," Trina said smiling widely.

"Trina, I also want you to meet my daughter, Sally Brown."

With a look of astonishment Sally greeted her.

Trina entered the house to give her a bit of time. She looked around noticing the simplicity. It was quietly elegant. Trina turned to watch Danny hugging and kissing Logan, while delightfully laughing at Logan's exaggerated bear hug.

This was also giving her time to prepare for Sally's comments. Trina knew from Sally's expression, that she did look the mirror image or a great likeness to her mother.

In the living room, Sally gazed fixedly at Trina again hardly breathing.

"Oh Dad, she is just like mother so much so that when you first set eyes on her, you must have thought it was mother returned."

"Yes Sally, I certainly did a double take. My eyes kept coming back to her so often and in such a way that it must have made her feel very uncomfortable. I couldn't help myself. I wanted to go over to her table, and touch her and call her Linda."

"Thank goodness you didn't. Although I did wonder at the time, why I was the focus of your staring expression. I was feeling strange when my eyes happened to roam in your direction, only for our eyes to meet in direct contact. Yours seemed to be devouring me," said Trina.

"Well you must admit now that you know the circumstances, that it was a natural reaction," replied Logan hopefully.

"Would you like a drink, Trina? I'm sorry for keeping you standing.

Please sit down and make yourself comfortable." Sally invited, then turning to Danny. "Danny, please give Grampa a break from your shenanigans."

"It's all right," said Logan sitting down on the sofa and placing Danny on the floor in front of him. "We'll just entertain each other, while you and Trina go in to the kitchen to get the drinks. That way you can get to know each other and talk a little bit." He grinned at Trina encouragingly.

Sally led the way through into the spacious kitchen with its gleaming modern appliances. It was sunny looking with flocks of little daisies splaying the walls artfully. She reached into the upper cupboard beside the enamel sink for the tall glasses.

"Is iced tea okay?" To Trina's assent, Sally went to the fridge to remove the lemon-flavored iced tea.

"Did my father tell you how my mother died?"

"No," Trina said cautiously.

"The shock of seeing her again, Dad must have been disturbed for an instant. It has been three years since she passed away." Sally's voice was soft.

"I will show you a picture of her later so you will see what we mean. My mother was not ill very long. She developed problems after she picked up a serious flu virus, that eventually turned into pneumonia. Our thinking was a minor situation at the time but turned out to be fatal," she said with sadness in her voice.

"Somehow mother knew she would never recover, so she made my father promise to only mourn her for a brief period. Then he was to find someone socially he could share his life with and eventually marry. So far, he has never met anyone and you are the first woman that he has shown an interest in. I know his social life has been active but only what is required of him as part of his position in the hotel community." Pausing. "Now you Trina, how do you feel about all this?"

Trina took a moment to think before answering. "Well I must say it has been overwhelming and quite disconcerting. Peculiarly when I learned, I drew your father's interest because of the resemblance to his late wife. He never said what happened to her." She paused still thinking. "It was not easy to accept that connection at first. Sort of a sick feeling in my stomach I guess, and a slight anxiety that the circumstances was sad."

Sally poured the iced tea into tall glasses with a slice of lemon floating around in each, placing them on a tray. She lifted the lid of the cookie jar sitting on the spacious counter, removing some to a floral plate, as she looked at Trina once again.

"I think my Dad is hoping I will be able to reassure you that he is a nice sociable man, after his unusual stares and fleeting recognitions. That is the impression I was getting from his conversations about you."

Suddenly it dawned on Trina that this young woman standing before her was quite formally dressed, compared to her own casual and slightly wrinkled attire. Sally's dress was a paisley print sundress that flowed around her as she attended to the orange juice drink for Danny. The light multi shades of blues complimented her blond hair and her blue eyes similar to her father's.

"Please excuse my outfit, your father picked me up at the tour boat. Casual wear was more appropriate for the viewing of the reef," Trina apologized.

"Dad did warn me that you were being picked up at the dock. I should have realized and dressed accordingly."

Trina hadn't meant to demean Sally so she quickly said, "I am pleased to meet you Sally, even though I was a bit apprehensive."

"I am glad you came. The fact that I knew ahead of time that there was a likeness to my Mom, made it easier for me to handle; than it was for Dad seeing you for the first time."

"Dad did tell you, we want you to stay for dinner. Oh dear, I see he didn't by your expression. It's just that I would like John, my husband to meet you too. He won't be home until after six. Shall we?" Sally started in the direction of the living room. Trina followed. Sally's voice floated back to her.

"Let's go in to save Dad, as Danny sounds rather exuberant in his playing. We perhaps can talk more this evening."

Trina followed her feeling slightly uncomfortable about letting Sally know that Logan had forgotten to tell her about the dinner.

After placing the tray on the coffee table, Sally with a gay laugh quickly caught Danny's arm during a diving and looping action with a red and white airplane. The propeller churning in a dramatic downward dive.

"What are you and Grampa being so noisy about?" She looked expectantly at her father although she was talking to Danny.

Logan was enjoying himself too as he stopped part way through a dive with his fighter plane, glancing in their direction. He concentrated on their expressions to see if he could determine how well their talk had gone.

"Grampa is trying to shoot my plane down but I keep getting away from him." shouted Danny accompanied by giggles of laughter.

"Danny sit on the sofa beside Grampa and try to be extra careful so you do not spill your orange juice or you will have to sit in the kitchen to have your drink."

Danny scurried up onto the sofa so close to Logan that their legs and bodies were touching as though that would stabilize his body from spilling anything. He then gave his mother an infectious grin, giving him an angelic look with his deep blue eyes and blond curly hair.

Trina approached the sofa where they were sitting. Logan was studying her face intently. He removed his rapt gaze as he accepted the glass Sally was giving him. He reached out to place it on a coaster so as not to mar the black ebony table with its magnificent highly glazed surface. He then placed the small glass of orange juice in Danny's hand. Danny quickly clutched tightly squeezing it till his knuckles showed white as though this would help, the no spilling threat.

Logan said thank you followed by Danny's parroted thank you. Taking a couple of cookies for Danny and him while smiling winningly up at Trina.

"I hope the talk in the kitchen went well? Knowing Sally, I am sure it did."

Before Trina could possibly answer Sally piped up. "Of course, Trina and I got along fabulously. Dad, I feel so comfortable with her, it's as though I have known her for years. And not because she looks like mother but because she is a gracious lady."

Trina smiled down at Logan. "Your daughter has a flare for putting one at ease."

Sally said, "Trina, I set your drink on the table near the sofa chair."

Trina took the angled sofa chair Sally indicated.

"Dad, you didn't let Trina know we were having dinner here tonight and that she would be expected to join us," Sally admonished.

"Sally, I didn't know how this was going to go. I didn't want to place Trina in a difficult position, or what your reaction might be to her." Logan looked at Trina thoughtfully.

"Besides, I vaguely remember mentioning having dinner together, while asking her to meet with you. Knowing the similarity to your mother must have been a concern, she probably didn't take it in." Trina felt a bit embarrassed because that was probably what happened as she remembered him talking but her mind not absorbing all.

Inclining his head towards Trina, Logan asked, "would you like to come back for dinner to meet John?" He added a hopeful. "Please."

Trina glanced from one to the other, smiling she replied, "I would like that very much and I also would like to meet John."

Sally inquired if seven o'clock would give them enough time to return. Logan relaxed his body for the first time since he entered the house. He had not been aware of how tense he felt. Letting out a sighing breathe he said, "that should be fine." Looking to Trina for confirmation, noting her nod yes.

Patting Danny's head lovingly Logan reiterated. "Well Danny, Mrs. Grant must like me after all to agree to come back, and I know she must like you too." No doubt in his voice.

Danny looked up at Logan with worshipping eyes. "I like her too, Grampa but can I call her Trina?"

Sally interjected, "You may call her Auntie Trina. I'm sure she will not mind, will you?" Looking at Trina.

"I would like Danny to call me Auntie very much. You have made me feel part of the family already," Trina replied easily.

"Auntie Trina will you stay and play planes with me and Grampa?"

"No champ not right now." Logan stood up carefully as Danny was still plastered against him even though he had finished his juice and cookies. Logan held out his hand to Trina in an inviting way saying, "we had better leave now to give Sally time to prepare the dinner."

Trina placed her hand in Logan's trustingly. Standing up while glancing at Sally. "Thank you Sally and Danny, for making my visit so enjoyable. I look forward to being with you for dinner."

Danny piped up, "I really like you Auntie Trina."

Logan said proudly, "that's my boy, you have good taste."

Sally inserted after this exchange. "You're welcome Trina any time. I want you to feel like you could be part of the family. Don't we Danny?" Who was now beside her clutching her hand in the doorway.

"Goodbye, come back soon Grampa and Auntie Trina." Giving them a winning smile and then looked up at his mother for approval.

"Goodbye Danny," said Logan and Trina in unison then they all laughed.

Logan leaned forward to drop a kiss on Danny's upturned face then one on Sally's cheek. Slipping his hand under Trina's arm he guided her towards the car.

Danny was enthusiastically waving and swiveling his head back and forth between his mother and the car, while Logan and Trina pulled away waving.

Smiling Sally waved too.

chapter
TEN

"Are you sure you want to return for dinner? I could always phone and cancel if you are the lease bit uncomfortable with it. Sally would understand after all I'm sure this is entirely overwhelming for you."

Taking a deep breath Trina faced Logan.

What was she getting into and where was this heading? She was supposed to be on a relaxing fun filled vacation, instead she was on a roller coaster ride of emotions. She could end it now or wait until after the dinner.

Logan was concerned. Her hesitation was not good. He was waiting with an inner churning. He wanted to give her the time she needed but he was dreading the answer might be to end it now. All he knew for sure was that he did not want to end it quite yet. He gave a half grin and concentrated on his driving, knowing the Tradewinds Hotel was appearing on the horizon.

Trina was studying the hotel's shape growing larger and larger as the car was quickly approaching their destination within seconds.

Was it to be goodbye? Was there any point in continuing their meeting? The trip was to end in two days and she would be going on to Darwin.

No, she couldn't justify doing that to Sally and Danny by refusing. They were both expecting her to return for dinner. She just would not feel right letting them down, as Sally wanted her to meet John.

She knew she had to say something. Logan pulled into the hotel parking lot. He turned off the motor and just sat there not looking at her but just waiting with trepidation. He lightly drummed his fingers on the steering wheel, a habit of his.

She gushed. "Yes, I will go for dinner." saying it so fast as though she was afraid she might change her mind.

Logan gave an audible sigh of relief, grabbing her hand, bringing it to his lips to kiss it gently. Trina laughed nervously. His gallant kiss made her heart soar. He smiled in relief.

The arrangements were made for Logan to meet her at 6:30 for a drink in the lounge. She approached the hotel entrance knowing Emma would pounce on her, for all the details.

She was now regretting the decision to have her in the same room. She had so much to think about. Emma and her prattling would distract her. Just maybe she was off somewhere with her camera or with the others from the group of six. She knew it was too much to hope for, as she opened the door.

Emma raced to her and dragged her towards the chairs beside the window.

No escape here, although she wanted to spend the time getting ready for her dinner date.

"Tell me, tell me what happened? Did the daughter agree with her father? How did she respond to you? Are you seeing Logan again? Does this relationship have a future?"

"Hold it Emma." Trina looked down at her watch. "Yes, I am seeing Logan again, but I have to get ready now as he is picking me up soon, to take me to dinner at his daughter's house." Rising to make a smooth exit to the bathroom, while grabbing her one and only dress from the hanger. She wanted to shower to relax a bit.

Emma could be overpowering at times but then Trina probably would be too if their positions were reversed. She wasn't sure she wanted to share all, at this point in time.

After a quick shower and her makeup applied, she viewed herself in the mirror. The dress had survived the trip quite well, considering the continual packing and unpacking. The green nylon dress with a floral pattern of pale lilac flowers looked striking on her. The low-rounded neckline and cap sleeves showing off her glowing tan.

Her eyes were glowing too, grey shot through with green highlights of color. Her hair was next to be attacked. All this sea air and wind was playing havoc with her usual wavy hair, that was now becoming unruly curls. Taming the hair was a challenge, but was successful finally.

Entering the room, with a tiny bit of guilt at ignoring Emma's questions. She felt she should address them. Walking over to Emma still sitting in a chair by the window.

"Yes Sally, his daughter was stunned at first but she quickly recovered, and made me most welcome. Her overtures of friendliness, is the reason I am going back for dinner tonight. I am not sure about Logan or where that will lead, as I am leaving Cairns in two days to go to Darwin. There doesn't seem to be much point in continuing. Logan at least put my mind at rest as to why he had been staring at me so intensely."

Emma didn't agree. "Logan is such an attractive man. I think you had better rethink that. I can certainly visualize you as a great couple."

"Emma, this from you who spurns the opposite sex, at each and every turn on this trip. Except for Max and Ron who are already taken."

"I know Trina but this is about you. I think you are ready for some romance in your life. After all you have been divorced for ten years. You certainly don't pine for your ex, so what's the problem?"

"Distance," Trina replied. "Now I have to go. I promised I would meet Logan downstairs for a drink at 6:30."

"Well, have a great dinner and don't hurry back on my account," Emma said.

Trina stepped from the elevator, her eyes drawn immediately to the vivid blue eyes watching the elevator doors. She smiled answering the wide grin as they moved towards each other. She could tell by his look that he was still affected by the closeness to his wife's image. It must bother him when she first appears, as she was sure he must have loved his wife deeply. Especially because her illness seized her so suddenly. They had never really discussed that part.

Trina sort of drew back, but there was no reserve in the way Logan greeted her. "You look lovely, my dear. That color brings out the green highlights in your eyes." He grasped her elbow lightly, as they turned towards the lounge.

"We should have time for at least one drink before we leave, as I arranged with Sally to be a little bit later than we previously planned."

The lounge was busy but there were still seats available. He chose two sofa chairs near the window, overlooking a water fountain under soft colored lights.

After placing their order for drinks, Logan inquired. "How do you feel about the strange circumstances of our meeting?"

Trina replied smoothly, "I am handling it fairly well now. However, Emma keeps bombarding me with questions about you."

"We will have to keep you out later, so she will be asleep when you return. I think I can handle that without difficulty. What is scheduled for your tour group tomorrow?"

"We are going on the Kuranda Rail Train ride to Kuranda Village."

"You will enjoy that. I wish I could go with you, but unfortunately, I have a business meeting."

Trina hesitated while the waitress placed their drinks on the table.

"What exactly do you do?"

"My family owns a hotel chain of family style smaller hotels. We make them inviting with a friendly ambiance and decor. Our congenial staff offers an alternative to the classness of larger hotels, that are so popular with the tourist trade."

"Every three months, I tour from one hotel to the other checking on their management, clearing up any problems and address their needs. It just happens this was my regular time to make the trip north. That is why you have seen me in several places on your tour, and why we kept missing each other on the way."

"Otherwise, I am mostly at the Kingfisher Bay Resort on Fraser Island, as that resort, I do own personally. I also spend time in Sydney as that is where the administration is for our hotels," Logan asked with a pleased voice, "by the way, what did you think of Fraser Island?"

Trina smiled with a special faraway look, visualizing her stay there.

"I liked it very much, in fact at one point during the tour of the island, I felt so content I wanted to stay on the island forever. Your grand gesture of wine added to the ambiance." She picked up her glass and sipped her drink, while she waited for his reaction to her comment.

Logan's wide grin appeared instantly. "Would you like to go back again?" he queried hopefully.

"I certainly would if I had the time, and I would love to return to

Sydney also," Trina said longingly. Rather sad that the trip was drawing to a close. Just five more days. Sighing Trina continued, "I always dread the last day of a tour because you quickly make such good friends intermingling daily. Tomorrow is the last day, and really the last day you will spend with that person in your lifetime. It is always sad for me." She gave another sigh. "I have kept a few friends over the years, that I've met on other trips. I have either been to their homes or met them some place closer to me but it is difficult living so far apart. Maintaining distant friendships is difficult."

She knew she was trying to explain the sadness she was feeling about Emma and the others but also the undeniable distance of their own connection.

Logan did not reply but stood up indicating they were leaving. Having finished their drinks as time was passing. "Are you ready?"

As they sped through the night, the bright lights of Cairns surrounded them.

He was quiet as though he was contemplating her departure and the distance. She commented on the sights of Cairns in order to try to draw his thoughts back to the present. She knew she had given him an explanation that involved them too. There was no conclusion other than parting.

But she also knew, she had to lighten the mood, as they would be arriving at Sally's soon. Thankfully Logan began exchanging an easy dialog with her. She was relieved as Sally's house came into view.

Danny must have been watching for them because the door opened with a jerk, as Logan was opening the car door for Trina. Danny was yelling.

"Hi Grampa. Hi Auntie Trina." They walked quickly up the sidewalk to the house. Logan caught Danny, knowing he would do his usual flying leap, amidst giggles of glee.

Trina was watching with pleasure, seeing Logan had a good relationship with his grandson, knowing each other well. So often grandparents did not live near enough, or were too busy to form this kind of closeness. The thought struck her that she missed her own family. She really hadn't thought of them much on this trip, as a bit of guilt set in.

She looked up at the laughing couple under the glow of the veranda light. Like Sally, John's reaction was a hesitation in a breath before he greeted Trina.

Acknowledging her introduction to him, she accepted his outstretched hand. Sally stepped back. "Come in, dinner is almost ready." Logan exchanged kisses with her, shaking John's hand in greeting.

Sally asked, "John don't you agree it is startling the ironic likeness Trina has to my mother?"

"Yes. It must have been hard for you to handle, Dad. The first few times you saw her," John replied wonderingly.

"I am afraid my stares were making Trina quite uncomfortable to say the least. I certainly wanted to go over and address her as Linda." He paused. "Trina must have thought I was a stalker or something, the way I was pursuing her and watching her with stares," Logan disclosed.

Sally looked at Trina for her reaction to Logan's comments.

"Did you really think that Trina?"

"Yes, he was so intense the times when I encountered his eyes upon me. I even tried a smile once but that didn't change the intensity of his eyes. I just didn't know what to think." She gave a little laugh.

Logan breezily said to lighten the mood.

"I was pleased she allowed me to explain myself, when we finally met. I also wanted her to meet you Sally. Knowing after what I said, you were intrigued to meet with her."

"I was certainly amazed at the likeness." Sally directed them towards the dining room, as dinner was ready to be served. The table had an attractive flower arrangement in the center, which must have come from her garden. The china pattern of the dishes was similar to the one Briana possessed.

Logan was carrying the squiggling Danny. He certainly adored him, thought Trina.

"Will you sit down here Trina, Dad, you and Danny can sit across the table from her."

Danny who had not had much opportunity as yet to address Trina said. "You look pretty tonight Auntie Trina. Isn't she Grampa?"

"Yes, Danny she is very pretty tonight," watching Trina warmly.

"Danny, you are a man of my heart." She laughed gaily.

John and Sally arrived with the dinner.

During the meal Trina recognized with the free-flowing conversation, an indication that Logan shared their company frequently, with a good rapport with John.

Danny asked. "Auntie Trina, Mommy said you live in Canada. I don't know where Canada is. Is it far?"

"Yes Danny, far-far away. I came by plane. I don't know how to explain the distance but it is like leaving after breakfast and arriving the next day after breakfast."

"That is far. You sleep on a plane?"

"Yes, people sleep on planes at night."

"I would miss Teddy and my blankie." Danny said sadly. Trina laughed.

He really didn't get the significance of the distance but she did only too well. She would be going home soon, never to see this family again.

Logan looked over at her, wondering how can I see her again with Canada so far away.

While Sally got Danny ready for bed, Trina studied the picture of her mother that Sally had given her. Linda was indeed remarkably like her. In fact, it was like looking at a picture of herself as she was a few years ago. The resemblance was uncanny. No wonder Logan had such a strong reaction to her, when he first saw her in the dining room at the Hotel Samatra.

"Don't you think it is like you?" Sally's voice startling Trina.

"Yes. They say everyone has a double in this world and your mother must have been mine," replied Trina placing the picture carefully back on the dresser.

"I haven't seen Dad so happy for such a long time. Thank you, Trina, for that at least. He was so shocked at mother's passing. He hasn't shown interest in anyone until he met you. I wish you could have met her. I am sure you would have become good friends."

Trina continued to look at Linda's picture thoughtfully.

"Shall we rejoin John but first Danny wants you to stop in to say good night. Dad is reading him a bedtime story."

Trina hesitated at the door of Danny's room listening to Logan reading in a melodious voice as Danny was drifting into sleep. He stopped when he felt her presence, looking towards her while patting the bed inviting her to join them.

"Looks like this young man is just a nod away from slumber, so I will say good night Danny and leave you both to finish the story." Danny put his arms up towards her longingly so Trina leaned over and hugged him.

Logan said teasingly, "do I get a hug too?"

"Are you sleeping with me Grampa if Auntie Trina hugs you?" asked Danny.

"No Danny," said Logan while tussling the boy's blond curls lovingly. "I just thought I could get a hug that's all." She stepped back smiling.

Logan continued with the story, Trina joined Sally on her return to John.

Over coffee and liqueurs Sally asked Trina about her tour, while John and Logan discussed something regarding hotel business. Logan shortly brought the conversation back to Trina, by telling them about the ribbing from the tour group when he had greeted her at the docks. "They knew I intended to whisk her away."

"Yes, Max and Ron love to tease me but it is meant as a harmless teasing."

"You sound like you get along well with your tour group. Can I get you anything else?" Sally inquired.

"No thank you."

Logan stood up. "I think it is time to go. I should return Trina to her hotel."

John and Sally immediately expressed their pleasure at meeting Trina. Sally invited, "drop in if you have any free time before leaving for home."

Trina specified, "tomorrow's lengthy tour will make that impossible but I will at least phone you to say a final goodbye."

"Good I will look forward to that."

She was included in the goodnight kisses by Sally and John.

———

During the trip back to the hotel, Logan kept up an easy conversation, as though delaying the inevitable closure to their connection.

Trina was deep in thought. *I have met this man, granted in the beginning he appeared sinister. But only because of her similarity to his wife. Now I know him and his family my views have changed. To think I will be saying goodbye with no possibility of continuing this connection. I will be leaving for home soon.*

He felt so alive since they had met. Do I want this to end? His feelings for this woman seemed fonder somehow, than his feelings had ever been for Linda. These thoughts were running through Logan's mind. He pulled the car into the parking lot of a hotel with glittering lights twinkling in a gay dance of sparkle.

Trina came out of her revere and looked around realizing the car had stopped. "This isn't my hotel."

"I know but I don't want the evening to end yet so please come in with me for a nightcap? It can be Perrier water or a soda if you would rather but please come in with me." On a lighter note he said, "Emma won't be asleep yet, will she?"

"All right, you convinced me with that last comment."

Logan held the door open, reaching in to help her out he said, "I would rather celebrate with something special. Our meeting should be toasted in grand style."

When they were seated with the Dom Perignon the maître d had served, Logan raised his glass.

"To a lovely lady that has graced my thoughts for the past two weeks."

Logan touched his glass to hers while looking deeply into her eyes. Then he raised it to his lips, never releasing eye contact. *Can this be the end for us? Like ships that pass in the night. Will it be a lifetime of wondering what ifs...?*

Logan realized he wanted more but how could it be possible.

Is this how it ends? Does he still yearn for Linda? What am I thinking, he is only about fifty and I am about eleven years older? But secretly, the desire was there for more she had to admit.

Logan said "Is... as Trina said "Can...

They both stopped waiting for the other to continue. Then they both laughed.

Logan said. "I want to see you again after tonight so I will give you a call tomorrow evening, when I am free. Is that alright with you?"

"Yes, I would like that too," she said without hesitation.

"Well I had better take you back to your hotel now as it is getting rather late."

As they parted at the elevator in her hotel, Logan leaned forward to place a light kiss on her lips, then quickly backed up and said, "until tomorrow."

She stood there looking at him leave. He glanced around from the door and waved at her. She continued to stand there, mixed feelings playing havoc with her mind until the elevator pinged.

She was hoping not to disturb Emma when she arrived at her room. This night should have ended differently. What is the point in delaying their goodbye? Yet…?

Trina opened the door cautiously and tiptoed into the room. There was a light shining from the bathroom with the door only partly open. The room was emitting a light sound of easy breathing, thankfully Emma was asleep.

chapter
ELEVEN

As the Tour Group arrived back at the Tradewinds Hotel there was a feeling of a day well spent and yet a feeling of regret that the tour was ending. They would depart tomorrow for their home destinations. They leave with good memories and good friends they have left behind.

Like the memories of today when they went on the Kuranda Rail Trip. The spectacular rail journey winds 21 miles from Cairns to Kuranda Village with 15 tunnels, climbing over 9800 feet in the last 13 miles. Trina was excited with the train ride, at the amazing way the train went around the base of the mountains, seeing the tail-end of the train coming out of a tunnel and its many cars forming a complete arc. Ever wending until they reached the Kuranda station decked out with flowers and ferns. "Emma, I feel like we are in the sky entirely separate from the world, so far below us that we no longer can see."

"Yeah, I feel like that too."

During the Tjapukai Aboriginal Show, Max tried the didgeridoo horn but was not successful. Ron was kind enough not to make comment, probably because he was not sure he could do it either.

After having lunch and they were wandering around, a man approached Emma and Trina because they had on their Canada pins. He asked, "where are you from?"

Emma said. "I am from Calgary, Alberta."

Trina said, "I am from Qualicum, Vancouver Island."

He laughed. "It's a small world after all. I live in Parksville."

She joined in his laughter, explaining to Emma, "Parksville is our neighboring town just fifteen minutes from Qualicum. My daughter lives there. Yes, a small world," ended Trina.

All too soon, they boarded the train, to take them back down to Cairns. The trip down was like you were falling from the sky going quite fast. Arriving at the bottom, only to see Marc's greeting smile and the coach for our further journey.

The next stop a ride on an airboat. They were skimming over the sedge filled water, gliding through the tranquil everglades. Witnessing crocodiles basking in the sun. Thank heavens the sun made them euphoric as most of them were quite huge in size. The airboat guide brought a small crocodile on board. It was approximately 3 ft. in length. Some of our group were holding the small wiggling creature.

"Trina, he wants you to hold it while I take a picture."

"Are you kidding, I'll forgo that picture. I can take your picture if you want."

"I take the pictures not you."

"Admit it Emma you don't want to touch it either." Trina grinned broadly.

Emma chuckled she had been caught.

A stop in Port Douglas for tea break completed the final day, as they would be returning to their hotel and some free time.

———

Emma and Trina had arranged to go to the Hogs Breath in Cairns for dinner, with the now famous group of six. Friends of Max and Elaine owned the restaurant. Trina certainly wanted to spend her last evening with her friends. They had become the "compatible six" throughout the journey that had passed all too quickly.

She had not let on that she might be meeting Logan, as nothing definite had been arranged. He would call with details once he knew them. She would have to deal with that when and if there was a message from him.

While Emma was saying her lengthy goodbyes to the rest of the group, and setting up the time they would meet for dinner. Trina went to the desk to enquire if there were any messages for her.

· The clerk handed her a folded message, which Trina took with a lifted heart, which quickly sunk as she scanned the message.

Trina
I am sorry I won't be able to meet with you tonight. I
had to leave, as an emergency came up.
Regrets Logan

Trina quickly crunched up the message in disappointment, that it had come to an end just like her trip. She walked to the elevator with dragging steps, her sprightly gait gone. It was just as well it ended this way because the distance was impossible to breach, besides maybe he intended to say goodbye tonight anyways.

Fortunately, she had avoided saying anything about tonight's possible encounter. Emma did not question the reason for her delay in arriving at their room. Trina wanted to keep this letdown to herself. She was thankful for the time spent preparing for their evening out.

Off to the Hogs Breath went the compatible six. The owner and his fiancée greeted them with exuberance, with a special hi to Max and Elaine.

"We will be serving you personally." This added to the gaiety of the evening.

Although Trina was putting on a brave front, fooling the others. Her disappointment at Logan's leaving was reflected in her extra merry laugh. Would this evening ever end? She was feeling sad for two reasons. Not saying goodbye to Logan and having to say goodbye to these special friends, and tomorrow to everyone on the tour.

———

The day of departure had arrived after an early morning tour of Cairns. Also, they made a visit to the Flying doctor ending up at the Botanical Gardens. Trina was ready to go home but she was booked to go on to Darwin.

At last they were on their way to the airport. Trina's three-day side trip to Darwin was upon her. At least she would be alone and hide her sadness leaving the friends she had made, and the disappointment of not seeing Logan the prior evening.

She had phoned Sally last night to say her promised goodbye. Sally had tried to talk her into staying in Cairns instead of going on to Darwin. Pleading her case by saying Danny had been asking for her. Trina had still said no. She did not want to let on about her failure to deal with Logan's sudden departure from her life, along with the fond memories in Sally's home.

She knew she would breakdown and confess her disappointment to Sally, putting them both in an unhappy predicament. Besides it wouldn't change anything. She still lived too far away to form a proper friendship with this family.

As the airport came into view, her mind was in a turmoil. She just couldn't leave. Maybe being with Sally and Danny would make her feel better. Last night, Sally's persuasion to stay with them in Cairns had been hard to refuse.

These thoughts were tumbling around in her head along with Logan, considering how short a time she had known him. Just outside of the airport, the group stopped for a last opportunity to pick up souvenirs for their love ones. She took the opportunity to look for a phone instead. She excused herself letting the others think she was interested in looking for a washroom.

In answer to her decision to stay in Cairns after all, Sally happily said, "you can have the guest room for as long as you want."

Trina answered, "I still have to go to the airport to say goodbye to everyone, and cancel my flight. I will arrange another flight home in three days' time. I can take a taxi to your place."

Sally was adamant. "I will pick you up at the airport, as Danny likes to go there anyways to see the planes land and takeoff." Trina wondered if she was coming just to make sure that she didn't change her mind.

The airport was a bustling hub of activity. Passengers overshadowed by voices on the loudspeakers announcing the incoming and outgoing flights. Their Tour group was milling around arranging luggage, tickets and addresses of those wanting and needing to continue contact with their new friends, they had gained on this excursion.

No time for thinking, as Trina was joining in on the goodbyes, before she made the changes necessary for her altered transportation home. She still had not let on that this is what she intended to do.

Emma and Trina were exchanging heartfelt hugs and kisses for the special friendship that they had formed. Expressing, they would get together sometime to exchange pictures back in Canada. The others were waiting to say their goodbyes.

Trina hugged each of the two couples and Ron's hug included a message. "If it hadn't been for the group of six this trip wouldn't have been nearly as wonderful." They all cheered at that heartfelt statement. Ron slipped a card into her hand with Sandra and his address saying to keep in touch, and he gave one to Emma too. Elaine had already given them her address at breakfast before Ron and Sandra arrived at the table. Eventually, they all went their own way to their scheduled flights, while Trina headed for the ticket counter.

She was still not sure if she was doing the right thing by staying in Cairns. *Was it going to make it harder to leave being with his family? And what about Logan. There had never been any romantic overtone in his attraction other than one light kiss by the elevator. Was she being fanciful wanting romance at her age?*

After Trina completed her change of travel arrangements, she collected her luggage and proceeded to the departure area where she had arranged to meet Sally and Danny. As she exited the automatic doors, they were at the fence nearby. Danny ran towards her and leaped at her with squeals of delight. Trina knew she had made the right decision, smiling at Sally over Danny's head.

———

The next three days were a whirl of sightseeing, playing with Danny and confidences shared by Sally, about her mother and father. She also talked about the grandparents that didn't come often, being so busy with their many hotels. Trina was feeling her position was between a sister and an aunt. By the way she was being unified into the family by John and Sally each evening, and especially by Sally during the day.

She told Sally all about Briana and her family, about her happy times with them. The births of Scott and Kathie and the life she led on Vancouver Island. She touched on her collapsed marriage and the feeling of failure as a result.

Sally spoke freely about her Mom and the way she grew up with her. Her teenage years, when they shared good times together. How her mother helped her arrange her wedding to John and be there for Danny's birth, staying a month to help with the baby. She expressed how much she still missed her mother. Trina and Sally never seemed to run out of conversation, but they did run out of time each day.

Logan was phoning each night knowing she was spending time with Sally. He had tried to rearrange his commitments to be with them. The conversation always ended in his disappointment in not being there with her.

Sally wanting to delay her departure. "Won't you stay longer so Dad can come to say goodbye personally?"

"I can't, my family will be awaiting my return. I don't want to disappoint them."

Danny put in, "I don't want you to go Auntie Trina."

"I know Danny. I loved being with you," giving him a hug.

"Sally, I am glad I met your father despite the circumstances that brought us together. Your Dad is someone that I found easy to talk with and comfortable to be with. In fact, I am glad I was the mirror image of your mother so that I came into both of your lives. I feel these three days together, was the best part of my trip. The time I spent playing with Danny has been special. He is quite the little charmer. I will certainly miss all of you." Reaching for Sally's hand, she was so overcome in feelings. "I have certainly felt like one of your family. You have a knack for making a person feel comfortable."

Sally said warmly, "it was such a pleasure to have you Trina."

"I am sad that I live so far away, as I wish I could continue to see, Danny, John and you. I will miss the opportunity of being part of your everyday lives. I shall also miss knowing your father."

Sally gave her a hug. "You can always come back again, or just maybe someday we will all come to Canada to see you."

Trina was wishing she had seen Logan one more time before she left for home. She had enjoyed his nightly conversations and his easy humor. Last night's call had been difficult during their final goodbye.

Was this wishful thinking on the part of an aging woman, to want this man in her life in a romantic way. It was interesting to hear at that moment,

Sally say, "my father has shown no interest in one particular woman, until you arrived on the scene.

Wishful thinking or not Trina couldn't help the flutter in her heart at Sally's comment.

———

The next day once again Trina was on the way to the airport. This time for the long journey home. While Sally unloaded her luggage, Danny and Trina were saying their goodbyes.

Danny tearfully strangled her with hugs and kisses. She almost broke down, it tore at her heart. This little boy was very affectionate in his goodbyes.

She tried to disengage herself from his clinging arms with the help of Sally, pulling him into her own arms. "It is all right Danny, we will go in with her so you can see her plane take off. We will find a window to see the plane." Trina knew Sally was trying to distract Danny but she did appreciate Sally's help with her luggage. She had collected extra souvenirs during her stay in Cairns. Danny wanting to help, was holding onto the strap of her carryon with her.

They entered the automatic doors, to be swallowed up by the large space within, amongst the bustling travelers dragging their luggage along with them.

Concentrating on finding her ticket counter. Her ticket was for Qantas Airlines via Honolulu enroute to Vancouver and the island. At the Qantas desk, the cheerful attendant took Trina's ticket to check for her flight record.

She got a startled look on her face. "Mrs. Grant, this is odd but you are scheduled to fly home via Sydney, which is highly unusual."

With a great deal of puzzlement in her voice she continued.

"I have never seen this before. However, that is the way the computer reads. I will try and correct it." She continued keying into the computer.

Was this a computer error or had she unwittingly made the tickets via Sydney. Impossible she wouldn't have done that surely.

"Oh dear, all the flights are fully booked except this one via Sydney. Do you still wish to continue with this flight? Otherwise, the best I can do is put you on a direct flight tomorrow."

Trina looking a little disturbed. "No, I might as well go via this route if that is what my booking says. I just wouldn't feel very comfortable having to plan for another night's accommodation in Cairns. My luggage and I are here now, so we might as well just take this flight."

"Your flight will go from Gate 11 in thirty minutes. You had better go directly to Gate 11 for boarding, as they probably have already started." The attendant looked at Trina with commiseration for the computer error.

She picked up her carryon case and bag, looking for the overhead signs for the direction to Gate 11. Going back to Sally and Danny she said, "that is strange, they have me booked via Sydney. Then I change planes for Honolulu. I thought it would be a direct flight via Honolulu to Vancouver from here."

"Yes, that is strange, too bad you couldn't meet up with Dad while you are there." Then they followed along with the many passengers moving slowly towards their different gates. Some looking intently for the sign directions and others moving along as if they knew exactly where they were going.

As they approached the security area Sally said, "we will try to find a window to watch your plane take off."

Danny grinned at Trina. "I will wave at you; will you wave back?" Bending down Trina hugged him. "Of course, I'll wave."

Sally picked up Danny. Trina hugged them both, exchanging kisses and goodbyes.

With a final wave Trina approached the security line. The long line helped remove the tears that had formed in her eyes at the goodbyes, with that sad parting knowing they might never see each other again.

When she arrived at her gate, they had started boarding. Some entering through the door to the plane, while others were still sitting or standing awaiting the announcement for their assigned seats to be called for boarding. Trina looked at her seat number as the flight attendant announced further blocks of seats ready for boarding, her seat number was included in the latest announcement.

As she walked the long ramp in the direction of the plane, Trina thought, wouldn't it be nice if she could afford to stop over in Sydney for a few days. What a foolish thought, it would be best just to keep going and not let herself in for more sadness. After all she didn't think she could be in Sydney, knowing that Logan might be there and not seeing him.

The Steward and Stewardess at the open door of the plane were waiting with messages of welcome, requesting to see her boarding pass wanting to direct her to her seat. She walked down the aisle glancing at numbers on the overhead luggage compartments looking for seat 20A. When she finally arrived at the seat assigned to her, she glanced at the man sitting in seat 20B, to see if she could get his attention, to enable her way to the window seat. He seemed to be fumbling with the seatbelt buckle.

Trina took the opportunity to put her carryon bags in the open overhead luggage compartment. Hoping that the man with the casual attire and beard would notice her standing there, and make access easy to the window seat.

He was young and hard looking. Noticing her finally. "Is this your seat?" he inquired pointing vaguely to the seat beside him.

"Please excuse me while I climb past you," Trina said, trying not to step on his feet while crossing in front of him as he half stood up. He seemed to be watching her face intently. She hoped he wasn't going to be a problem during the flight. She quickly pulled her book out of her purse, to indicate that she was settling down to read during the short flight. Then she gave her attention to the window so she could wave to Danny.

———

As they were landing in Sydney, Trina looked at her boarding pass for the next flight to Vancouver to learn the gate number. Gate 23, would it be near or far from her arrival gate? There would be plenty of time to find it as she noted that she had a couple of hours between flights. Slowly she inched her way into the aisle as the line of passengers were slow in moving. She had to get her bags out of the compartment above. At last she had made it to the doorway and the stewardess, said goodbye as she exited the plane.

The passengers were walking quickly down the long plane ramp as though they were glad to be released from the plane's confinement. She kept pace with her fellow passengers, who appeared to know where they were going. She was hoping they did as she was following them.

They were being funneled into the airport departure area and she assumed gates to connecting flights. When she looked ahead, she noticed some people watching the passengers for love ones and friends by the smiles of greeting on their faces. She then looked towards the direction where all the others were heading. Her eyes zoomed back to see a familiar face. No, he couldn't be here.

Logan was standing there with the biggest grin on his handsome face. She stopped dead. People bumped into her, which made her move from her frozen stance. She sprinted towards him as he moved past the rope to where he could reach for her with wide-open arms. She went into them like a homing pigeon to be engulfed in a loving embrace. Logan was laughing at her enthusiasm.

"What are you doing here?" Trina exclaimed. "How did you know I would be coming here on my way home?"

"Sally called me about the ticket mix up. Thank goodness I was here in Sydney and not on Fraser Island. When you decided to stay in Cairns with her, she phoned me and I wanted so badly to return but it wasn't feasible. When Sally called today, I couldn't believe my good fortune, you were headed my way. The change in your travel plans redirected you back to me in Sydney. I just knew I had to see you again."

"I am glad I decided to go along with the change. They did give me another opportunity to take a direct flight tomorrow."

"I am glad too. Now we will have to arrange with your airline to have your luggage removed, as you are staying at the Hotel Samatra for the week. If you would like, that is?" Pausing for her reaction.

"Yes, oh yes." Grinning and nodding her head.

"It was a crazy thing to do booking you into the hotel for a week, presumptuous on my part. But I just couldn't come to say goodbye. Quite honestly, when your plane was directed here, I had to take advantage of the opportunity to get to know you better. The very thought of never seeing you again bothered me somehow." Dropping a light kiss on her lips.

Taking her hand and her carryon with his other hand, they headed for Qantas Airlines to recover her luggage. Trina was talking a mile a minute about her wonderful stay with his daughter. How much she enjoyed Danny and his antics. Jabbering along in her excitement.

The airline's ticket attendant was very cooperative, indicating that it shouldn't be a problem with recovering her luggage as there was a two-hour stopover in Sydney between her flights. She also arranged Trina's new flight home with a smile. She could see the happiness these two were sharing in each other's company.

"Sally didn't mention to me, that she was calling you about my changed travel plans."

"She knew how disappointed I was not being able to be with you during your extended stay. She is happy that I have finally taken an interest in someone." Logan squeezed her hand affectionately. "I have cleared my slate so I can spend the next week with you to show you Sydney from my perspective." They headed to the baggage carousel.

The conveyor belt finally started circling in a wending passage through one high trapdoor down and around in front of the waiting passengers and then snaking out another trapdoor. Finally, luggage of all shapes and sizes in various colors came spewing out, with baby stroller, boxes and golf clubs in between. They waited expectantly. Some became second time around luggage when their owners had missed them on the first time around. The belt traveled so quickly, you have to grab your luggage rather speedily. No more luggage was falling.

Did they not manage to capture her luggage? After a slight delay, the trapdoor ejected out one more piece of baggage. She pointed at the luggage with its little crocheted pink bunny ornament tied to the handle for easy recognition. Logan reached forward and retrieved her suitcase.

He swung the strap of her carryon over his shoulder, as he wanted to capture her hand again as they headed for the car parking area. It was a grey Mercedes. He easily maneuvered the powerful car out of the parking lot, leaving the airport behind, heading towards Sydney and their surprising week together.

chapter
TWELVE

On the way to the hotel Trina expressed her concern that Briana would be waiting at the airport for her but Logan said, "you can call her when we get to the hotel."

"I will say I am extending my holiday but I don't think I will mention us. I will give her the details when I get home. Otherwise there will be too many questions, making the call too costly. Briana is a stickler for details."

"Whatever you think is best. I am just glad you agreed to stay." They arrived at the hotel.

Darcy, the same receptionist from her last visit greeted Trina at the desk.

"Good morning, Mrs. Grant. Welcome back to the Hotel Samatra. Your same room is waiting for you."

"Good morning Darcy. I am happy to be back."

"Good morning, Mr. Hunter. Your father wants to see you in his office. He asked me, if I saw you to let you know immediately."

Trina looked at Logan. "This hotel is one of the family hotels? I should have realized." Trina said laughingly.

Logan smiled. "You can get settled in your room first. Then come down to the dining room, I'll meet you there for lunch. Besides I want Dad to meet you as well."

"Okay. I will phone Briana while I am up there. I will be down after that."

The call to Briana was still lengthy. Her curiosity was aroused. "Why are you staying in Sydney again?"

Trina hedged as best she could. "I enjoyed it so much on my last visit."

Briana was being persistent for more but couldn't get Trina to commit to anything else.

When she reached the dining room there was a cheerful Wiley waiting to greet her. "Hello Mrs. Grant back for another stay?"

"Yes, thank you Wiley, for remembering me."

"I must confess Darcy let me know you were back. I understand you are dining with my Uncle Logan and you are friends."

"Yes, I met your Uncle in Cairns while I was there."

Wiley led her to the same table that Logan had been sitting at when she had first laid eyes on him or he laid eyes on her. Trina sat down rather nervously looking around trying to be casual but dreading the introduction with Logan's father.

What had Logan told him about her? What would he think of our association under the circumstances? Was she putting the wrong interpretation on all this?

Then she saw Logan heading her way with a gentleman following him. He was of the same stature and looks but shorter than Logan. The man's grey wavy hair was a tribute to his appearance.

Trina was grasping her hands tightly in her lap, while she watched their slow progress towards her, stopping occasionally to greet other guests.

Upon reaching the table, Logan came to Trina's side.

"Trina, I would like to introduce you to my father, Charles Hunter and Dad this is Trina Grant."

Charles eyes fixed on her with awe, but without hesitation as he regained his aplomb quickly. "I am pleased to meet you Trina."

Turning to Logan he said. "I am glad you prepared me or I would have thought she was Linda."

Trina felt she should say something. Quickly before she could even think she blurted. "How do you do Mr. Hunter?"

"None of that Mr. stuff, just call me Charles," he said trying to cover his comment to Logan, knowing it must have been embarrassing for her.

"I would love to join you both but I have to get back to the office but it was nice meeting you Trina. Logan, I want you to bring Trina out to meet your mother perhaps for dinner."

"Yes Dad, I think we could arrange that as she is staying here for a week."

Looking once again at Trina, Charles smiled. "Excuse me now but

I look forward to seeing you again, when Logan brings you to meet my wife, Martha."

After saying goodbye to his father, Logan walked around the table to sit across from her.

"Dad is trying to gracefully retire but he hasn't succeeded yet. He keeps finding reasons to stay around. Mother is hoping to do some travelling soon but it hasn't happened as yet. I can understand his reluctance to be put out to pasture, as the old saying goes."

Wiley arrived with a bottle of wine in a bucket. "Just to let you know Uncle, I highly approve of your lady friend. You have good taste." Joking with Logan, while he removed the bottle for his uncle to inspect the label. Then uncorked it with an expert manner. Logan laughed good-naturedly and winked at Trina. After pouring the wine, Wiley bowed to Trina with a gallant air and left them to their dinner.

Raising his glass Logan said, "to us and our week together." She picked up her glass, clinking lightly against his with a smile.

The waitress arrived with their food, Logan must have pre-ordered their meal.

The conversation started off about her visit with Sally. Trina teased Logan on his plan to waylay her in Sydney. "What would you have done if I had insisted on a direct flight?"

"Besides cry you mean," he joked.

"You were just lucky that I felt I couldn't put Sally out again, for another night's stay. If she hadn't come into the airport with me, you would never have known my change of plans. I never dreamed she would call you, when I mentioned the change via Sydney."

"Are you glad there was a change?" Logan asked wistfully.

"Yes, I am glad to be here in Sydney once again."

"Just glad about Sydney?"

Trina laughed but didn't take up his innuendo.

The meal was enjoyed while Logan relayed plans for her stay. "One day we will go to Bondi Beach and another day to The Blue Mountain National Park."

"That will be nice I haven't been there."

The week progressed with Logan showing her his Sydney with many places new to her and some she had been to already. But enjoyed them more sharing with Logan. He took her to Paddington's outdoor market, which was well known and quite crowded. It was fascinating to see all the stalls with their colorful array of goods and bargains.

"Paddington is one of the most attractive residential areas." Logan told her. "It was restored in 1960 with Victorian terrace style homes for the 'trendy in crowd'."

Trina asked, "do you have a place there?"

Laughing he said, "no."

One afternoon he took her to Bondi Beach which was packed with sun worshippers. Neither had brought their bathing suits. "Let's wade at least," he said as he proceeded to remove his shoes and socks. Then reached over and helped her remove her sandals. They strolled along the beach talking.

Trina was taking in the many ways Australians enjoyed themselves in the sun. Sydney was a whole new experience having Logan as a guide.

The evenings were relaxing. They spent most nights in various outdoor bistros or restaurants so she experienced the busy city's nightlife.

Logan was attired in dressy casual clothes for these occasions, that were every bit as imposing on his muscular body as when he wore suits. Trina had purchased a couple of dresses for these outings. He had enjoyed the opportunity to comment on the purchases during her shopping spree.

One evening when they were enjoying an outdoor bistro Logan said, "my social interest is mostly business oriented."

Trina wondered if the reason was the overshadowing of Linda's death? While he had been trying to portray his interest in her in a subtle way but noted she gave no reply.

Logan chatted about parts of Australia. "Not far from here is a place called Melbourne. They hold a major horse race in November, and everything stops for five minutes while the race is being run. This is the only country that ever does that."

"You mean even people not at the race track?"

"Yes, they are usually either listening to the radio or watching it on TV."

Logan mentioned. "Another enjoyment is the Aboriginal paintings some over a century old, that I saw in Kakadu outside Darwin. You probably would have seen them had you made your trip to Darwin."

"As much as that sounds interesting, I am glad I spent the days at Sally's place instead."

"I am glad too. Oh, so glad." Placing a kiss in the palm of her hand he was holding.

"Another place you would like is Alice Springs, the camels run wild there, and it is fun watching the camel races they hold there each year."

"I didn't realize you had camels here. I always connected camels to places like Saudi Arabia."

"Most places that have a desert like terrain have camels, because of the lack of water. Another place I like is famous Ayers Rock with its 1140 ft high dome shape that continually changes many colors with the sun's reflection. Particularly at night when the sunset is a blaze of red. Well enough of the travelogue. Let's get you back to the hotel for some sleep." Logan stood up pulling her up with him.

Heading for the car and the hotel.

—

One of the days, Logan drove Trina to the Blue Mountains outside of Sydney in the National Park. That morning, over breakfast, they had perused maps making plans for the day's trip.

He wanted Trina to experience as much of his country as possible, taking different twisting roads through the hills rather than the usual direct route. When they arrived, they took a walking tour to see the spectacular views from the top of the cliffs. Then following the trails to take in some spectacular waterfalls in the park.

While in the park they stopped for lunch. Logan built a bonfire in the pit provided. He said it was to add to the atmosphere needed while he talked about the famous outback. He sat down leaning his back against a tree and drew her close to him while they enjoyed their sandwiches and the bonfire.

"Picture a place that can be drought ridden for 3 or 4 years, where it can be flat and dry. Where some places habitation ceases. Then the rains come the following season with so much flooding. The roads become rivers and station homesteads become islands in a shallow sea."

"It must be a hard life for those that experience that type of conditions."

"Yes, they are hardy people, preferring the Outback no matter what the conditions."

Logan also set the scene. "Now in the extreme north within the monsoon belt, that is tropical. The Far West, there is a mountain range and a fertile coastal strip on the Indian Ocean. That is where petrol and water form the bulk of your travelling supplies."

His arms wanted to close around her. He wasn't sure she was ready for that yet, so he kept talking instead.

Regaling her with tales of the Australian Pubs characterized as social clubs and a refuge from heat, where male bonding prevails. "The lingo is 'fair dinkum' means okay and 'brekie' means breakfast, 'cut lunch' means sandwich, 'lolly water' means soft drink and a beer is called a 'stubby'. It is normal in the outback to see signs that read NO WATER FOR THE NEXT 180 KMS." Trina knew from the way Logan talked that he was proud and content with this vast land of his.

"Now it's your turn," he said.

Trina shared her special part of Canada. "My beloved British Columbia, has fast-flowing rivers, with salmon runs for spawning in the fall. My favorite hiking is up the Notch and Mt. Washington. On the west coast I love going to the famous Long Beach on the Pacific Ocean and the nearby town of Tofino. It is known for whale watching, the big grey whales traverse north or south according to the seasons."

"Sounds wonderful. Do you have whales near you?"

"Yes, only our whales are more colorful and called Orcas. You can see them from the beach in March during Herring season."

The fire was snapping and crackling, burning down gradually while they talked.

She continued. "I live in a quaint little town called Qualicum. The charming shops and the greetings from the friendly villagers make it pleasant daily. When we go to our beach, you see weaving seagulls of gray and white against blue skies along with majestic eagles and the blue heron standing in the water. Across the Georgia Strait looms the impressive snow-caps of the Rocky Mountains on the mainland. At night, we often go to the beach to view the sunsets, transforming the water into a sea of shimmering color."

He could almost picture being there with her. The love in her voice for her homeland showed in the way she conversed about it.

"So, you are a small-town girl."

"Yes, but if I feel a need of the big city, I go to Victoria. Its romantic horse and buggy rides, that meander the streets that I have had fun riding in."

"Romantic buggy ride? Who did you go with?" with a big grin.

Now I've done it, how do I explain David? "I went with my girlfriend Amanda for fun." Half-truth but she left it that way. She went on in the hopes he wouldn't question her further.

"Victoria's waterfront has boats of various shapes and sizes. The Empress Hotel overlooks the harbor. Its majestic appearance draws tourist inside to have their notorious Afternoon High Tea. When we want to feel extravagant, we have lunch in the lounge."

Logan was beginning to realize from the warmth in her voice that it would be hard for her to leave her homeland.

Turning to him, Trina gave him a big smile. "Do you think I love my piece of earth as much as you love your land?"

Logan kissed the tip of her nose. "Yes, but now we have to get back to Sydney." He gently helped her to stand by heaving her upwards. She turned, playfully pulling him upright.

He carefully covered the ashes before they headed back to Sydney.

Even though they had had a full day together Logan insisted that night they go on the Sky Train to Darlington Harbor. Trina was happy to see it again with Logan.

"I came here one night. I sat with some people named Wendell. I danced..."

"Yes, go on." Logan knew why she had stopped and he was jealous but not that she had danced with other men, but that he hadn't been there with her.

"Nothing else, I danced." Trina tried to get out of describing that night, looking around at the lights and the water.

Logan let her off the hook with a conversation sharing his family and their history. Relating antidotes of his growing up especially with his Uncle

Adam. She found out that he was fifty-one. He was kind enough not to inquire as to her age.

"Would you like to dance?" Logan stood up with his hand out.

"Yes."

As Trina was led on the dance floor Logan said, "no comparing me to your last Romeos." She looked at him startled, saw he was smiling and laughed.

Gliding around the floor enjoying the rhythm of the music.

When they were back at the table, the talk was about Linda. He kept it brief the role she played in Logan's life slipping in about the shock of her sudden illness and death. Instantly, he put out his hand as though it was her turn. Trina said. "Devlin's attitude was the reason for our parting. He now has a new lady in his life. Maybe we didn't try hard enough to make a go of our marriage." She stopped, taking a sip of her wine. *Does he still love Linda, he didn't sound that sad?*

Logan was standing again inviting her to dance.

———

After a few messages from Charles enquiring when Trina was coming to meet Logan's mother, they finally made the trip to their place for dinner, the night before Trina was leaving.

The introduction of Trina to his mother went smoothly. She carefully hid her reaction to Trina's strong resemblance to Linda.

Logan's mother commented. "Please call me Martha, as we never stand on ceremony in this house."

Logan explained why this was the first opportunity to come.

Charles teased Trina. "I really thought you might be avoiding us."

Logan had filled his parents in ahead of time, that they were just friends. Trina felt comfortable as there were no personal questions other than about her family.

The evening passed quickly with many anecdotes from Logan to his father, about his feeble attempts to retire and his mother talked of her hopes of travelling soon.

When it was time to leave, Trina felt relieved that there was no reference to Logan and her relationship. But sad that she had met this very pleasant couple, only to leave knowing that they would probably never share this experience again.

After the goodnights were said, Logan handed Trina into the car with a possessive hand. When they were ready to drive away, they both looked at his parent's house to wave.

His parents were standing framed by the light within and without. They were holding each other in an embrace that spoke of good yesterdays and good tomorrows together. Logan and Trina answered their wave.

Trina fondly said during the ride back to the hotel. "Logan, I really like your parents a lot. I felt so comfortable with them. Your close relationship with them is evident."

"They are super parents and I love them. Dad tries to bluster me at times but that is because he is fighting retirement," he replied giving her a loving look.

"I envy you that you have both parents as mine are gone. I do miss them both so very much. Especially because they never saw Briana's children nor had the joy of watching them grow up. Many times, I have gone towards the phone to call my mother about something special only to realize that it is no longer an option. We were quite close."

He took her hand and squeezed it comfortingly. He continued to hold her hand. "Would you like to see my place? We have never been there and this is our last evening together."

"Yes, I would like to see it." Trina closed her hand around his more firmly.

It seemed only a short time before they were in the residential area. The houses were luxuriant, charming, and inviting, but it seemed that the car kept slipping through the well-lit streets to another destination, without slowing down.

Ahead was an inspiring high-rise with lush terrace gardens bearing trees and shrubbery on each level, lights glowing throughout the foliage.

She was not surprised when he turned into the underground parking. The automatic door opening and closing after them sealing them within. They entered the elevator and Logan pushed the top floor button.

Trina looked at him slyly. "The penthouse?"

"No," he replied. "Just the top floor. The two top floor condos are similar."

The elevator climbed silently up the building. Doors opening gently into a hallway, like the foyer to a grand home. There was a closed door ahead to the right and the hallway continued to the left.

Logan put his arm gently around her waist, drawing her with him to the door. Keying the lock. His hand guiding her on her back into the automatically illuminating room. Soft leather furniture was in front of a fireplace. It was a place with a used look of comfort, with bookshelves on one wall and an entertainment unit on another.

As he drew Trina from room to room she was thinking. *Did Linda live here with him?* The decor did not seem like a bachelor pad. The warm colors throughout could be a female choice.

Is she thinking that I have ulterior motives in bringing her here? She admitted once that there had been no one since Devlin.

As he headed back to the kitchen, he inquired if she would like something to drink. Trina was taking in the kitchen, which was obviously well used by the gadgetry displayed. Logan took down brandy snifters for the drink she had indicated she would like.

"Do you cook for yourself?"

"Oh yes, mother made sure I was good husband material and taught me to be useful around the house. I have since taken an interest in gourmet cooking not that I get a lot of time for it with my business travelling."

He led her back into the room that they had first entered into. Specifying she should sit on the sofa. He went over to the bookshelves, and pushed a button on the edge of one of the shelves, opening up a recessed liquor cabinet.

He took out a bottle of Napoleon brandy and poured some into the brandy snifters.

"Well you haven't said what you think of my place," Logan said glancing over his shoulder at her.

"It is well laid out and very comfortable looking. I particularly loved the terrace and the grand view of the city." *Did Linda help pick this out or did he move here after?*

"Thank you," Trina said taking the glass from his hand.

He sat down beside her raising the snifter. "To a wonderful week together. This has been the best time I have had in a long time."

"I too have enjoyed this week together."

They clinked their glasses their eyes holding each other's. His blue and her grey eyes were entranced. 'Mr. Eyes' was gone, as his eyes were looking at her so warmly.

Neither was ready to say goodbye. They both raised their glasses to their lips taking a sip.

Logan broke the moment by saying, "this is our last night together. I wish you could stay longer."

"I wish I could too but Briana is depending on me being home for the children. I promised to look after them while she goes on a business trip with Ken and I can't let them down."

"I am really thankful you were detoured through Sydney and were willing to stay. I wanted to see you again. It felt unfinished when I left you in Cairns so abruptly, when I was called away unexpectedly."

Logan removed her glass from her hand, putting it on the polished table in front of the sofa.

Then he drew her to him and kissed her lightly. Pulling back, he gazed deeply into her eyes. What he saw was this lady he had pursued relentlessly, was lying willingly against him. With a moan his soft kiss was more passionate this time. She was responding to his tormenting kiss. He folded her close into his body. She lay against him like this was where she wanted to be.

He rained kisses on her closed eyes, her ear and down to her neck and then returned to her mouth, which was hungry for his.

She was returning all he offered with such passion, that her inner core was causing a craving of a nature that was too long buried. He gently placed his hand on her breast and felt the fullness beneath his hand and the nipple hardening in ready response.

She dropped her head back. He kissed her neck in a tantalizing nuzzle, she gasped. He knew he wanted all of her but was she ready for this? She made him yearn.

Looking down into her smoldering eyes, he studied her deeply. *Was it too soon to take this any further? His desire was being hindered by his caution but he had to know if she was truly willing.*

He drew back and stood up. Putting out his hand in invitation. Trina easily responded by placing her hand knowingly in his.

The bedroom bathed in soft light was large and held a king-sized bed, its mahogany headboard glistening in the lamp light he had left on when they had visited earlier.

He pulled her into his arms and kissed her. While his hand drew down the zipper in the back of her dress. The dress slithered down her arms when they slowly parted. When their bodies lost contact, the dress slipped to the floor. He continued to gently remove her bra, holding her eyes, keeping the contact. He watched for any hesitation.

Then he gently laid her on the bed. Her breasts protruding whitely against her exposed tanned skin. Their eyes locked in a smoldering gaze, he removed his shirt and lay down beside her. Their lips met in an all-consuming kiss.

He broke the kiss trailing his mouth over her face, kissing lightly as he went. His lips made a slow forage to her breast.

Trina was running her hands over his body getting to know him more intimately, as he was getting to know her. Feeling this is so right and yet...?

Had Logan made love to Linda in this bed? As this thought filtered through her mind her body reacted.

She managed to smother her thoughts, because the desire of her body was overpowering her senses. Logan sat up and looked down at her with lust in his eyes, but instead of continuing to caress her body, he backed away from her.

Why did she appear to freeze ever so slightly? Was Devlin still a factor in her life? Was she having second thoughts about intimacy? Was it just too soon in their relationship?

Trina's body, so untouched by a man for such a long time, was now primed for love making. But she noticed Logan's slight hesitation. She looked at him with bewildered eyes.

He had sensed her doubt and desire at the same time but Trina's instant of disquiet overrode his lust. "I think we had better stop. I want you very much but I feel something came between us, perhaps Devlin or Linda, and this just wasn't meant to be."

He got up from the bed and stood with his back to her then reached for his shirt. Trina had closed her eyes. *Was she hurt or was she relieved?* She laid there in confusion, her emotions visible.

He straightened his shoulders as he shrugged into his shirt. "I wanted to make love to you Trina but I sense you are not ready. Was it the ex-husband or possibly my late wife or just too soon in our relationship? I am sorry I went beyond the boundaries of friendship. That was never my intention when I brought you here. It just seemed to happen."

He moved to the bathroom. "I'm sorry this didn't..." continuing inside to shut the door giving her space.

Trina removed herself from the bed and dressed quickly needing to be away from the empty rumpled bed before he returned.

He was leaning with his head down, his hands bracing him on the vanity. *How can I recover this situation? I wanted her so much but something was not right for her.*

Trina was back on the sofa where this had begun. She was looking uncomfortable. *Why had she thought of Linda at that moment? His making love to Linda in that same bed.* Trina thought she had been ready. She had responded fully oh so fully. She could still feel the warmth of passion tingling throughout her nerve ends. *Why had he backed off?*

He appeared at last in the doorway, looking pleadingly towards her.

"Perhaps I should take you back to your hotel now. Are you ready?"

She reached for her purse she had set on the table by the sofa. "Yes, I am ready," her voice strained.

He came over to her and offered her his hand. "Friends?" Logan asked inquiringly.

"Yes friends," placing her hand in his with some relief.

He pulled her up into his arms and kissed her gently almost a feathery touch on her swollen lips. Pulling back Logan said, "Hi," laughing shakily, studying her at the same time. Trina gave a weak smile, hoping they could continue without too much embarrassment. He took her hand and proceeded to the door.

Tomorrow they would part and maybe it was for the best that things had ended this way.

chapter
THIRTEEN

As the elevator descended towards the ground Logan smiled. "Trina, I want you to know I did not bring you here with any plan of seduction. Believe me that was not my intent. I had just enjoyed our week together so much I didn't want it to end. We had always met with others around us and I wanted to be alone with you." Trina was standing straight beside him.

"To have taken you back to the hotel right away seemed to be so final. I just couldn't bring myself to do that. Then there you were looking so adorable and it seemed only natural to kiss you. Once I started kissing you, I wanted more." Logan paused. "I felt that you did too or I would never have taken you into the bedroom. Then I sensed a hesitation. My mind clouded by passion cleared and then I knew that it wasn't right. This is our last night together. I wanted it to last in your memory but not this way. I'm sorry." Logan paused. Silence.

"I'm sorry if I have offended you in any way. Help me out here, say something," he said in a drowning voice.

"Logan, you're doing fine." pause "I was not offended. I wanted to be loved, that is why I let you take me into the bedroom. Maybe I wasn't ready yet. My leaving tomorrow must have made the situation more pressing for us. I will be sorry to leave, and not see you again."

He responded. "It may be just me wanting this but I got the impression neither of us wanted to let go of each other. I think maybe that was why the kiss meant so much and led us to the bedroom."

Trina replied, "maybe making love would have been like bonding our souls. The reason for our first encounter certainly was not the usual circumstance under which two people usually meet." She turned smiling up at him. "When I arrived back in Sydney, seeing you standing there as though we had known each other forever. In truth, we were basically strangers. This week together, I felt an enjoyment that was wonderful. You did that for me, just being with you." The elevator door opened. They made no move or inclination towards escaping from its confines. The door glided closed silently encompassing them both within.

"Trina, I am so glad you felt that way as I felt that way too. Linda made me promise to meet someone so I could put my life together again. You are the first one I have had any desire to know more deeply. I am not saying that because of your likeness to Linda. But that fate has brought us together and I am having difficulties saying goodbye. We live so far apart which will be an insurmountable obstacle."

"Logan, do you believe in destiny?"

"I'm not sure, why?" he replied.

"When I knew I was coming on this trip, I kept getting this feeling that something would be very special or something special would happen. For some reason, I felt my destiny was involved so I had to come alone. Now I know why. Our time together has been very special. I will always remember you with a warm feeling in my heart. Someone who made my stay here more memorable, and gave me a bond of friendship."

Logan took her into his arms and kissed her forehead and hugged her tightly. Then as if he just realized that the elevator was not moving, he kissed her lips lightly and pressed the door open.

"Trina you are a very special lady. I am glad that we had this time together. I do feel I can go on from here. Maybe we will meet again and destiny will be kinder next time."

"I know despite the distance, I still want to keep you as a friend," replied Trina. They stepped out hand in hand.

———

Arriving back at the hotel, which was not too far from his place, Logan turned to her. "Tomorrow you will be leaving. I will be busy all morning but I will meet you for our last lunch together, if that is okay with you? I want to take you to the airport. Parting is going to be difficult for me but I know you have to leave for other commitments," Logan said regretfully.

"Yes, I would like to have lunch with you and I appreciate your offer to take me to the airport. Parting will be difficult for me too."

He made ready to open the car door. Trina stayed him with her hand. "Don't come in with me. Now is not the time to say goodbye. It will come soon enough. I had a lovely time this evening and I also enjoyed your parents. I just feel so sad that I will never see them again."

She leaned forward placing a kiss on his cheek. Opening the car door, she slipped outside, then quickly entered the hotel. Disappearing inside without a backward glance, tears flowing down her cheeks.

Logan did not try to stop her, but sat watching her through the thick glass door, that distorted her image as she disappeared. She had looked so sad and he felt so sad too. How do you say goodbye to someone, that has touched your heart in such a way that you feel bereft without them?

He continued to sit there looking towards the door, that no longer showed evidence of her departing figure. That door that had closed between them, just made him feel sadder. He didn't know how but he just knew, this could not be the end.

He started the car and swung out onto the road for the lonely trip back to his condo. Tomorrow was going to be difficult. How do you say goodbye to someone you don't want to leave, but you know there is no other choice?

He did something out of character for him, he started talking.

"Linda, I have at last met that someone you wanted me to meet, but the circumstances are such that it won't be the conclusion you wished for me. We will be living an ocean apart, that will stop us from having the life you wanted for me. I thought when I made the promise to you that I would never meet that someone, but I did and now..."

Then as if coming on a breeze he heard the words. "Give it time and it will happen."

Logan squared his shoulders, as he pulled off the road into the underground parking and his lonely condo.

———

"Good morning, Mrs. Grant. I hope you enjoyed your stay here? Darcy told me you were leaving today. We are sorry to see you go. You are such a charming lady. I bet Uncle Logan is sorry too." Wiley said audaciously with a twinkle in his eyes. "Your usual table is available. Right this way. I will let Laura know you are here for breakfast."

Laura arrived with her usual cheery smile and greeted her. They passed the time of day in a friendly manner. Trina mentioned, "I plan to take a final walk on the Circular Quay after breakfast."

Laura had enjoyed serving this lovely lady. "That will be nice, that you will have the time. I want to say; how much I have enjoyed serving you this week. We will miss you when you leave."

She did not dawdle over breakfast, as she was feeling melancholy about leaving Australia.

She spent the morning walking the Circular Quay of Sydney Harbor. Getting her last look at the setting that she would sorely miss. This past week in Sydney would always be something extra-special in her heart.

She was going home to resume her life, which for her had always been happy. Now she had the knowledge that there was someone out there in the universe, that had touched her heart in a very special way.

She knew it would be difficult having lunch with Logan, but she couldn't avoid him nor did she want to. It would be so hard to keep up a natural conversation, when she knew an airplane was waiting to separate them. She had to see it through, to be casual and light. So, he would not know how much her heart was breaking. Especially when he took her to the airport.

It was poignant what happened last night but she knew it was for the best. If they had shared their love to the fullest this parting would be so much more devastating. But then, if their lovemaking had continued to completion. It would have been a remembrance, in her heart forever.

She didn't really see all the activities around her, as she was too deep in her inner thoughts. On this picture-perfect day, Sydney harbor was displaying its many colorful sails bobbing and circling about. Yachts skimming the surf to the delight of the tourists. On parting from her thoughts, she looked at her watch, it would soon be time to meet Logan.

She arrived back at the Hotel Samatra and paused at the desk to say a special goodbye to Darcy, who had been so courteous. Her welcoming smiles and her encouraging manner which made her stay at the hotel so perfect.

She continued to her room with lagging steps to complete her packing. Preparing for her departure. She placed an envelope on the desk with a card of thanks for all the staff. It would soon be time to go down and meet Logan. She stood at the window for her final look. She looked at her watch. It was time.

There was a knock on the door. When she opened it, Samuel was standing there smiling at her. She let him take her luggage. Giving the suite one last glance, its memories of a wonderful stay.

"I will put your luggage near the reception desk, for when you are ready to leave," Samuel said as they exited the elevator.

"Thank you, Samuel. I will miss being here."

Wiley greeted her warmly at the entrance to the dining room.

"Good afternoon, Mrs. Grant. Uncle Logan is waiting for you." He sent her a sparkling grin and with a flourish of his hand, led her towards the table overlooking the terrace.

Logan stood up looking at her with a loving smile. Walking towards him, she remembered she had called him 'The Eyes'. There certainly was nothing sinister about him now. His clear blue eyes were seeking her features as though he wanted to freeze them in his memory. To bring them out when he most needed to remember.

Wiley greeted his uncle with a playful grin. "I have found a special lady that I think you would like to meet. May she join you?"

Logan took her hand and said, "I would be delighted to dine with her." Waving Wiley away laughingly.

He was trying to keep a light note, during the short time remaining together saying. "Hi. I missed being with you this morning. How did you spend the time?"

Seating her, he looked at her questioningly.

"I went down to the harbor to take my final look. To lock the scene and its pleasures in my memory."

The lunch progressed with a cheerful conversation reminiscent of the times spent together during the past week. A normal meeting and soon to be an ending.

All too soon it was over. Logan stood to take her hand. "Shall we?"

Leading her out of the dining room, leaving the place where their chance meeting had first begun.

Several of the employees were gathered in the lobby to say goodbye. They expressed their hopes that she would come back again in the near future. Trina gave them all her heartfelt thanks.

Charles came from his office to say farewell. "I will say goodbye now but hopefully some day you will return. Martha also extended her wishes for a safe journey."

"Thank you, it was such a pleasure meeting you both."

Logan picked up her luggage and after she said her warm goodbyes, took her out into the sunlight and the final journey to the airport. She had such a lump in her throat, she hoped he would give her some time before engaging her in dialogue.

After they had been driving for a while, Logan expressed his concern, "I hope your reservation will be okay this time. I don't want you to run into any more problems after I delayed you for a week."

"I hope not either. I can't disappoint my daughter again."

At the airport he parked the car. He fully intended to be with her right up to the security scanners lineup. He wished he could keep her in Sydney longer. She had promised to look after her grandchildren, while their parents were on a trip, so that was not an option.

The attendant at the check-in counter took her ticket assigning a seat on today's flight. Presenting her with a boarding pass, she told her to be at Gate 18 no later than 2:30, boarding is at 3 o'clock. Glancing at his gold watch, it was 2:15 Logan stated. Looking up for the gate indicators direction.

"I will walk you to the gate but I won't be able to stay, as I have to get back for a meeting," Logan said regretfully.

Trina was sort of relieved that lack of time would facilitate their parting. Following the signs to Gate 18, he took her hand and held it lovingly. He knew he had no alternative, he would have to let her go. Gate 18 appeared on the overhead sign and they slowed their pace as they approached the long line up for the security scanners.

He turned towards her stopping her. "Let's say our goodbyes here and we will walk away from each other as though we will be seeing each other tonight or tomorrow."

"Yes" she murmured, "that is the way I want it too." Trina lied.

He leaned forward and kissed her lips firmly saying, "Goodbye my love."

Their hands parted reluctantly and Trina said, "Goodbye" her breath catching.

Turning Logan walked away just like he said. Trina stood there but he didn't look back and then she turned to take her place in the depleting line up. Her carryon and purse passed through the security scanner and she picked them up on the other side as the machine expelled them. With a heavy heart, she entered the waiting room for her Qantas flight home.

———

The trip went smoothly even though it was taking her farther and farther away from Logan. Could there have been any other conclusion to their parting?

She entered Qualicum airport, Briana and the children were there to greet her. With enthusiastic hugs and kisses, they made her glad she was home. She laughed, seeing the signs of love and missing her. She too loved them dearly and had missed them too.

Briana asked her, "did you have a good time? What was the extended vacation all about?"

Trina laughed putting on a happy front. "Not now darling, it is just too complicated to tell you at the moment. I just want to talk to my little ones and hear all their news as I've missed you all very much."

After picking up her luggage, they proceeded to the car with Scott and Kathie trying to outdo each other, in the telling what had happened since Trina went away. Excitement at seeing their grandma giving little skips to their feet.

Briana was chomping at the bit to find out the reason for the extended trip to Sydney. Was there some intrigue here? Her phone calls had been very vague. As she watched her mother chatter with the children, she noticed changes in her.

There was certainly something there that Briana couldn't quite put her finger on. Something causing her mother's manner to seem quite different and somehow more tranquil.

Briana was finding it difficult to maintain her silence which Trina was aware. She knew her daughter was just dying to know. However, she had to concentrate on her driving as the traffic exiting from the airport was moving slowly. Helping Trina postpone what Briana wanted most to hear.

She listened to the children, bringing her up to date on their important news as they swapped turns in the telling. She looked around at the scenery as her mind compared the island to the scenes of Australia.

Australia had its beaches and sun but so did this island. The bustling cities would not draw her; she had avoided them by moving here to this quiet island. Australia had its islands and rainforest. But this place held its own beauty. She looked at the snow-capped mountains, knowing it was good to be home.

When they arrived at Briana's place in Parksville, the children had exhausted all their tales. Anxious now to see their playmates. They burst out of the car to run and find their friends. To share their information about Australia their Grandma had imparted.

When the door of the house opened Neptune leaped out and began circling Trina's legs. Loud meows reprimanded her desertion. Trina picked her up, following Briana's voice into the kitchen. While stroking Neptune, to her loud forgiving purrs.

Briana put on the kettle for tea. They kept up small talk until the tea was poured and put on the table, which gave Trina a chance to relax and gather her thoughts. She was absently stroking the cat, deciding what could be told to her daughter.

Briana passed a cup and saucer to her mother. She again looked intently at her mother's face, noticing the look of contentment that seemed to make her glow. She couldn't wait any longer.

"Mom, I am dying to hear about your trip and particularly why the long stay. Please tell me?"

Trina told her about her journey up the coast of Australia and the nice people she had travelled with. The scenery that had enchanted them. Briana was not patient, she interrupted and demanded to know what had really happened. She was sure that there was definitely more than her mother was willing to let on.

Trina finally made up her mind to ease Briana's curiosity. Taking a breath before she started to talk. Neptune butted her hand powerfully in a wish for more attention.

"I met a man in Sydney the night I arrived there. He kept staring at me during dinner, which I thought was a bit sinister at first. It sort of intimidating me, knowing we were both staying at the Hotel Samatra."

"Hotel Samatra?" queried Briana her attention jolted. "That wasn't where you were supposed to be staying."

"I know but the other hotel gave away my room because my plane was delayed and I missed my expected arrival time by five hours. All the hotels were busy because of a big chess tournament being held in Sydney. They referred me to the Hotel Samatra, which I grew to love."

"Continue," commanded Briana.

"Well as I was saying this man kept staring at me the first couple of days in the dining room during meals. But made no effort to speak to me nor give me any explanation. Then he disappeared. I then enjoyed my stay both in the hotel and Sydney."

"I joined my prearranged coastal tour only to stop at the Surfers Paradise. He was there again staring at me intently as he got into a car. After that I saw only fleeting glimpses of him but he never made contact." Trina stroked Neptune absentmindedly.

chapter
FOURTEEN

Briana asked her mother if she wanted another cup of tea although she hated to interrupt this most intriguing story. She knew there had to be more by the way her mother had blossomed and her eyes were glowing.

Trina thanked Briana for the tea and proceeded talking.

"The tour went to Fraser Island and I saw him as Emma and I entered the lodge for dinner. Emma was to become the closest friend and my roommate as the trip progressed."

"MOTHER! I don't want to hear about Emma right now." Briana said firmly.

"It turned out this man owned the Kingfisher Bay Resort where we stayed."

"Did he contact you?" Briana inquired eagerly hoping to move the story along more quickly.

"No but he did send a bottle of wine to our table for the six of us that were eating together. I must tell you about them."

"Mother, please just get back to the story, that you can tell later." Briana pleaded getting exasperated but unable to move her mother along more speedily.

"All right. When my fellow travelers finished dinner, we didn't see him around but I did ask who he was at the desk. The helpful receptionist disclosed the fact, that Mr. Hunter owned the resort. When I got back to my room there was a pink rose, a chocolate and a message on my pillow."

"What did the message say?" Briana probed.

"The message was in bold masculine writing and just said *SWEET DREAMS* and it was signed *L. Hunter.*"

"The next day when I enquired at the desk, to thank him for the wine. They said, he had left the island on business. However, I did see him when I got to Hamilton Island a few days later. I caught a glimpse of him as he entered a quaint little church, where he was attending a Japanese wedding. I came back late to our room as Emma, a camera buff, kept me out snapping pictures until after ten."

Briana fidgeted in frustration.

"He had seen me too because he left a message for me to page him at the wedding reception, but by the time I called; a plane had whisked him off the island. My chance to learn the reason for his interest was gone."

"We finally did made contact in Cairns and it was so nice. I was at a Kup-Mari Feast watching the dancers gyrating to drums. When a hand reached for mine. and when I turned there he was smiling at me. He led me away from the feast, because it was too noisy to talk with the loud drums. We went into the resort. The feast was being held on the resort grounds."

"When we were inside, he introduced himself as Logan Hunter. He soon conveyed the explanation of his interest in me. Apparently, I was the mirror image of his late wife, Linda. That was why he had stared so. He couldn't believe his eyes thinking at first that Linda had returned."

"His late wife. Mirror image." Briana was amazed, she never would have thought of something like that happening.

Trina did not acknowledge her comments but went on with her story.

"The next day he took me to meet his daughter, Sally and her little son Danny. Sally was amazed at my likeness to her mother. I ended up staying three days with them instead of going on to Darwin. She showed me a picture of her mother and it was uncanny. If I hadn't known it was another woman, I would have thought it was me."

"Sally and John made me most welcome and Danny was adorable and fun to be with. I enjoyed my stay with them."

"On with the story what about Logan?" Briana cried impatiently.

"Well Logan and I planned to be together for dinner at Sally's that first night to meet Sally's husband. It was a very nice dinner and evening. They made me feel so welcome, that is why I stayed with them for the extra three days, instead of going on to Darwin." Briana was staring at her mother intently.

"Logan and I were supposed to meet the next evening. But the message, when I got back from the day's outing was, that he had to leave on business again."

"How did you feel about that?" asked Briana handing her another cup of hot tea. Trina looked down and stroked Neptune, purring erupted loudly before she continued her story.

"I was disappointed, I couldn't believe Logan did another disappearing act and I couldn't believe it would end that way."

"Then you didn't get to say goodbye to Logan."

"I talked on the phone each night with him, during my stay at Sally's. It wasn't the goodbye I thought we would share." She continued.

"After the three days with Sally and Danny I thought I was heading home. When I went to the airport I discovered, my reservations had been fouled up somehow and I was going home via Sydney." Trina hesitated in memory of the surprise meeting in Sydney.

"It wasn't until I reached Sydney to change planes, I thought I saw him." Briana noticed the animation of joy when her mother said this.

"Looking back, I stopped dead on the plane ramp, people were bumping into me. He was standing there with the biggest grin. I was thunderstruck and then he opened his arms and I flew into them." Briana felt at last that she was finding out the important details now.

"Logan retained my hand as though we might get separated again. He wasn't about to let that happen. He inquired if I would consider staying for a week? We were lucky, because of the long delay between flights, we were able to arrange the removal of my luggage from my connecting flight. Logan took me back to the Hotel Samatra, which is one of the several hotels his family owns."

"We had a wonderful week together. The last night we had dinner with his parents. They agreed that I was the mirror image of Linda. The week went by ever so fast. Too fast really. Then I came home."

"Mother that can't be all," Briana said in disgust.

"Yes, we parted as friends with no promises."

"A man does not spend a week with a lady then just says Goodbye," said Briana wistfully wanting more for her mother.

Trina paused, picked up her cup to take a sip of tea, before saying.

"We parted as good friends and no commitments were made by either of us. We recognized the impracticality of living an ocean apart." Her tender feelings showing in her voice.

"I can tell by your face that you would have wished for more, if he had suggested it. Do you think he will call?"

"He didn't say he would, but I just don't know the way we left it," Trina answered quietly.

Briana got up and came around to hug her mother and said how much she had missed her with a little sympathy mixed in. Trina said she missed them all too and started clearing the table.

Briana went to the kitchen window to see if she could see either of the children. Kathie was playing on the swing set with her best friend Patty. They were talking and giggling but Scott was nowhere in sight. He was probably at Kyle's house.

She walked back to the fridge to pull out the vegetables and meat in order to make dinner. Trina was staying for dinner, as she knew there would not be much in the way of food, at her place. Briana watched her mother as she peeled the potatoes. Trina looked sad, reality had set in after telling the story.

In the melee of dishes being passed around and the children's voices raised excitedly telling their father the events of their day. Trina was able to recover her happy mood, which she had lost during the conversation with Briana.

She was able to talk about her trip with Ken without letting on about Logan, as she romanticized the wonders of Australia instead. Then she directed the conversation to the care of the children, during their upcoming trip to Whistler.

Briana said, "Kathie goes to dancing classes Tuesday while Scott will be playing sports after school Monday and Wednesday. They would have to be picked up at 4:30 on those days." The children piped up with more suggestions as to time spent while Grandma was to be there.

The gifts Trina had purchased for each of them in Australia were oohed and aahed about and more stories ensued as to the gifts' origin. The evening flew by. Briana left to take Trina home, while Ken supervised the children's bedtime activity. They had been allowed to stay up much later than usual because of Grandma's return.

Briana took the opportunity on the drive to satisfy her curiosity.

"Mom, will you contact Logan in any way now that you are home?"

"Briana, I just got home I haven't had time to think about anything. I will probably write to Sally as we did form a gratifying connection, and she did ask me to keep in touch. Logan is a separate matter. I think it may be best left that we parted as just friends."

"No, I don't," Briana prompted.

"Think Briana, he lives in Australia and I live here. We are just too far apart for anything else to be practical. Besides I am not sure he wanted to develop our relationship anyway."

"That's true the distance does present a problem and I would certainly hate to lose you to Logan, as that would mean you would move so far away," Briana said less cheerfully. She switched to a discussion about the children ending the thought of Logan. Not wanting him to take her mother away from them.

"Now while we are gone, don't let Scott and Kathie stay up too late at night. Especially Scott, he plays so hard during the day at everything he does. He needs his sleep or he is impossible to get out of bed in the morning."

The rest of the ride was spent discussing the things expected of Trina while she was away and about the plans Briana had made for their trip.

—

The first week flew by during which Trina hardly had time to think. Running a household with children, was quite different for her. However, she did so love the quality time with her grandkids. She had certainly missed them, while she had been in Australia.

She had a busy life with them while Briana and Ken were away. Keeping house, planning interesting meals, shopping for things for special meals she wanted to make. Trina spent the balance of her stay enjoying the children tenfold.

She particularly liked their mealtimes. Of course, their meals started out with the usual incessant chatter, trying to outdo each other in stories about school, friends, dancing and sports. Typical of all children.

Scott, two years older than Kathie gave his male perspective in their talks, but Kathie never one to let her brother outshine her, put in her viewpoint too. These two were at a stage where they were discovering life and what it could hold for them. Trina was amazed at the knowledge they had attained. They seemed so much older than when she had left, or had she not noticed they were growing up so fast.

Even though she was always busy, she took time off the day Amanda came over to visit. The few phone calls they had so far, Trina had kept them to a minimum. She had decided not to tell her about Logan until they saw each other in person.

Amanda came in looking striking in a pink blouse and navy pleated skirt. She was fifteen years younger than Trina but today she looked even younger. It had always amazed Trina that their friendship was so close considering the age difference. Amanda was ecstatic about something so Trina gave her a brief synopsis of her trip, in comparison to Amanda's trip to Australia. She barely got finished when Amanda said, as she stood up in her excitement.

"Guess who's getting married?"

"Who?" Trina asked eyeing her with curiosity.

Amanda continued breathlessly. "You know that trip to Nassau you won at New Years and David sold to Ted."

"Yes," Trina said pensively.

"Well Ted has decided to use it for his honeymoon and he asked me to marry him," she exclaimed eagerly.

"Amanda that is wonderful." Jumping up Trina went around and hugged her friend. "Tell me all about it. When did he ask you and where?"

Before Amanda could reply Trina said, "I'll get the coffee so sit down then tell me all." She poured two cups of coffee, that she had made knowing Amanda was dropping in. She picked up the mugs and spoons, returning to the table.

She watched the animation in her friend. Amanda had an undeniable radiance.

"Well," Amanda started, "one night we were discussing the trip as to when it would be the best time for us to go. After several ideas were bandied about Ted got down on his knee. I thought he was going to beg me to hurry and make a decision as to the date of the trip."

Trina placed the cups and spoons on the table then sat down. Amanda was ready to continue. She could hardly contain herself.

"When in fact Ted said, 'Amanda, we have known each other for three years now and we seem to have gone out exclusively for this past two years. Do you think you would consider marrying me?'"

"I was dumbfounded. I asked in awe, 'Are you really asking me to marry you?' My voice almost abandoned me as it came out in almost a squeak."

"Yes love, I want you to marry me very much. Can you love a guy like me, do you think?', Ted asked me. I replied, 'Oh yes! I love you and I want to marry you."

"Ted said 'Good' and got up off the floor and asked 'Now when are we going to Nassau for our honeymoon' and we both laughed and laughed."

"Trina, can you believe it?" Amanda asked breathlessly.

"No, that's great," said Trina wistfully.

Amanda went on discussing her plans for their marriage in August and the honeymoon that they would take. She didn't notice how Trina was reacting, sadness marring her face thinking of Logan and missing him.

Trina got up for the muffins she had left on the counter hoping to give herself time to recover her composure. She glanced out of the window as if looking for something, to delay facing her friend right away. She knew she was envious of her friend's proposal. She walked back to the table and offered a muffin to Amanda.

She was still talking about her plans for the wedding trip and getting time off from work. She was so deep into her own excitement, that she didn't notice Trina's withdrawal.

Trina expressed her happiness for them. She was glad that she did not have to share Logan and her experiences with him just yet. She wanted to keep him to herself for a while longer as her feelings were still too vulnerable. Especially in light of this wedding announcement. She just would tell Amanda that she didn't want to take away from her excitement, when she finally told her.

After Amanda left Trina went into the living room and sat down on the sofa to read for a while. Although she held the book no pages were turned. She was thinking deeply about Logan.

I miss him and I wish I could call him. Just to hear his voice. I wonder if he ever thinks of me. Could he forget me that easily?

Logan had entered her heart, during that last enjoyable week together. What would have happened if they had taken their love making to conclusion in bed that night? Would there have been a different ending to her stay? Instead they had parted as friends, with no definite plans to contact each other.

This is unreasonable, she chided herself concentrating on the fiction book reading several pages. Then again, the pages did not turn.

We are an ocean apart. He is still pining for Linda. I am ten years older than he is. I put a romantic connotation on his interest during the trip. But it so backfired because I fell in love with him in Sydney on my extended holiday. He is a very handsome masculine man with a wonderful personality. Surely, he would meet someone else soon.

Shaking her head, she straightens her body and concentrated on the book again, which was about a couple of hopeful women who kept getting into the craziest situations with the men they were meeting. She wasn't sure this was the kind of book she should be reading right now in her emotional state. But she did enjoy this author, who wrote on various topics.

After several more pages she set the book down and gave up on the pretense of reading. Sitting there thinking.

Logan was not going to meet someone, because she wanted him. Positive thinking, sitting up straight and squaring her shoulders, but how could it possibly work? Her shoulders slumped again. Logan lives in Australia, she lives here and she wasn't ready to give up her family. She would work out the pros and cons of it. She got up to look for a piece of paper.

Pros	Cons
I think I love him	Ten years older
Compatible together	Ocean apart
Enjoy his company	Linda
Like his family	Leaving my family

I love him	Leaving my friends
I miss him	Leaving my community life
	Leaving my homeland
	Changing my way of life

Trina knew the cons were winning so she might as well forget it, besides Logan may never call. She certainly wasn't going to spend the rest of her years waiting by a phone. Plus, she wanted to be with her family. She had enjoyed her stay with Scott and Kathie. She doubted that she could handle the emptiness in her life without the children or Briana and Ken.

She was now ready to get on with her life. The final decision was made to file her experiences in Australia into her memory bank, where they belong.

———

When Ken and Briana got home from their trip, Briana asked Trina to stay an extra night, she said yes. Trina knew Briana needed this time together to fill her in on their trip activities.

Over coffee the next morning, after the children caught their school bus, Briana started to reveal more about her trip when Trina put in. "Briana, guess who's getting married?"

"No not you. Did he call?" Briana shrieked.

"No, it isn't me. It is Amanda and Ted. That trip to Nassau that David sold to them at New Year's will be their honeymoon trip. Isn't that remarkable?"

"Yes, it is remarkable but how does that make you feel?" Briana looked intently at her mother.

"I think it is terrific and I am happy for them."

"Oh Mom, that isn't what I meant and you know it."

"Well Briana, I repeat I am very happy for them. I don't come into the picture at all. In fact, Amanda, Ted and David came over one night for dinner with the children, while you were away. Sort of an engagement party for Amanda and Ted. David mentioned that maybe we should tie the knot too."

"Marriage! You and David. What did you say?" asked Briana hesitantly not sure if her mother would do it on the rebound from her experiences with Logan.

"It's okay Briana, I just laughed it off like he was just joking."

Briana relaxed. "I like David but I don't think he is the man for you."

Trina picked up her coffee cup to head for the dishwasher. "I have a feeling that he was very serious but I hope the conversation doesn't reoccur anytime soon."

Trina changed the subject to Briana's being late for work if she didn't hurry. Distracting her, neither David nor Logan were to be part of a discussion right now.

chapter
FIFTEEN

Another week flew by with time disappearing trying to catch up on all the happenings over the month she was away, plus the two weeks looking after the grandkids. Friends to call, people to see and meetings to attend and her volunteer work. She certainly had a busy life here but a comfortable one.

Why did she even consider leaving especially when she went hiking with her hiking group? The hikers had stopped on the top of the Notch looking out at the snow-capped peaks of Mt. Moriarty and to the west to Mt. Arrowsmith. While they were eating their lunch, they enjoyed the view of the expanse of water below them. And the distant Island Highway, with its crawling traffic of matchbox cars and trucks, plus the train in miniature wending its way by. Emma should come here for a photo shoot.

Trina commented to her friend Eleanor who was sitting beside her, "What a wonderful place we live in."

"This view is well worth the climb." Eleanor replied in total agreement.

Trina was linking up with Amanda, Ted and David regularly these days also. David was still making overtures of a dual wedding when he talked to her. So far, she was able to evade the situation by laughing and joking. At least he wasn't bringing it up in front of Amanda and Ted.

She didn't know whether that was because she kept laughing it off and

David would be embarrassed. She knew that she couldn't keep laughing it off much longer. She had to tell David about Logan and her feelings for him but she still wasn't ready, mainly because she hadn't heard from Logan.

However, the night Briana invited both Trina and David for dinner, the subject came up again.

"Briana, what would you think if your mother and I got married?" David asked audaciously.

Briana hesitated passing more vegetables to give herself time to reply.

"Well I don't know. Did Mom agree to marry you tonight? I was unaware that she was thinking of marrying again," Briana said cagily.

"I have asked her to make it a dual wedding with Amanda and Ted." He looked at Trina and took her hand and squeezed it lovingly. "She hasn't given me a definite answer yet. I felt maybe it was because of you Briana, that she wouldn't commit. Thinking perhaps you weren't ready for your mother to marry again."

Kathie and Scott both chimed in. "Grandma are you getting married?"

Trina who had evaded things too long knew she was caught at last but let Briana carry the conversation.

Unfortunately, it wasn't to be that simple because she turned to her mother and said, "Mom, do you really want to get married again?" At least this gave Trina an out, rather than making David the issue.

Ken joined in by saying, "well children, looks like wedding plans are in your Grandma's future."

Scott queried, "but Grandma, how come you never told us when you were minding us?"

Trina knew that she was cornered, what could she say and not hurt David's feelings too much in front of the family.

"I had just got back from my trip and I really hadn't got back into my life here yet. David, your proposal of marriage was overwhelming to say the least, so I barely know what to say. I have not really thought about getting married again, particularly not right now," Trina said elusively.

"Are you sure it doesn't have anything to do with Briana's feelings on your getting married? After all I am fully aware some children have concerns about their divorced parents tying the knot again."

Before Briana could say anything Trina quickly said, "not really. I have been so busy since I returned, after being away for so long. I really haven't had much time to do a lot of thinking on the subject. Besides I really thought you were just joking. I am sorry I didn't take you seriously, David."

Still holding Trina's hand David raised it to his lips and gave her hand a gentle kiss then said, "Darling, I would very much like to marry you. It is certainly not a joke on my part. I am sorry that I didn't ask you long before now. I really wanted to ask you on New Year's Eve at the Castle Inn dance."

Now Trina was really put on the spot and she was sorry she had delayed telling him about Logan. She did not want to offend David, especially in front of her family. She wished that she had been able to address this in private, but she had delayed the inevitable too long.

"David, I really like you very much but I am not ready to make such a commitment. Besides I don't think we should take away the limelight from Amanda and Ted's wedding. I want to help her carry out her plans, as she is hopeless in these circumstances. You've known Amanda long enough to know that." Trina was still trying to evade. "We can discuss this after their wedding, which is next month."

David looked crestfallen but had to make the best of the moment.

"You are right Amanda is rather dithery when she gets too excited."

Trina gave a slight sigh of relief. Getting up she started clearing the table. "Can I help you with the dessert, Briana?"

But as she left the dining room, she could hear Kathie asking. "Does that mean Grandma isn't getting married after all?" No one answered her, instead David started talking to the children about current school activities and Scott's sports to cover his embarrassment at the rejection.

Briana was only too glad to corner her mother in the kitchen, as she got out the deep-dish apple pie that had been warming in the oven, while Trina prepared the tea.

"Mother, are you really going to marry David? What about Logan have you filled David in on what really happened on your trip?"

There was that 'Mother' again. Trina knew her daughter was upset about what was going on whether it was for David or herself.

"Briana, I am having trouble sharing Logan with Amanda let alone David and Ted. She is my best friend and I still haven't told her yet. They all will be deeply hurt that I held back, but it seemed like I couldn't discuss it with anyone at the time. Unfortunately, I have deliberately avoided the telling ever since."

"You are right. You have left it too long and they will be hurt but I know that you are vulnerable where Logan is concerned. That makes me feel bad for you," Briana stopped to reach in the freezer for the Ice Cream. "But Mom, you have to tell them sometime especially David."

"I know, I know," Trina lamented weakly.

"You love Logan, don't you?" requested Briana. "That's why you don't want to discuss him with anyone. You also know you're in a hopeless position. That's it isn't it?"

"Yes Briana, I love Logan or at least I can't seem to forget him. But I know it isn't practical to feel this way. He will never call me. although I want to be more than friends. Which is the way we left it when I came home. I'm not sure but I don't think he is completely over Linda, and my likeness was disturbing to him."

Briana started towards the dining room with the desserts on a tray, passing her mother who was pouring the boiling water into the teapot. "Mom, I am so sorry that things couldn't have worked out for you with Logan. He sounded very interesting, and from what you have said, he enjoys being with you."

She left it at that, as she didn't want to go into the possible separation of their family should her mother marry Logan and move to Australia. She thought she had better leave things alone and just sympathize with her mother's feelings.

Trina picked up the teapot and followed Briana. They both continued into the dining room Briana asking in a cheerful voice. "Who wants dessert?"

The children both yelled with half leaps off their chairs. "I do, I do."

Trina was glad that the subject had ended for now but she knew that David had to be told tonight.

David and Trina left shortly after dessert was finished. She had every intention in telling him, but when they were alone in the car, he kept up a running conversation on his bowling game, and the tournament he had played in that week. So, Trina let it slide once again.

———

Wednesday, the following week, Trina ran to the ringing phone, as she entered her house. She hated missing calls. She had an answering machine but sometimes people didn't bother to leave messages. Then she didn't know who had called. Maybe she should get caller id. That way the number at least would be recorded. She leaped for the phone still in high hopes that the person on the other end was persistent enough to hold on.

"Hello."

"Hello to you Trina."

She dropped into the chair in a weaken state, it was Logan. She didn't say anything.

"Trina are you there?"

"Hello Logan. How are you?" Trina asked breathlessly.

"Fine. Fine," he replied. "How was your trip home?"

"Fine. Fine," was all Trina could say like a parrot.

"I missed having you around after you left," Logan said. "Mom, Dad and Sally told me to say Hi if I ever contacted you."

Why was he calling? Does he want to continue our relationship?

"Tell them Hi from me the next time you are speaking to them," Trina replied inanely.

"Trina, I wanted to know if the whales are in the waters around you, I think you mentioned the Georgia Strait has Orca whales in them. I think they are called Killer Whales too. I bought a book on whales for Danny and mentioned to him that you talked about the whales around Vancouver Island."

He only wants to talk about whales. Is that the only reason he is calling?

"The book is on Orca Whales and Danny asked if I could call you to find out if you had seen or if there were any close by. I remember you did mention Grey Whales off Tofino," Logan confided.

Danny asked him to call. She felt really let down.

"Yes, we do have Orca whales in the Strait of Georgia which can be seen from shore on occasion, particularly during the herring run each year and yes I have seen them there," Trina replied brightly to cover her disappointment.

"Danny will be pleased to hear that. It will make the book more real to him, knowing you have actually seen them. He mentioned to me, how much he misses seeing you."

There was a pause in the conversation. Then they both started talking together.

"How are...?" asked Trina

"Are you...?" asked Logan

Then they both laughed. She asked, "what did you want to know?"

"I was going to ask if you were recovered from your trip?"

"Yes, I have settled back into my bridge clubs, hiking, swimming and volunteer work," replied Trina mindlessly.

"You sound like a busy lady."

Why don't I tell her the truth I want to see her again? Why am I making this ridiculous conversation?

"How have things been going for you, Logan? Keeping busy going from hotel to hotel still?"

"Yes, it's that time of the month again and that is why I am with Danny."

This is ridiculous why don't I just tell her I want her in my life.

"I don't seem to get time to relax I am on the go a great deal right now," Logan continued.

"When will you be going back to Fraser Island?" Trina asked.

"I did so love the island when I stayed there. I wished we had met there instead of Cairns then you could have shown me your island like you showed me Sydney."

"It was unfortunate that it didn't work out that way, but I wish that now too." He paused. "I have to go now but I may call you again if that's all right with you?" Logan asked tentatively. *I definitely intend to call you again.*

"Yes, I would like that."

Why don't I tell him I wished I was there in person talking to him? Maybe next time I will tell him how I really feel.

"Goodbye Trina take care."

"Goodbye Logan don't hesitate to call anytime," Trina said optimistically.

She sat there feeling deflated. Logan had finally called and all he had talked about was whales. Didn't he care anymore? He didn't even sound like a close friend, that we supposedly parted as. She got up from the chair and went out to the car to retrieve the groceries, she had left in her hurry to answer the phone.

When Amanda invited David and Trina to join Ted and her for a BBQ dinner about a week after Logan phoned, she knew she had to tell them about the rest of her trip, which was Logan.

The evening started with Ted and David being the professional BBQ cooks. Ted the live action and David giving advice. Amanda and Trina were enjoying the entertainment.

The back patio was sheathed in a warm sun and the odd cool breeze, made a perfect mix. The soft air bathed them in the scent of roses and cedar. An elusive breeze brought the aroma wafting from the steaks to them.

The dinner went well with the usual laughing dialog. Although the others did not seem to notice that Trina was abnormally quiet.

After dinner, they were having coffee and liqueurs in the living room. There was a sudden lull in the conversation. Trina was fearful that the wedding would be introduced as the next topic. She knew Logan's appearance in her trip had to be addressed first. So, she took the opportunity to make her narrative.

Still avoiding David, she addressed Amanda instead, thinking it would be easier that way.

"Amanda, you know my recent trip to Australia, which I enjoyed very much?"

"Yes."

"Well there was more to it then I previously related to you all," Trina looked around at everyone.

"Well this sounds kind of mysterious," said David, "out with it. What happened while you were there?"

"At the beginning of my stay which was in Sydney, as you already know, there was a man who was staying at the same hotel, as I was."

They all looked at her with renewed interest. David, who was relaxed, sort of stiffened.

"I saw him in the dining room a few times," Trina continued. "He never spoke to me only stared. Then he disappeared. Over the next two weeks, while I was on my coastal tour, I saw him stare from a distance but again never had a chance to talk to him. He seemed to be at some of the hotels I was staying at, on my way north. It was kind of eerie." She paused taking a breath.

"It wasn't until I got to Cairns that he appeared once again, drawing me into a conversation with him."

David really sat up right now. He knew he wasn't going to like this next part somehow. He had an inkling that this was why his proposal had never been answered but left up in the air.

Trina was anxiously twisting her untouched liqueur glass. She took a large gulp that took her breathe away, coughing as it burned its way down her throat. Trina waited for her throat to clear before continuing.

"His name is Logan Hunter and he is in the hotel business. That was one of the reasons I kept seeing him on my travels. He explained his reason for staring at me. Apparently, I was the mirror image of his late wife, Linda. The likeness he said was so uncanny that he was astounded and therefore could only stare at me as though Linda had come back to life."

"Logan asked me to meet with his daughter, Sally who lived in Cairns. I agreed. Sally too had almost the same reaction to my appearance, except that Logan had forewarned her about the likeness. We became fast friends and no doubt you will recall I spent an extra three days there. Instead of going on to Darwin as I originally planned."

"Well, I spent that time with Sally and her family. She has a son; Danny that is adorable and we had lots of fun together. Logan had disappeared the day after he took me to see Sally. I never saw him again while I was staying in Cairns."

David felt relieved for a second but he still felt there was more to come, and he was not going be happy.

Amanda piped up, "what happened after Cairns? I recall you said you went back to Sydney. Did you see him there?"

David and Trina both shifted uneasily.

"Did you see Logan again?" David wanted to know.

"Well, Sally took me to the airport to come home but there was some mix-up in my plane reservation and I was routed home via Sydney," she looked guiltily at David then back to Amanda.

"When I arrived at Sydney, he was waiting there for me. Evidently, Sally had phoned him about the change in my flight, and that I would be going home via Sydney."

"He talked me into staying for a week at the Hotel Samatra, where he had first seen me. He also wanted to take me to meet his parents."

"I agreed to stay." Trina took a small sip of her Kahlua in the hopes of bolstering her courage to go on. "The dinner to meet his parents was on the last evening before I left for home. Again, I noticed their surprised reaction to my appearance. Apparently, I did look identical to Linda and they said it was phenomenal."

"What did you do for the week?" Ted asked. "There is evidently more to this story than you are telling us, isn't there?"

"Logan had a free week which we spent in Sydney. Hotel Samatra is owned by his family and various other hotels on the Gold Coast, which was why he appeared every once in a while, during my tour. He travels once every three months to each of the hotels to oversee their problems or the general operation of them. That is his job in the family business."

Amanda said, "that doesn't explain what you did all week."

"During that week, Logan showed me his Sydney. We spent a lot of time together discovering places I had never been to on the first visit."

"And?" Amanda asked inquiringly.

"Nothing, that was it and I came home."

"Then why do I get the feeling that there is more to tell?" David asked apprehensively.

"We parted as friends. Nothing happened. In fact, he just phoned me a week ago and all he talked about was whales and how he had bought a book on whales for his grandson, Danny."

"Whales," Ted queried.

"Yes, he bought a book about Orcas and Danny wanted to know if we had any here, so Logan phoned to ask."

"And?" Amanda prompted.

"That's all there is to the story." Everyone looked skeptically

"Really that is all there is," Trina said a little too brightly.

"There must be more," David said looking at Trina expectantly.

"David, I am ten years older than Logan and he is still pining for his wife Linda. Even though it has been three years since her death. There is definitely no more." She stood up to put an end to the discussion by gathering up the coffee cups, hoping to escape to the kitchen.

David was not satisfied. "Tell me, is this why you have been evading my proposal?"

She turned and looked back towards David, stopping her unsuccessful exit.

"Sorry David, I should have told you about Logan sooner," Trina said weakly.

"Obviously, because you didn't. It has been two months or so since you were in Australia, he must mean something special to you." David looked intently at her.

"Yes David, I let him get into my heart but it will never come to anything. Like I said he is still in love with his wife. I remind him of her and that was the only reason he wanted to be with me was for her likeness and nothing more."

David came over to Trina and took the cups and set them on the table near the armchair, then he took her into his arms. "I'm sorry I acted that way, grilling you like that. I sense that you have deep feelings for this man. He doesn't even know how you feel, does he?"

"No, I don't think he does."

David gave her a hug then kissed her forehead not knowing what else to say. Then stepping away from her, he picked up the cups and walked towards the kitchen. Then he said breezily, "let's get these dishes into the kitchen and say our goodbyes, it is getting late."

Everyone started moving at once picking up cups and glasses, trying to soothe the uncomfortable situation. Trina was glad it was out at last. She felt bad, mistreating her friends, withholding information about Logan for so long. Although all were thinking their own thoughts about Logan, they did not share them at this particular moment.

Trina finally said, "I'm sorry I didn't tell you all sooner. I know I am being foolish about Logan, but I just couldn't talk about it." Looking sadly at David.

chapter
SIXTEEN

L ater in the car Trina once again apologized for not telling him sooner.
 "That's okay, I understand you were feeling vulnerable, and you
weren't ready to share it with me. I guess I won't get the answer I want to
my proposal now, will I?"

Trina looked at him plaintively. "I can't say yes when I feel this way
about Logan even if he doesn't share my feelings. David, you wouldn't
really want me to, would you? You are too nice a person for me to do that
to you."

Knowing full well that Trina was hurting inside David wanted to say
something encouraging. "Maybe I should call him and let him know what
a wonderful person you are. What he is missing out on. Tell him, if he just
called you would be his."

"Don't you dare. Don't even think such thoughts, do you hear?" Trina
said horrified. "Being continents apart, it is an impossible situation, also
sizeable age difference and Linda in-between."

"That does create problems doesn't it?" David said fondly.

They had reached Trina's place and he pulled into the parking space
near the door of her house. He turned the key and the sound of the motor
faded away. He then reached for Trina and pulled her into his arms. They
sat that way for a little while, both drawing comfort from each other.

He drew back and looked into her face. "It is time to go in Trina. Are
you going to be okay?" David asked kindly.

"Don't worry I'll be okay, you don't have to come in."

He got out of the car and came around to help her out. Then he leaned forward and kissed her gently on the lips. "Logan doesn't know what he is missing. I wish I could tell him."

They proceeded to the door with her hand firmly in his, lending his support although he was hurting inside. They parted at the door with their goodbyes.

———

The next day when Briana came home after picking up Scott from school, her mother was waiting for her in front of the house.

"Where is Kathie?" Trina asked.

"She went off with her friend Stephanie, her mother picked them up at school. She will be staying at their place for supper," Briana replied, as Scott jumped out of the car spilling books in his hurry.

"Mom, I am going to Kyle's place, okay?" Picking up the dropped books and heading for the house. "Hi Grandma." He threw back over his shoulder.

"Hi Scott." Trina said with a laugh.

Briana led the way to the side door while calling after Scott to be back by five and no later.

"We are having an early dinner, I want to go shopping at the mall after we eat and Ken is meeting us there, as he wants to pick out a new TV. Our TV bit the dust last night," Briana explained as she opened the door.

"Won't Ken want to come home first?"

"No, he phoned before I picked up Scott to say he had a business lunch and would snack later. His business lunches are always so late for some strange reason, and he never feels like eating much after. So, he is going to stay to get caught up on some work. Then meet us at the mall later."

"Sit down and I'll put the kettle on for tea." Briana headed for the stove and picked up the bright red kettle perched on one of the burners.

Walking to the sink she said looking towards her mother. "We can't really afford the TV so soon after our trip but Ken feels it is a necessity. You know him and his sports. I would just as soon that we all did without a TV for a while. You know, to do family things like play games or just have lively conversations. I doubt the children will agree either."

"I know what you mean. Television consumes too much of our lives now. Unfortunately, family activities are a thing of the past," Trina said regretfully.

Briana came and sat down across from her mother after placing cups and saucers on the table, waiting for the kettle to boil for tea.

"Yes, but I try to limit the children's viewing of TV. Drawing their attention to their friends and the good times they could be sharing. Fortunately, they don't bother with TV as much anymore. After dinner, of course, comes homework before recreation. I shouldn't complain really. They are very good kids most of the time. Now what brings you over today, Mom?"

"Last night at Amanda's dinner party, I finally shared my story of Logan with them," Trina said pleasantly.

"Oh dear, how did that go over after all this time? I bet you really shocked David with your confession of the missing part of your vacation."

"Actually, he took it quite well. In fact, they all did because they knew I was different since I got back and this shed a light as to the reason why. I guess my tender emotions did that. There is something I haven't told you yet Briana."

Briana looked anxiously at her mother as she got up to take the boiling kettle off the stove. She poured the boiling water into the teapot and carried it to the table.

"Logan called."

Briana noticed the disappointing note in her mother's sad voice. "And?"

"All he talked about was a book he bought Danny on whales."

"Whales."

"That was the same reaction as Ted gave when I related the essence of the phone call last night."

"Oh Mom, I'm sorry." Briana was sad for her mother.

"Don't be after all, when we parted it was clear we were only friends." Trina picked up her cup by the saucer and held it towards Briana. She poured the tea that they had given time to brew, during their conversation.

She took a drink and looked at Briana lovingly knowing that she cared and was thankful for their close relationship. She felt comfortable, sharing her feelings with her daughter.

Briana asked, "do you think he will call again?"

"He asked me if it was all right if he called again, but I don't really know if he will bother or not," she said woefully.

Briana said decisively, "you know I would like to call him and tell him he is missing a nice person, that is for sure."

"David offered to do the same thing. But I quickly dispelled that idea," Trina said adamantly. "I really think I should forget him. I thought it over thoroughly, when I got home last night. I will just have to hide Logan away in a corner of my heart and get on with my life." She gave a sigh.

"Briana, I do have a wonderful full life here. David, although I shattered his illusions and his hopes for marriage, will still be my friend. Probably, he hopes I will eventually forget Logan entirely. He will just know now, that we can only have this kind of relationship. Maybe that will be enough for both of us. I certainly hope so. I do like David very much and I would hate to lose him as a friend."

After discussing the plans that were being made for Amanda's wedding, Trina got up to take her leave. Carrying her cup and saucer over to the counter, so Briana could get her dinner ready.

"Do you want to stay for dinner, Mom? It is a casserole I have warming in the oven."

"No, I think I will pass this time. Neptune is starting to complain heavily about my absences from home. She is feeling neglected. Neptune can be very vocal when she is displeased, and that is what is happening lately. At first, she tried ignoring me when I would arrive home, but then voicing her displeasure soon after. But not for long, she loves her petting too much. She purrs enthusiastically when I cuddle her. Listen to me going on and on about a cat, but I am thankful to have someone to come home to, the house is so quiet otherwise." Briana looked at her with concern.

Trina headed for the door, exchanging goodbyes. Entering her car, she headed home.

———

The day of Amanda and Ted's wedding arrived. It was a nice sunny day. Perfect for the planned garden wedding at the Castle Inn.

Trina was decked out in a beautiful turquoise dress carrying a bouquet of yellow roses and David was attired in a black suit. They slowly strolled down the path between the many guests leading to the rose covered arbor where the minister was awaiting the wedding party.

Amanda in a satin white dress with a lace veil carrying a bouquet of red and white roses strolled arm in arm with Ted in a black suit. Ted was beaming proudly. He gave Trina a wink as he arrived at the altar. Amanda passed her flowers to Trina with a happy smile.

Amanda and Ted exchanged special vows they had prearranged between them. During the interchange of their rings, they were looking deeply into each other's eyes. The minister pronounced them husband and wife to the cheers of the guests. Ted was kissing Amanda lovingly then they both laughed.

Ted yelled exuberantly. "My wife and I would like to invite you to dine with us in the Castle Inn Restaurant. I expect lots of ringing glasses so I can kiss my new bride frequently." Amanda was becoming a blushing bride to the delight of the guests. They all went inside to a special room decorated for the occasion.

Amanda, Ted, Trina and David greeted the guests before they were seated. The good wishes for the bride and groom were many with a few comments about Trina and David getting married thrown in. Much to their embarrassment as they both knew that would never happen.

After dining and lots of ringing glasses and cheers as Ted gave his bride kisses. Speeches were many and much laughter ending with Ted thanking everyone for their cooperation in the ringing of the glasses as he dropped another sweet kiss on Amanda's lips. There was only time now to throw the bouquet and their goodbyes as Ted and Amanda had a plane to catch for Nassau and their honeymoon.

—

Logan arrived in the afternoon on Friday at Vancouver Airport. He had purposely not let Trina know. He wanted to surprise her and now he was having second thoughts. Maybe this wasn't the right way to go about things. It wouldn't be easy to get to her as he original thought as he soon found out.

While Logan was driven to his hotel by taxi, he asked about Vancouver Island.

"Vancouver Island is a self-contained island," the taxi driver replied, "The only way to get there is either by a two-hour ferry ride or plane."

Logan didn't realize that the distance between the two places was so great when Trina had talked about her homeland with him. In her conversation about home she hadn't mentioned the actual size of the island and its distance to the mainland.

He was due to be in Vancouver for five days at the Worldwide Hotel Association Convention.

So near but so far. He would have to wait another six days before he saw her and that was not part of his plans. He had hoped to have her come to the Hilton Hotel where he was staying for a candlelight dinner in his suite, when he could get away one night from the convention.

Best laid plans go array when not aware of the time and distance involved. He felt so disappointed at this new dilemma. Why had he not checked into this before he came?

Should he call her and ask her to come to Vancouver? Should he call and make plans to meet her on Vancouver Island? But that meant waiting six days before that could happen and his patience was running out, he wanted to see her now.

When the taxi finally deposited him at the Hilton Hotel, he was feeling let down. In the lobby, he ran into Tom Jackson a colleague of his that had been to Fraser Island. In fact, Tom had been there while Trina was there also, Logan remembered as he greeted him. He mentioned to Tom he was unaware of the huge distance between Vancouver and the island.

Tom suggested. "if you want to go to the island there is a 20-minute airplane ride to Nanaimo and you can get transportation from there."

Logan said, "I am actually trying to reach someone in Qualicum."

Tom told him. "CalAir flies directly there. I have been to that particular area, a couple of years ago."

Tom continued, "I have looked at the schedule of events for the next five days. Tomorrow afternoon is an entertainment show, which is featuring, excerpts from several current movies or Broadway shows, appearing in the local theatres in Vancouver, followed by a dinner. After which we can go to the theatre of our choice. They have booked seats for each one of us. The purpose is, a sales feature showing a film of exerts of shows at local theatres. Surely you won't find this important enough to stick around for.

So why don't you take the opportunity to slip away to Vancouver Island? I am sure whomever you wish to see will be more interesting, than a trip to the theatre."

Logan said with revived hope in his voice, "yes, I can cheerfully miss the theatre. There is someone special I want to see while I am here."

Tom explained, "take a taxi to the south terminal airport where CalAir will put you on a flight to Qualicum."

Logan quickly said, "thanks, I will meet you for a drink in an hour." Then he proceeded to reception to check in, and asked if they could look into flight times for him to Qualicum by CalAir. Logan was anxious to get to his room, to make that all-important telephone call.

In his suite, he was reaching for the phone when it starting ringing. It was the reception desk with the times for the flights, he had requested. He thanked them and asked for them to wait to book his flight until he knew what time would be best. After disconnecting he called Trina, his first priority.

Will she be home? Will she be too busy to see me? Does she even want to see me? During his lengthy trip from Sydney, these were the types of questions he asked of himself and now they were back.

He certainly wanted to see her but the phone kept ringing and ringing. He was too anxious; he couldn't just hang up without any response. Where was her answering machine? Surely, she had one.

These questions were forming in his mind as the phone continued to peal, waiting for an answer. His disappointment rapidly deflated him and his excitement was dwindling. He took the phone away from his ear when he faintly heard a voice issuing from the receiver. His heart starting to beat faster, he started calling out to her. He was raising the receiver back to his ear. Then the disappointment set in once again, it was only Trina's answering machine that had finally accepted the call. He put down the phone with the saddest feeling, deciding not to leave a message after all.

No one could feel this bad and not care deeply for someone he thought. If he had any doubts on the flight to Vancouver, they were gone now. He just wanted to see her face, hear her voice and yes kiss her senseless.

Logan walked over to the window. There was a large body of water and he could see islands and mountains in the distance. He knew that Trina was over there somewhere, so near but so far.

He didn't want to leave the room until he had reached her in person.

He was rather sorry now that he had arranged to meet Tom in the lounge for drinks this soon after arriving.

With lagging steps, he headed for the elevator only to turn around and head back to his room. He would try once more.

Logan phoned once again but he only reached the answering machine and again disappointment. He headed out the door.

What if she is away? What if she doesn't feel as I do? Does this David that Trina mentioned have a strong feeling for her? Were they planning marriage now that he was out of the picture? Yes, David was the name that she had mentioned. Saying she was most friendly with him, along with Amanda and Ted.

Exasperated he pressed the down button firmly as he entered the elevator. He decided to put his doubts and fears behind him until he got back to his room.

He knew he couldn't wait that long. He would try again from a phone down in the lobby as many times as it took to reach her, hoping Tom wouldn't mind the interruption for a few minutes. This call was just too important to him to be put off.

—

Briana was with her mother at the mall on her day off. She was trying to talk her mother into watching the *Titanic* video with her that afternoon and stay for dinner. "Ken is willing to watch it tonight," Briana said. "I know that I will enjoy it more with you, mother. It is two videos long and Ken won't be able to sit and watch the whole of it before getting bored, and wanting to watch his sports."

Besides Briana knew her mother so well. They could share the movie and enjoy it better together and maybe cheer her mother up because she seemed so sad lately. "This movie isn't exactly cheerful but this is the film I particularly want to see."

Trina hesitated but finally gave in. "Alright I will stay. I hear it is a good movie." If she had only known her phone had been ringing at regular intervals, she would have been the happiest person on earth.

—

150

Logan was getting frantic, he was almost being rude to poor Tom that was trying to be understanding. Excusing himself almost every fifteen minutes. He returned to his seat looking dejected.

"No luck? Maybe this isn't a good time for us to talk?" Tom queried.

"I am sorry but the party I am trying to reach doesn't seem to be home and I don't want to miss talking to her." Logan sat down again.

"Her so it is someone very special," he said with a twinkle in his eye.

"Yes, someone I met in Sydney." Not expanding further.

He really didn't mean to be impolite to Tom but he also did want to talk to Trina. Where is she? Maybe I should not call until after dinner then I won't be continually let down if she doesn't answer.

———

Trina and Briana were deeply into the movie *Titanic*, having only watched the first part before dinner. Ken was teasing them both about their entranced stare at this movie. The picture was of a romance and a sinking ship, which wasn't something Ken really enjoyed. Not when there was a football game on that he would prefer to see.

Ken even got up and made popcorn to pass the time. He was willing to bet, they hadn't even noticed that he had left the room. When he placed a bowl in each of their limp hands, they sort of jerked into awareness long enough to say 'thanks'.

The picture was at the scene where the couples were saying loving goodbyes having to separate forever as the women and children only were getting into the lifeboats. There were not enough lifeboats for everyone. Ken noticed Briana and Trina had tears streaming down their faces. He went to get tissues for them both.

Trina's tears were not just for the picture's grief but for her own heartbreak. Logan whom she would never see again. Thank heavens this is a sad movie so Ken and Briana would think she was crying over it.

Could she ever be happy again? Was there any chance of his coming to see me? Should she call Sally then during the conversation inquire about Logan? Maybe he had met someone else, that he could eventually share his life with since she had left.

This is getting to be too much, she had to forget Logan once and for all. She was so wrapped up in her pain, that she had lost contact with the screen and its drama. She just wanted to go home and be alone. She needed to get a proper perspective. This feeling of a hopeless romance with a man that really didn't care for her. Knowing if he really cared he would be calling her.

Ken was holding out more Kleenex with a laugh, Trina took them thankfully.

She was glad when she noticed Briana get up to turn off the video, setting it to rewind. "It is getting late and I think I will head for home. Neptune will be waiting to go to bed with me, as she does nightly for her cuddle before she heads for her own bed," Trina said inanely. "Thanks for dinner and the movie. Ken thanks for being patient with us, two movie lovers even if all we do is sit and cry."

"Gee Mom that was really sad, wasn't it?" Briana wiping further evidence of tears from her eyes. "I could watch that again and still enjoy it."

Ken lamented. "No way, I am not sitting through that again. You and your mother can watch it tomorrow while I am at work."

Briana teased him. "Spoil sport, this is a real heart-rending account of a true event and the way the story unfolds reaches your deepest emotions."

Ken laughed. "Leave my emotions out of it. This is your kind of movie, not mine."

Trina watched the natural bantering going on between them. She was envious but at the same time felt blessed. That these two were so happy together and could kid each other, with a feeling of love flowing between them.

She just wished she had the same opportunity for this special type of relationship. She felt she could have had this with Logan.

"Thank you both for having me here, for the dinner and I did like the movie. But I don't think I am ready for a second sitting right now either." Trina said as she went into the hall to get her purse and jacket.

She kissed Briana good night and hugged Ken as he responded in a joking way. "It sure put you in a loving mood, didn't it?"

Trina patted his cheek. "Be thankful I am a loving mother-in-law, and not the forbidding ones most men complain about."

"That is right dear, Mom treats you really well." Briana laughed.

She gave her mother an extra hug knowing that her mother's sadness was more than a natural reaction to the movie *Titanic*. She hated to see her mother leave for her lonely house. Maybe this movie wasn't such a good idea after all, but she had wanted to see it and she had enjoyed it tremendously.

chapter
SEVENTEEN

Logan was now beside himself. He was calling almost frantically. He had refused a nightcap after dinner with Tom because he wanted to get to his suite and the phone. He wasn't ready to give up after coming all this way to be with her.

Where is she? Why doesn't she come home and answer her phone? Will I be so close and not even see her? Why didn't I phone from Sydney and let her know that I was coming here?

Logan picked up the phone with a prayer, this final call would be directly to her and not to the machine. It was getting so late but he had to talk to her or he knew he wouldn't sleep.

He dialed her number again with not much hope, prepared to hear her voice on the answering machine and was shocked when Trina picked up the phone and said, "Briana, did I forget something?"

"Hello Trina."

She couldn't believe the voice in her ear, sending her heart in flight. She was glad she was sitting down patting Neptune when the phone rang.

"Logan?"

"Yes, darling it's me," he said with some relief in his voice. "I have finally reached you. I have been trying to call you since two o'clock this afternoon when I arrived."

Trina was so excited she could hardly speak.

"Arrived. Arrived where?"

"I am here in Vancouver. I called you earlier. The phone just kept ringing. Where were you?" He half expected to hear her say with David.

"I was at Briana's and she talked me into staying to watch the movie *Titanic* with her. It ran so long that we broke for dinner and carried on after. It was five hours long. Ken wasn't really into it and besides he makes fun of Briana when she gets teary eyed over movies, even though this was from a true story. She wanted me there for moral support because I cry too. It was a good movie and I enjoyed it." She kept talking aimlessly until she calmed down.

Then it dawned on her he had said 'Darling' in his greeting. She felt uplifted and excited. She continued to ramble, "I am so glad you called. How are Sally and Danny?"

"Please darling," said Logan. "Give me a chance to talk." He laughed partly in humor and partly in happiness, that he had finally reached her. It was such a pleasure to hear her sweet voice.

"I am in Vancouver for a hotel convention. I wanted to surprise you by showing up on your doorstep and invite you to dinner in my suite. But I found out that Vancouver Island is so far away from here. I was so disappointed when I found out the distance on my arrival. I should have looked into that before I left Australia. My impression was that I could rent a car and travel to the island by bridge. I want to see you. I want to hold you again and I miss you, I need you in my life. Do you want that too?" Logan asked expectantly.

"Oh Logan. I want that too," Trina replied tenderly.

"Now I will have to change my plans. But I found out there is a plane that goes to Qualicum. I intend to be on it as soon as I can get away from here tomorrow afternoon. Can you meet me at the airport if I let you know the time? In my urgency to call you I didn't take heed of the times of my possible flights."

"Yes, I will be there. I will be the girl waiting impatiently for your arrival to have your arms around me," she said light heartedly.

"Trina, I have been so afraid this was one sided on my part. Afraid you wouldn't feel the same way about me. I knew you were seeing David. I thought that you might have formed a closer relationship with him after you got back."

"Logan, I never dreamed I would see you again. But David has never been a romantic part of my life, only a friend. Especially when you were in my heart still," she replied with tears of joy creeping into her voice.

"Trina, I wish I could skip this convention all together but there is some information that I need and I am scheduled to be one of the guest speakers. So, I can't ignore it. Fortunately, the program tomorrow afternoon and night, is something I can miss. Trina, I just have to see you without delay."

"Logan I am anxious to see you too. I will be there for sure when your plane lands, no matter the time."

"I haven't made any arrangements yet, as I wasn't able to reach you. I was getting rather frantic," Logan admitted. "I will call you tomorrow morning with the time. Sweet dreams, my love. I am really looking forward to seeing you."

"Logan, I have wanted to call you so many times, but I thought you might have met someone else so I didn't. I am sorry now that I didn't make that call."

"Me too," Logan replied. "Trina that time I called about the whales had nothing to do with whales. I just wanted to hear your voice. We had parted as just friends. I thought we had better keep it that way, until I had the opportunity to take this trip. So again, I will call you tomorrow as soon as I arrange my flight. It will be early morning. I have to go to bed as it is very late for me. The time change is playing havoc with my mind and I have to get some sleep. Good night, my love, see you tomorrow."

"Good night, Logan. I will be awaiting your call no matter the hour. I am so glad you are here."

Trina put down the phone with a happy heart, and the knowledge that Logan was back in her life. I will never sleep tonight, so how can I possibly have sweet dreams?

———

The next day a problem had arisen that was keeping the lovers apart. When Logan phoned for reservations apparently the fog over the Strait was so heavy that no planes were flying until the fog lifted. Because of the heavy fog, there was no time frame available.

He was unable to contain his frustration. He had to get to the island some way. He asked the voice on the phone did they think the ferries would be running? The answer was that they weren't sure as it was very foggy over the Strait and in Qualicum and Nanaimo it was worse. They had not checked with the other mode of transportation.

He went to the window and looked out like he had yesterday but he couldn't see anything in the distance, only smidgens of the water through fog.

Logan phoned the reception desk. He told them that it was imperative that they find a way for him to get to Vancouver Island as soon as possible after 12:30. The reply was not encouraging, they were sorry but the fog was very intense over the Strait and the island. They believed that the ferries would not be running either.

This was not what Logan wanted to hear. He said, "please have someone call around to see if there is any other solution to my problem." Then hung up the phone dejectedly.

He went back to the window and stared at the distant shore, which was deeply hidden in a thick heavy fog. Logan knew that it was worse than when he had previously checked a few minutes ago.

I know you are over there somewhere Trina and I am trying to get to you. I can't even let you know when or how.

The phone rang and he grabbed the phone quickly. The male voice said, "the weather bureau has no indication at this time of the fog lifting. However, the airlines said that the Comox area was not socked in with fog like Qualicum and Nanaimo area and planes were landing there."

Logan gave a heartfelt thanks to his uncle the spirit up there who was guiding him to his destiny. *Where did that thought come from?*

He got the young man to call and make reservations not knowing where Comox was but only that it must be somewhere on the island. He didn't know if Trina would have difficulties picking him up there. He just knew, he had to get to the island as quickly as possible.

After the young man provided him with the information for his flight, Logan immediately phoned Trina. Her voice answered on a short ring. She must have been sitting by the phone, anxious as he was.

"Hello. Logan?" Trina asked eagerly. She was aware that the thick fog was creating problems, he heard it in her voice.

"Hi, I have good news and bad news but I will be there. The good news is that I have a flight out at one, and the bad news is that it is to somewhere called Comox. Do you know where that is from you?"

"Yes, it is about an hour and a half drive from here. I was so upset when you didn't call earlier. I was expecting your flight would be cancelled. I have been watching the fog hoping that it would lift."

She continued, "it is unusual for fog to be so heavy here, although Nanaimo gets fog a lot. Maybe it will lift before the flight time."

He said, "I am not taking any chances of not getting over to the island. If you think there is no risk to you, could you meet me in Comox otherwise I will take a taxi to you or rent a car."

Trina had walked to the window, which looked over the water in the Georgia Strait. She could see a little further than before, so the fog had lifted a little bit.

"Logan things are starting to improve here so I should be all right driving to Comox, they seem to have less fog there for some reason."

"Well that is the way I will come over. I want to be positive that I will get to you. My plane is supposed to be landing at 1:30 so I will see you then. They said the ferries would probably be running sooner but the earliest I can get away is twelve. I want to know that when I am finished here, we have a firm plan in place."

Logan continued, "I have something special to tell you when I see you." There was an air of mystery in his voice. "See you at 1:30 darling. I have to run now as I am already late for the morning session."

Trina whizzed around, completing some housework she had started. She had avoided doing the vacuuming because she wanted to hear the phone. Not wanting to miss Logan's call. She had kept busy so she wouldn't be frantic about not hearing from him right away. Dreading the fact, the fog was going to keep them apart. She had occupied herself while waiting by emptying cupboards and reorganizing them. There was stuff all over the place, which she had to clear away before she could leave for Comox. She had promised to take some baking pans over to Briana this morning and that was in the opposite direction from Comox. She was in a frenzy to get to the airport now that she knew he was coming. She would have to make sure Briana didn't delay her.

On her way to her daughter's place her heart was pumping with excitement. He had sounded so uncaring during his whale call. That call had made her think there was no hope of their ever seeing each other again.

Now he was only three hours away until his arrival. She was going to cut her visit to Briana as short as possible, because she wanted to be on her way to Comox in good time. Visibility was getting better as she drove to Briana's but still the fog was lingering around. She was aware that the Island Highway could be under dense fog because of its location. She would have to take it slower when she got to the highway. She was going no matter what the road conditions. She was going to be in Comox, come hell or high water.

She chided herself for swearing. Ladies don't swear. Then she giggled. She was so happy. Logan was almost here, and her heart was bursting with joy.

After Briana gave her a hug and shoved her out the door saying, "Go for it, Mom. You deserve it." She was glad she had let her daughter know that Logan was coming after all. She originally had considered not letting her know until she took Logan over to meet her.

She took the connector to the highway knowing that at last she was on her way to Logan and the airport. The man she had never expected to see again. She shouldn't let the problem of distance between their countries creep into the equation. But just accept what time they would have together at the moment. Trina shook her head as if to clear it, knowing that she had to keep her eyes on the road and concentrate on her driving.

Pulling out onto the main highway she noticed the visibility was definitely improving. Thankfully traffic was not too heavy, probably due to the fog. She was able to keep up with the traffic, by following the red tail-lights revealed ahead of her through the fog. The road seemed to be never ending as it wended its way through the countryside. The only blessing was the fog was fading.

At last there was the sign for her turn off to Courtenay and the Comox airport. Trina noted that the fog had indeed lifted. When she finally drove into Comox, she could hardly contain herself. The road to the airport was just ahead. She could see where she would have to turn. At the red light, Trina stopped after putting on her turn signal indicating she was making a left turn. Impatient to be there, she wished the traffic lights would quit turning red and slowing her drive to the airport.

With a sigh of relief, the airport appeared. She pulled through the gates into the parking lot. She easily found a parking space close to the terminal and pulled into it. Glancing at her wrist for the time, she was three-quarters of an hour early, but she was definitely here. There was no fog in sight as she looked around, before gathering up her leather purse and opening the car door. Logan's plane would certainly be able to land here. Inserting money for the parking meter rapidly, then she headed across to the entrance.

Arriving in the terminal, she looked for the Arrival and Departure sign to see if the plane was delayed. Trina glanced at her wrist again, noting that the hands had hardly moved since she had last looked at her watch. She found a seat near the arrivals gate, which Logan would be coming through.

She had brought a book with her to help pass the time, but she was too excited to read. So, she sat there glancing around at the people anxiously awaiting the plane. She noted, they kept checking their watches too. Trina examined hers, the minute hand was just not moving fast enough. Hurry, hurry said her heart.

A sweet elderly lady struck up a conversation with her. She said, "I am meeting my grandson, Greg. My daughter has just gone to get some more information on her son's arrival time." Trina was having a hard time following what she was saying because some thoughts were whirling around in her mind.

What does he anticipate to happen? What does he have to tell me? Will this make any positive difference in our relationship? He is calling me darling and seems to be anxious to see me.

Trina continued to make automatic mumbling noises in reply, to the elderly lady who continued with her monolog of her wonderful grandson, Greg and his accomplishments. Trina must have looked somewhat interested as the lady was merrily talking away.

The loud speaker crackled to life bringing Trina's mind back to hear the awaited announcement that Logan's plane was landing.

Starting to shift around, everyone was craning their necks to get the first all-important sighting of their loved ones. She stood back from the rest of the people waiting. She was not sure what was the best way to greet him, after all this time. She wanted to watch his face as he approached her. Would it be the same as she recalled?

Logan stopped about a yard in front of her, dropping his briefcase; he opened his arms along with his heart to receive her. She was there in an instant.

He hugged her ever so tightly and kissed her temple lovingly. He didn't want to let go now that he had her in his arms at last. He knew that this was the way he wanted them to be. This close forever.

The luggage banging and thumping on the nearby conveyor belt brought them back to the here and now. He said as he released her and picked up his briefcase. "I don't have any luggage everything is at the hotel. Unfortunately, I have to go back tonight but I will be returning from Qualicum. They assured me that the weather would not be a problem for my night flight back to Vancouver."

He kept Trina firmly planted at his side with his arm around her as they left the terminal, and headed towards the parking lot. She steered him in the right direction, pulling the keys from her pocket.

Logan asked, "is there a restaurant close by, where we can talk privately without too many distractions? I want to tell you a story and it will explain why I am here."

"There is a nice restaurant that has many little rooms with nooks and crannies to give patrons privacy in their dining. It is called "The Cottage" but is quite large and set back off the road in the middle of Courtenay."

When they reached the car, Trina asked Logan if he wanted to drive but he said she knew the way and he didn't, so it would be best if she drove. They arrived at the Cottage parking lot.

He looked at the treed area surrounding a quaint old house. that had a stepping stone path leading to the entrance. "It was converted into a restaurant twelve years ago," she told him.

As they made their way on the stepping stones, the shrubs and trees gave the empty path a certain amount of privacy. Logan stopped to draw Trina into his arms. He kissed her gently on her lips and then he pulled back to look deeply into her eyes. He had a look of desire. He drew her back into his arms for a more intense kiss. They broke apart at the sound of the snickers of a young couple approaching behind them chuckling at their passion.

They let the couple past smiling at them. Logan waited until they went inside then he said to Trina. "I wanted to do that at the airport but I preferred to do it more privately, so that is why I waited."

She was thinking she preferred this moment here too. He took her hand and proceeded to the door of the restaurant, set back in an intricate latticework entwined with a profusion of jasmine flowers. Entering, the entrance was filled with old style decor. The smiling hostess was walking towards them with a warm greeting. Asking if they had a preference as to where they wanted to be seated.

chapter

EIGHTEEN

The hostess led them to a small room where there were only four glossy wooden tables, all were unoccupied at the moment. When they were seated, Logan ordered drinks for them both. Neither wanted food, they just wanted to talk. Trina's stomach was in too fluttery a state of expectation for food.

He gazed into her eyes and he saw the brightness there, he felt he could tell her his story. He still held her hand enclosed tightly in his.

"When I was growing up, I had an uncle who was very special to me. His name was Uncle Adam. He took me places. We did things that usually fathers do with their sons. He made sure I had the proper respect for my parents as he thought that was important. He never had any children of his own, as he had never married. He felt this was the way he would have influenced his son, knowing he would never have one."

"Uncle Adam had been in love with a wonderful lady, about the age I am now. But they had never married. My uncle was my father's oldest brother by a number of years. He passed away about the same time as Linda."

"Back to the story. Uncle Adam had met this lady when she travelled to Australia by herself on vacation in 1960 or thereabouts. They fell in love almost at first sight, and spent a full two weeks together before she went home to Canada.

He stopped while the waitress put their drinks on the table. Logan thanked her then looked back to Trina and continued his story.

"Uncle Adam told my father that he had been in touch with her several times after. But she would never consider leaving her family to join him in Australia. My uncle was devastated that she kept them apart. He later said to my father, he should have gone and just taken her away with him. But he was too afraid that if he had done that, she wouldn't leave with him. Or she would be so unhappy and pining for her family. If this happened, he knew he would feel badly, knowing he had more or less forced her to come to Australia."

"The story continues with her fading enthusiasm for his phone calls, and my uncle eventually died of a broken heart, although he never let on to me. It was my Dad who told me this story when I was pining for you. To think that as close as we were, Uncle Adam had never shared this special story with me. I guess he was too private a man."

He squeezed her hand tenderly while he raised his glass for a toast. "To us." Their glasses clinked lightly then they took a sip, his eyes held hers over their glasses.

Did he say pining for me? Popped into her head.

"My call to you on whales, was really wanting to hear your sweet voice again." Logan brought her hand to his mouth and placed a light kiss on the back of her hand. She felt quivery inside. "I went to see my Mom and Dad to relay your message to them. He knew the way I talked about you, the hopelessness of the situation. That was when Dad felt, I needed to know Uncle Adam's story."

"My Dad finished the story I have just told you, by saying not to make the same mistake that his brother had made. He told me to look within and if I thought I really cared about you, to go and see you and talk it out. And that is what I did. I just kept thinking about you and our wonderful week together. The happiness I felt being with you. How we seemed to be so well suited in everything we did and said. When we were together, I felt whole again. Which is something I haven't felt since Linda died. I was seriously thinking of flying here, when Dad mentioned the Hotel Convention in Vancouver."

She was sipping her drink slowly watching Logan, thinking about this incredible story he had told her. She felt she was almost devouring him with her eyes, gazing at him intently.

He continued with encouragement by her intense gaze feeling that she had appreciated his story.

"I didn't call you sooner because I still wasn't sure which way I was going to get here, until my father came up with the convention. Then I didn't want to phone ahead that I was coming in case you didn't want to see me again. Or if you and David were now a definite couple since your return."

Logan paused hopeful that she would say the right comment in reply to all he had told her.

"No, David and I are not a couple, although he did ask me to marry him last month and I declined."

He issued a sigh of relief. His heart started beating slowly again. He realized his unease about David being on the scene. The possibility of his wanting more than friendship. After all he knew, they had parted as just friends. Relief showing in his face as he continued. "There is more." Logan paused to take a drink of his wine.

Trina sipped her wine, waiting for him to continue.

"After I left Mom and Dad that night, I went back to my place to think over the story about my Uncle Adam. I was deep in memories of my childhood and the happy times spent with my uncle, when I had this strangest feeling come over me. This thought or saying popped into my head as though it was my uncle trying to communicate with me," Logan said with some hesitation.

"Don't keep me in suspense. What was it?" Trina implored.

Logan grinned at her and repeated what he had felt came from his uncle.

"*When you see your ladylove, will you please see if my own true love is still alive?*' At the same time, I felt this heaviness on my shoulder like a hand placed there."

"My uncle used to do that when I walked beside him, as a boy. It felt rather eerie to experience that feeling again. I have thought about the spirit world at times when people mentioned it, but never really believed in that sort of thing. But you know at that moment, I really felt my uncle was there."

"He was not a happy man but he was a proud man, not sharing his deep feelings. Probably that was why he never told me his entire story. Uncle Adam helped me grow to be the man I am today. My father was always too busy, being so involved with the hotel business to spend time with me during my childhood."

He paused, waiting for some response from Trina. She seemed to be digesting what he had shared, in the way she was deep in thought.

Her glass was set down gingerly, while she took a moment of contemplation.

"You know Logan, I have heard of these entities visiting others, but I have never experienced them myself. Therefore, I can't say it never happened but I think if you believe it did, that is what is important. You should try to find this lady. Do you know anything about her?"

"My father remembers her name was Doreen, Diana or Doris or something like that, but he wasn't positive. He also thought her last name could be Naismith. Dad remembers the last name because he knew someone by that name and had asked her if she had any relatives in Australia."

"Uncle Adam had brought her to our house to meet me but my mother and I were out at the time. My father had tried to get them to wait around but they were both anxious to be off alone or so he felt, at the time."

Logan paused thinking about how he could find this unknown lady. What else had his father told him?

"My father said he didn't know, if knowing her name would be enough, or whether she is still alive even. All I know from my Dad is that she lived near or in Qualicum and the coincidence of the same place had struck him when I had first introduced you to him. My father thinks she would be about seventy-eight or eighty because he seemed to be sure that she was younger than Uncle Adam by about ten years. My Uncle would have been ninety if he had lived."

Trina responded, "I can inquire around if anyone knew a woman bearing the surname Naismith and her first name starts with 'D' who lived in Qualicum. That at least would be a start."

Logan said wistfully, "I wish I didn't have to go back tonight but I have to be there to take part in tomorrow's activities about Worldwide Hotel practices, as they relate to today's market. After all that was the purpose that brought me here originally." Then he corrected himself. "No, you are the reason I came and only you. I will get away as soon as feasible. I definitely do not intend being there for the wrap-up of the convention on the last day."

"At the session tomorrow, I am the guest speaker, and I have to take part in the next three days. I really have no choice in the matter. My family is depending on me to bring back the findings of the convention's ideas. This is important to smaller family hotel chains like ours," Logan said regretfully. "On the last day I noted from the schedule of events that there are some talks I can skip, without missing any important information. The material relates more to larger hotel chains."

"I understand, but will you have any time when you finish to come back?" Trina asked optimistically.

"Yes, I have booked my return flight for an additional week, before I return home to Australia," Logan said decisively.

She gave a sigh of relief. Logan smiled at her and clasped her hand more tightly.

"While you are at the convention, I will see what I can do about finding this unknown ladylove."

"Thank you and let's get out of here. I want to go to your place where we can relax before my plane takes me away again. Thank heavens I have a booking back to Vancouver from Qualicum as that will give us more time together."

He dropped some money down on the table for the drinks. They headed for the door and the parking lot. Just before they escaped from the trees and shrub coverage, he pulled her into his arms and gave her a tender kiss. A kiss of expectation for their future was all there. She wound her arms around his neck and returned the kiss lovingly.

As they progressed down the highway the conversation was of an easy nature, about their surroundings. Tales of Danny and the hotel life since they had been apart. They seemed to have fallen back into a natural way of togetherness, that they had had in Australia. When they arrived at Trina's home it was as though they had never been apart.

Logan looked around with interest. He certainly felt that it was comfortable with a coziness. The decorations were simple but colorful. She had left the stereo on and tranquil music was invading the air.

She led him through the house with an easy grace. He particularly liked her bedroom that was very feminine in dark and light pinks with white blended in. There was a cat sprawled out on the bedspread lapping up the rays of the bright sun slipping through the curtains. The curtains were lacy and the view was of a mountain top way off in the distance.

She called his attention to the cat that she introduced as Neptune. The cat opened her eyes but continued her lazy sprawl enjoying the sunbeams cloaking her. Logan reached over and gave Neptune a pat, which started her purring but she still did not change her position in the sunrays.

He said facetiously, "so, you do have someone in your bed, where you know I would like to be." Trina laughed and her face took on a pink glow. She pulled him away from the bedroom.

She headed for the kitchen while Logan headed back into the living room where there was a fireplace with a mantel in the corner of the room. There was a large formal family picture above it of an attractive young woman, that looked a bit like a younger version of Trina. He assumed this was the much talked about Briana and her family.

He glanced out the window at the view of the water in the Georgia Strait. There in the distance were the snow peaks of the Rocky Mountains she had mentioned while she was in Australia. He thought her place was well situated with its striking view. He started to hum with the music. He was just thankful to be here.

When she came out of the kitchen with the tea that she had prepared, she noted he had made himself at home. His jacket was slung over a chair, his sleeves were rolled up and his tie was loose at his neck. She smiled to see him standing silhouetted against the window. The way he was standing was reminiscent of her father that she had been very fond of.

Logan quickly came forward to help her with the tea tray. The last thing he wanted right now was tea, as he was ready for more than making conversation. Thinking he would rather make mad love to her instead. Trina was too much a lady for that kind of conduct. He would just have to be patient. Time was running out, soon he would have to be on his way back to Vancouver. He had a lot to say to her before then.

Accepting the cup and saucer she held out to him she mentioned, "I enjoyed being with Sally and Danny during that special visit."

"They know I am here. Sally says hi and that she misses seeing you. Danny sends his love. He wants me to tell you to come back with me."

"Tell Danny I would love to but it is not possible."

He kept up his part of the conversation until the cup was empty. He then got up and removed her cup and saucer from her hand and placed them back on the tray on the coffee table. He drew her up into his arms, his patience had come to an end.

He lightly kissed Trina while she made purring sounds. Her arms came up to encircle his neck. He deepened the kiss gradually and their love flowed.

Logan knew his emotions were going too fast. He respected her too much to cause her embarrassment, especially after what happened that last time, they had almost made love.

Trina was in a dilemma. It had been years since she had met someone, she could possibly make love with. So, intimacy had never been a problem or even a thought in her relationships until Logan. She felt like an inexperienced teenager.

Can I do this? Will he love me and then leave me again? This is beyond friendship this time she was feeling. There is that old question, is he really over Linda? Should she broach the subject?

Logan gave her one last kiss putting warmth and caring into it to show her how precious she was to him and always would be. Then kissed the tip of her nose and placed her back in her chair saying. "We better call a halt to this before it gets completely out of hand."

He went over to the couch and sat down, the love they were both feeling, was vibrating throughout the room.

"Is there somewhere we can go for dinner close by? I have to get my plane at seven." Logan said quietly, trying to bring back his control of the situation.

Trina started listing the restaurants in the area. She too was trying to ease the emotion they had found themselves in.

Logan suggested, "something like the place we were in earlier would be nice."

"We could go the Castle Inn it has a nice cozy restaurant with little rooms off the main dining room. The atmosphere there can be very romantic," she said grinning in his direction.

Logan grinned back, "That would be fine. Do we need to make reservations?"

Trina went to the phone to make reservations then asked, "do you want to see something of Qualicum beforehand as there is time?"

"Yes, that would be nice."

As they drove around in the village, Logan was impressed. "I understand now why you had such pride in your voice when you talked about your home and its surroundings. The village is quaint and the mountains majestic, the huge trees and forest encircle you. So different from Australia."

Over the candlelight dinner, Logan said, "I like your choice of restaurants. Are all the places here like the two you have taken me to, so far?"

"No these are special. I wanted to be with you in more intimate private surroundings."

Logan's eyes were luminous at her reply. He picked up her hand and placed a loving kiss in her palm. "The waiting is still between us for a few more days but I will return, as soon as possible. Then we will renew the days we were together in Sydney, here on your island."

He raised his glass. "To you, my love, and our special week together." Looking deeply into her eyes. Trina smiled with happiness.

He was very attentive and they discussed plans for his stay. She made suggestions. "We can go to Cathedral Grove and Qualicum Falls. A longer trip will be to Long Beach and nearby Tofino. I can come up with other suggestions. We will just see what we feel we want to do during the week." She was pleased that things were coming together at last.

He kept touching her hand at every opportunity and raising it to his lips with a twinkle of mischief, then he would touch the palm of her hand with a kiss. These caresses were making her tremble inside. Making her wonder what next week would bring.

Over tea and dessert Logan brought up the subject of his uncle and the mystery lady in his uncle's life again. She offered, "I know some older residents who I can call who have lived in the area for a considerable time to see if anyone is able to recognize the name."

"Thank you for the offer."

"I am looking forward to the challenge of finding her. It will make the time go faster."

At last, it was time to head for the airport and the plane that would carry him back to Vancouver. They both were sad about their separation but they knew they would soon be together again. Four days isn't too long or is it?

The parking lot was full of cars when they came out but seemed deserted of people so Logan embraced Trina and kissed her lovingly with the promise of his return.

She hugged him and laughingly said, "is this what is known as a parking lot affair?"

Logan laughed too, saying with honesty. "No but it seems that is the only convenient place where we can have privacy without running into difficulties of bedrooms being too near." They continued to proceed to Trina's car for their ride to the airport.

When they got to the airport Logan held her hand. "Trina you know of course where this is heading and I want you to think seriously about this while I'm gone. To me you are my love and you *will* be my only love and we *will* be together. Our problems will be resolved somehow. Please keep an open mind and let your heart tell you what is right for us," Logan said hopefully.

All too soon their time had run out as he kissed her goodbye on the tarmac.

"I will be back on Tuesday evening. I will try to get the first flight out but I'll let you know for sure. I will be calling you each night before you go to bed. Tuesday seems a long way off when I want so much to be with you. We will continue our conversation on our being together when I return, so you don't have to say anything now." He released her and walked quickly to the plane not giving her time to say more than goodbye.

He nonchalantly turned around at the top of the steps and gave her a wink and a wave then disappeared into the plane. She saw him framed in one of the windows, and raised her fingers to her lips and blew him a kiss. Tears had formed in her eyes as she thought of his declaration of love.

She knew where it was heading and she did want it too. But she also knew she would miss her family so much. Would she be able to leave them? When it came right down to it, was she ready for the bedroom scene? Had it been too long since Devlin? She felt like a love crazed teenager thinking these crazy thoughts, wanting to be loved at the same time.

His plane was ready to proceed to the runway for takeoff. They had both been staring at each other as they waited for the plane to ready itself, each with their minds racing with similar feelings. She lifted her hand to wave. He waved back as the plane moved to ready for flight. The plane jets roared as the blue and white plane hurdled down the runway and leaped into the sky.

Trina stood watching until the plane was a tiny speck in the distance.

chapter

NINETEEN

Trina had been wandering around aimlessly after getting back from the airport. She should be happy that he was coming back but she felt disconnected from him with the expanse of water between them. She was thinking that expanse of water represented the ocean that was between their two countries. Insurmountable. What would this week be like for them? Will it really bring us together or will it just mean more heartache in parting?

Logan was being so positive why wasn't she? I want him and I need him to fulfill my life. I know that, especially after today. BUT?

Blue eyes had followed her. Destiny had caught up with her. But was she able to cope with the family separation that would come with it?

She must have been stewing over this doubt for over an hour without a solution. When the phone's trilling penetrated her thoughts, she glanced at the clock a natural reaction at night. Her heart started to quiver with excitement she knew it was him.

"Hello Logan." A chuckle greeted her.

"No Trina it is Sally."

"Sally, how are you? It is nice to hear from you."

"Fine. I know my Dad is with you as he phoned last night to say he would be there."

"I am sorry he just left a while ago. He had to go back tonight as he is speaking at the convention tomorrow."

"That's all right, it is you I want to talk to."

"Is there a problem? Is Danny okay?"

"Danny is okay, there's no problem. I was going to write you a letter. But when I thought Dad was to be there, I thought I would phone instead."

"Now you have me curious."

"While Dad was here on his last weekend, we were discussing you and my mother came into the conversation. Dad is pretty taken with you. He indicated if things went well between you two, and he is hoping it will. Then he will be very happy.

Then we were talking about my mother and their relationship. He said Mom was never the love of his life. He proceeded to tell me how they met. She worked with him at the hotel. Their relationship was based on her helplessness and they drifted into marriage. Apparently, my mother was adopted and as a result was insecure." Trina was wondering why Sally was relating this information to her.

"The only reason they stayed together was because of me. It was after this conversation that things started making sense. The lack of open affection between them which was noticeable. Don't get me wrong, he cared for her mainly because she was a nice person. He did say, he felt sure her insecure feelings were a result of being abandoned by her mother."

"I'm sorry to hear that," Trina said still wondering where this was heading.

"Dad said you don't live with someone for years without feelings of caring for them. He also said he never met anyone that he could love until he met you. He said he couldn't explain it exactly, but you were the only woman he felt that way about."

Trina was relieved to hear this but felt there was more to this phone call yet to come.

"Did you by any chance have a sister or is it possible your mother had another child that was put out for adoption? Is there a possibility of a family connection? Your resemblance is so similar to my mother. I can't help but wonder if there is a possibility of a family connection?"

"Family connection? Not that I am aware of. My mother never said anything to me about a sister."

"It was just a thought." Sally was hoping Trina wasn't taking offence at her questions.

Trina was frantically thinking is there a possibility here? "Sally, I seem to remember in my childhood, mother sent me to live with my grandmother. She said her job had sent her to head office in Seattle in the States on a special job for six months. It was shortly after my father passed away in a car accident. I really have no idea if there is any connection between my mother and Linda. I know mother was sad but I thought that was because of the car accident in which my father died."

"Trina, I know there is a big if here. IF she is your missing sister that is why you look so much alike. I also want to say that if she isn't your sister that you understand, Dad cared for her but he really didn't love her."

"Thank you for that information. I wondered if my likeness to your mother, was the reason your Dad seemed to care for me so much. You have put my mind at rest on that point. Do you think I should mention your conversation about your mother, when I talk to your father later?"

"I rather you wouldn't he will think I am having fanciful thoughts but you can tell him I called. I'm sorry I missed talking to him before his plane left."

"I won't mention it then."

"I had an ulterior motive when I made this call with the hopes that you and my father were able to share the same feelings, that he will persuade you to come to Australia. I wanted to put your mind at rest about the relationship between my parents." Adding, with a chuckle, "Danny misses you and so do I."

"Thanks for the sentiment, I miss you both too." Trina didn't respond to Sally's wish for her to go to Australia. She was keeping an open mind until the week with Logan was over.

"I better let you go perhaps Dad may be calling."

"Goodbye Sally. Thank you for putting my mind at rest about your mother's relationship with your Dad. It was always at the back of my mind when we were together that he might still love her."

She did not have any time to think over the conversation with Sally before the phone rang. Before she could say anything, Logan said, "my darling, I love you."

Trina gave a shaky laugh. Logan was a more compelling man than she was used to.

"I love you," Trina replied mistily, "and I miss you."

"Darling, you finally said the words I have longed to hear. Trina, I was beginning to think it was all one sided. I knew you liked me a great deal but I wanted so much to hear you say those words."

She was glad too that she had been daring enough to say them. "Logan, I have felt like a lost soul since you left. I can't settle, and I just know I won't sleep."

"Darling, I know and I feel the same way, but we will be together in a few days. We will work out all our problems, I know it. They are not insurmountable and I know we were meant to be together. Remember what I said. Please keep an open mind and let your heart tell you what is right for you," he stressed.

She accepted what he was saying and replied, "I will try. I want you back with me as soon as possible."

"First plane out of here after the conference ends Tuesday. I will be on it for sure. I checked when I landed and it will be at six, so please be there waiting for me at six-thirty. Now look out the window across the water, as I am looking out towards you. We are together linked by the water, think of it as a powerful force, joining not separating us."

She walked over to the window with the phone pressed to her ear and looked longingly towards Vancouver.

"I'm looking," Trina said wistfully.

"Now love, do you feel that I am with you?"

"No but I want to."

Logan chuckled. "I agree it isn't the same but I tried. Goodbye love and I will call you tomorrow night. Sweet Dreams"

"Good night, Logan and I will be looking across the water to you until your return." The phone went dead and she just stood there yearning for his return. Her mind slipped in the direction of Sally's phone call. She forgot to mention the call. *Could Linda be her sister? How could she find out?*

The next day Trina got on the phone to try to find Uncle Adam's lost ladylove. She called a friend who had been in the area for all his life. Trina asked, "do you know anybody by the name of Naismith that lived in this area?"

Brian was from one of the first families that had settled in Qualicum.

"I recall that there was a family by that name but I never had occasion to make their acquaintance. So, I have no idea what happened to them or whether they are still here. Did you try the telephone directory?"

"Thank you for that suggestion. I will see you around town no doubt. Goodbye."

Next Trina tried the telephone book for the whole district and surrounding towns. She found three Naismith listings. There were two in Nanaimo and one in a neighboring town.

She called the one in the neighboring town first. They were very friendly towards her quest but they said, "we nor any of our relations had ever lived in Qualicum to our knowledge. We have only been here for ten years."

"Thank you for your help."

She dialed the numbers of Nanaimo Naismith but again they were both helpful but not able to shed any light on this unknown woman that had lived in Qualicum. Nor did they think there had been relations of theirs in that area.

What to do next? Trina sat pondering the situation while glancing across the water towards Vancouver. What was he doing now?

The thought suddenly came to Trina that perhaps this unknown lady may have been married and she was not known by her maiden name when and if she left Qualicum. Perhaps she had moved back after she and her husband separated or she was widowed.

If she is approximately eighty, she just might be in a retirement home and that is why she couldn't find a listing for her. She turned to the nursing homes in the index of the telephone directory. There were six in this general area. She made a uniform list of names and numbers with spaces in between for comments.

Trina was getting a bit distraught, after she had called four of the numbers without avail. This too could be futile and maybe a dead-end. The next one was Mountainview Retirement Lodge. This was up island from Qualicum in a nice area overlooking Mount Arrowsmith according to the big ad in the telephone book. She had glanced at the ad while checking for their number.

The voice that answered was cheery. Trina asked. "Is there a D. Naismith residing there?"

The answer came, "I am not familiar with all the names of the residents, as I am new. Then the voice started to say, "no…"

When she recalled the lady in Room 305. Doris Reilly was a great storyteller and she had spent time with her listening to her stories, whenever she could get free time to do so. Doris' stories were of her good times and also her bad times with her ex-husband and family but she made them interesting so that you wanted to hear more. She remembered her telling stories of her father and she seemed to recall that his name started with 'Na'. Doris also would spin tales of a certain lost love that you just knew it was someone she missed significantly.

Trina was wondering why the voice had said 'no' without saying anything further. "I am sorry to bother…"

The voice interrupted, "there is a lady here that used to be married but I don't believe she goes by her maiden name. She once told me a story about her ex-husband giving her father a hard time. Her story telling of the occasion made it quite humorous. At the time I vaguely remember she mentioned the father's name, I think it started with 'Na'. I am Karen and I will contact you after I speak to Doris Reilly. If you give me your name and number, I will call you back and let you know."

Trina's heart skipped a beat when she heard the 'Doris'. That was one of the names Logan had mentioned. She gave Karen her name and number and suggested, if it would help, this lady I am searching for travelled to Australia at some point in her life.

Trina made a cup of tea and almost tripped over Neptune. She had been so preoccupied; she hadn't noticed the circling motion of the cat hoping for tidbits. Her loud meows brought her back to awareness. She reached down and picked the cat up.

"Neptune, I am sorry I didn't mean to ignore you but I have a lot on my mind right now." She lovingly rubbed her cheek on the cat's fur. "I will get you a treat." Reaching into the cupboard, Trina removed a box of cat goodies shaped like fish. While Neptune settled into eagerly eating, she returned to her thoughts of what she would do next if this turned out to be the wrong person.

She jumped when the phone pealed beside her, as she came quickly out of her problematic thoughts. Tipping her cup with her arm but it righted itself without spilling in the curved saucer.

"Hello," Trina said with an expectant voice.

"Hello, Mrs. Grant this is Karen. I spoke to Doris and yes her maiden name was Naismith and yes she has been to Australia."

Trina felt her breath catch with excitement. This was the lost ladylove she felt sure. She thought she should make sure this Doris was well enough and able to receive visitors. She knew that Logan would want to see her so she inquired.

"If you can tell me without invading her privacy is there any problems that would be a reason for her not having visitors? My friend from Australia and I would like to come to see her."

Karen replied, "no, she is in a wheelchair but her faculties are good and she is bright as a shiny penny but frail. That is why Doris is here because she can't fend for herself anymore but she is a real sweetheart. Everyone loves her and her stories in particular, of which she has many. When will you be coming to see Doris and how can I prepare her for your visit?"

"I don't exactly know when we will be there."

Karen added in a concerned way. "How do you know of her or are either of you a relation? I know you mentioned your friend was from Australia and she has been there."

Trina didn't know how to explain the circumstances of their visit, as she wanted Logan to tell Doris in his own way. She hesitatingly said thinking as she spoke. "This friend visiting from Australia thinks he may know someone she has met, during her trip to Australia back in the sixties. My friend, Logan would like to talk to Doris himself, and find out if she knew a member of his family. He is on the mainland until Tuesday but he will be here for a week. I know he would like to meet her if it can be arranged. What are your visiting hours?"

"They are ten a.m. till eight p.m. daily," replied Karen.

"I'm sure Logan will be there right away to see her or sometime on the weekend. I will phone to let you know exactly when we will come. Do you think it will harm her in any way, the excitement of meeting strangers? You did say she was quite frail," asked Trina in a concerned voice.

"No, she is not flustered by anything. She always takes things in her stride. It is only her body that is fragile. I am sure she would love to see you both, as her family live in Victoria now. Although they do come to see her fairly frequently considering the distance. In fact, they were just here this past weekend. They did consider moving her to Victoria but Doris was raised near here and she loves her mountain too much to leave it."

"Can she see it?"

"Yes. Doris is in the end room and her picture window looks out on Mount Arrowsmith, and she sits there daily admiring the view. She calls it her strength that keeps her alive."

Trina disclosed. "Well this is a visit we are looking forward to. Just to see her reaction to this story Logan has to tell her. I am certainly glad I found her for him. Thank you and maybe we will see you then."

"I won't be working Saturday; it is my day off. I hope your visit goes well because she is a sweet dear lady and deserves every bit of happiness that comes her way."

They said their goodbyes. Trina replaced the receiver on the base with an inner excitement that she had found Doris (Naismith) Reilly. Now she just had to wait for Logan's call.

She went into the living room to look out across the water and think about Logan and visualize him giving a speech at the conference podium. He has such an assured manner about him, she had noticed.

Then her mind flipped to Sally's call. *Did she have a sister? Could she find her as easily as she found Doris?*

———

Trina phoned the company's head office in Seattle, WA that her mother had temporality worked for. She spoke to the receptionist knowing full well that this might pan out to not reveal any information. The receptionist was trying to be helpful, by putting her through to Human Resources. The girl there, looked back in the records of employment to the year Trina believed her mother worked there for six months. She came back on the phone to say yes that there was a woman by that name that worked there for a short period. Thanking her, Trina hung up.

Now what? If there was a birth record would it be under Linda Grant? If her mother was putting her up for adoption would the baby have the new parents name on the birth certificate? Trina thought and thought while these questions played around in her head.

She called the birth records people in Seattle. They couldn't find a record of a Linda Grant unless I had more information as to a date or at least an actual month and year. She told them the approximate date as best she could recall. They came back with the answer, "no, are you sure of the date?"

"Thank you for trying but I don't know the date for sure nor can I obtain more positive information."

Maybe it wasn't in her mother's name? Now that her Mother and Grandmother had passed on, there was no way to find out the date they were requesting or if the name was correct. Definitely not as easy as finding Doris.

———

That night, Logan was later calling her than usual He apologized for being so late, "I was out with a few of my colleagues for drinks after dinner."

Trina said, "it is all right, as I was at Amanda's. In fact, I was afraid that I would miss your call. I had difficulties getting away from her."

"How are you? Did you miss me today?" Logan asked hopefully.

"Yes, I missed you. It was hard telling Amanda about your visit because I really didn't want to say too much. Since she got married, she wants everyone to be in love the way she and Ted are. She is a good friend and I understand how she feels."

"Were Ted and David there?"

"No, it was just Amanda and me. Ted and David went to the Rotary Club meeting." Trina changed the subject quickly. "Now I have some good news for you." The excitement in Trina's voice was evident. "I found Doris Reilly, which is her married name."

"You did? Where?" Logan's voice leaped through the phone excitedly.

"She is in the Mountainview Retirement Home up island not far from here. Apparently, she loves to tell stories and the girl on the phone, Karen, was fascinated by her tales. She remembered Doris had said her father's name started with 'Na' and she has been to Australia."

"Australia?"

"Yes, Karen said she also tells stories about a lost love."

"You're right it does sound like she is the right one." Logan was thrilled that Trina had found her.

"I will be getting the six o'clock plane Tuesday as I thought I would. So please be at the airport to greet me." He wanted her to be there when he landed.

They continued talking about his daily happenings and then it was time to sign off. "Good night, Trina. I miss you very very much and I am impatient for Tuesday to get here," Logan said plaintively.

"Good night, Logan. It is difficult for me too, being patient for Tuesday to arrive." She didn't want to hang up so she waited for Logan to break the connection. The buzzing of the phone is such a deflating sound, she was thinking, as she put the receiver down.

———

Monday, Trina spent the day with Briana. She was off work because she had gone into work on the weekend to finish an important project that was needed for today.

Trina's spending time with her daughter, would help past the dragging hours.

Briana knew Logan was coming Tuesday and she wanted to meet him but at the same time she didn't. This man could take her mother away from her. Would she like him? She had feelings of resentment against him already. In reality it was unfortunate, and not fair to Logan.

She knew that her mother loved this man because she could see the love shining in her bright sparkly eyes as she talked about him. This was her mother who usually was very down to earth in everything she did. This was going to be a visit that would cause some difficulties.

When the children arrived home from school, Trina gave them big hugs and they were planting kisses on her cheek. They excitedly talked about their day at school and their friends. Briana watched reservedly, because this was something that would be missing from her children's lives if her mother married this man and moved to Australia. She wondered if she would be able to be impartial towards this man when they finally met.

A knock came on the door, Scott bounced out of his chair. "That will be Kyle calling for me. Goodbye Grandma. Goodbye Mom." He headed for the door. Scott promised, he would be home in time for dinner. Kathie headed down the hall to change her clothes before going to her friend's house.

Briana talked her mother into staying for dinner, she just couldn't let her go home yet. She resented the possibility that these dinners may be a thing of the past very soon.

Trina stayed and tried to be cheerful. She knew her daughter only too well, and knew that she was thinking of their possible separation. There would be a time they would have to discuss this quandary. All day the air had been gradually getting thick with anxiety. She had been putting off the discussion since nothing had really been settled between Logan and her.

She remembered the pictures, she had received that day from Emma. One was of Logan and Trina when he had met her at the dock in Cairns. She was unaware Emma had taken that particular shot. It was the picture where Logan had put his arm around her and pulled her jokingly close to his side in an amorous manner, as they were saying goodbye to the tour group.

She reached for her purse. Maybe this picture will help Briana think better of Logan. She looked at it with critical eyes. They did make a wonderful looking couple as Emma's letter indicated.

She handed it to her daughter. "Briana, this is a picture that arrived today from Emma of Logan and me at the dock in Cairns. It was taken the day he took me to see Sally and Danny. Emma and I were supposed to get together to exchange pictures but it never worked out, so she sent these by mail instead."

Briana looked at the picture and knew right away that this couple was meant for each other. His look of affection said he wanted her by his side forever.

"Logan looks like he could be a very caring man. It is certainly a nice picture of you both," Briana said too brightly. She knew now why her mother was interested in this man. She handed the picture back to her mother still feeling sad inside.

Ken knew that Briana was not her usual self when he arrived home from work. The talk of Logan's coming was the reason for her quietness. Although he was concerned for Briana, Ken felt Trina deserved her happiness too.

He was trying to keep the conversation going during dinner, when the children ran out of things to say. Finally, he suggested he would supervise the kids' bedtime activity. They leaped up and gave Trina and Briana hugs and kisses and trouped upstairs chatting happily to their father. Ken listened, thankful that the children were unaware of the atmosphere like a heavy cloud, that he had left behind.

Trina got up and started removing the dishes. Briana joined her picking up some of the dishes and heading for the kitchen too. She started stacking the dishes into the dishwasher. She knew it was time to get her feelings out in the open.

"Mom, you are probably aware that I am not feeling too amenable about the fact that Logan is coming here."

Trina went over to Briana and took her into her arms. "Yes, I know but I don't really want to discuss it right now because nothing has been settled between Logan and me, other than he is just a friend," Trina said elusively.

"I don't want you to move to Australia and never be with you again. I watched you with the children, and they need you as a grandmother not a distant relation. I know I am being selfish but I can't help myself. I want you to be happy. I really do but not so far away." Briana's voice was full of tears and her eyes were over bright.

This was the very issue that Trina had been avoiding all day. How could she reassure her daughter when she wasn't sure herself?

"Briana let's just leave this for now until you meet Logan, and see what a wonderful caring man he is. But I have to tell you that I think I am in love with him. I have had some reservations about leaving too. It isn't easy to think about the distance between us if I do decide to go with him."

Briana stepped back and gave her mother a weak smile and said, "I will wait to meet this man you have fallen in love with, hopefully with an open mind. Mom, honest I want you to be happy but I can't help being a bit selfish in wanting you in our lives."

"Me too, darling," Trina responded, "me too."

They cleared the rest of the table, filling the dishwasher each with a sadness in their hearts. Only Trina's feelings were mixed because she knew now that in her heart, she loved Logan deeply.

That night when Logan phoned, he said, "I have decided, that we should spend time together first. To define our promising relationship before making the trip to see Doris."

"I agree and I did mention to Karen it might be the weekend before we came."

Trina knew he was truly anxious to be with her, because he said, "I am going to the airport sooner hoping to get an earlier flight but I will not change my ticket until I am sure I have a definite seat on the plane. Would you mind meeting the earlier plane, in hopes that I made it?"

"Yes, I am willing to meet every plane tomorrow just so long as you get here."

Logan asserted, "it is good that we will spend time together and enjoy each other. How can we be sure that we want to spend the rest of our lives together until we really talk, such as getting our idiosyncrasies out in the open." Logan concluded happily. His voice was very loving.

Trina was more reserved after knowing Briana's feelings on her leaving. He could detect reserve creeping into her voice, fearing her feelings had altered. He continued talking in the hopes of dissolving her apprehension. Sometime later when they rang off, he was at a loss at the sound in her voice that had changed since her eager comment about meeting his plane. This week ahead together was not going to be a breeze after all.

She sat looking out towards Vancouver and her love, knowing that the time of decision was coming all too soon, tomorrow he would be here.

What can I do? What can I say to convince him I am not ready to leave my family yet and not hurt him? When will the right time be? No time. The choice she had to make was so hard as she really loved him.

chapter

TWENTY

Neptune had not been happy that there was no time for her usual loving and stroking from her mistress. She meowed loudly but Trina was too busy getting ready to leave for the airport to notice the disgruntled cat. When she finally left the house, Neptune sauntered off to bed in a huff.

Trina was at the airport early. Logan was due in at 5:30, as he had managed to get the earlier flight. He just had enough time before takeoff to call her.

She was very happy that she was to see him again. She had missed him very much. If only there wasn't the distance between their two countries. No one could change the situation but herself and she was still unable to come up with a possible solution. Her thoughts of Logan and leaving her family seemed to be with her all the time now.

He was watching the terminal as his plane landed. He saw Trina silhouetted against the building, a beautiful smile and a wave. Her outstretched hand appeared to be drawing the plane and him towards her. He was here and her joy was escalating.

The pilot exited the plane and he proceeded to remove the luggage from the baggage compartment. Logan followed the other passengers' departure as quickly as he could. He paused on the step to give Trina a big smile, as she stepped forward in anticipation. Logan stepped down the stairway and reached for his luggage which had been placed close to the stairs. Turning he walked towards her. Trina had moved aside instead of directly towards him. So that they wouldn't hamper any of the other commuters in their departure.

Dropping his luggage, he drew her into his arms and kissed her with a lover's kiss. He clearly wanted to give her this message right from the start. The message that he wanted her with him in Australia.

He knew he was leaping ahead of what she was expecting but seeing her again he couldn't help himself. He placed his hands lovingly on each side of her face and said, "I love you, my darling. I hope you will let your heart show you the way into my arms, to become my loving wife." Kissing her tenderly to seal his proposal of love and marriage.

She stepped back and sighed. This was not the time to bring up the problems with Briana's concern about leaving the island. "Darling, we need to discuss some things before I can make the promise to become your wife."

This was not what Logan wanted to hear. However, he did think they should hold this conversation at Trina's place, not here on the black tarmac at the airport, with people milling around. He picked up his luggage and followed her to her blue Toyota Camry. Logan looked at the car. "This is new isn't it?" He realized he hadn't noticed the car the last time he was here.

"Yes. Ralph Appleton, my ex-boss gave the car to me for so many years of faithful service although I had left my job for retirement a year ago. I was so surprised, I had never believed that Ralph had appreciated me so much. He had always seemed to take me for granted, or so I thought. I guess he must have realized my worth after I had been gone for a while. This arrived about three months ago with a letter of appreciation. Isn't that amazing?" Trina was glad of this small talk to get them away from the proposal Logan made on his arrival.

"Trina that is incredible but I too appreciate you, and I want to show you how much in this coming week."

She opened the trunk so he could stow his luggage and then went to the driver's side to open the car door. Logan slid in beside Trina and glanced at her longingly.

Not being able to wait said. "I get the feeling that this is not going to be easy after all. What about the 'I love you', you gave me on the phone was that not true? I do want you for my wife." Logan said resolutely.

"I know I said that I love you and I do. But I got to thinking about leaving Briana and the children. When I had dinner with them last night, I realized more fully how much I would miss them, causing me to have second thoughts."

Logan took her hand as she went to put in the key in the car's transmission.

"Don't start the car yet. Please tell me how I can make this right between us. I don't want you to be unhappy. I want you to love me as I love you and be with me for the rest of our lives." Not giving her a chance to deny him he rushed on, "Trina, I know you will have to give up a lot to be with me but I have to return to Australia because my father is retiring soon. It was mentioned at the dinner at my parent's place, when you were over there. I am the only one proficient enough to take over in his place. My Dad is counting on me to keep the business running. I do have a lot invested in the hotel business. You know that my mother is counting on his retiring soon." pausing. *What can I say now to convince her?*

"Trina, will you be willing to consider giving me four years until we can make plans to include your family somehow in our future? I don't know, maybe we can move here to the island."

Trina sat still resisting in her mind. "Logan, I wish it was that easy. I am just afraid this is too good to be true and we will regret being so hasty in our decision and our marriage will become a failure."

"No Trina I am ready for this. I don't want to make the same mistake as my uncle. You know why he never married. He never could forget his ladylove. Do you want that for me too?"

"No Logan I don't. Please I am just asking for a little time. We have only had one week together plus a few days. We are still literally strangers."

"All right," Logan replied drawing away from her. "I am here for a week. I promise I will not pressure you again, but the time will be used for getting to know each other. We will have fun. We will laugh. No crying though." Logan chuckled. "You will see at the end of the week, that we are well suited to each other in every way."

"Besides I have a grandson that thinks his grandfather is really special and can do anything. Danny wants you back and so do I. You do still want me to be special to my grandson, don't you?" Halting his plea. "That was unfair of me," Logan chided then looked repentant. "One week without pressure. Okay?"

Trina started the car. She breathed a sigh of relief at this reprieve. She was ready now to accept the week together.

Pulling out of the parking space, Logan asked where he was staying, hoping it would be at her place.

"Well I thought of putting you in with David," Trina said with a chuckle. "Then I thought of Briana's but I think you would be happier at my place. I do have a second bedroom."

"No, I would prefer to bunk in with David," Logan said giving her a grin.

Trina swiveled her head quickly and saw his grin and laughed.

———

They went home and settled in for a pleasant dinner that she had prepared that afternoon. It had been cooking in the oven while she picked him up. Roast beef with onions, carrots and potatoes around the roast. She heated peas while she made the gravy. Logan sat watching her move around the kitchen, visualizing her in his kitchen in Australia.

She handed him the wine and the corkscrew to open the Borsao red wine. She asked, "Would you mind slicing the roast to speed the dinner along?"

"I was hoping you would ask."

She was filling bowls with the vegetables and put the gravy in its china gravy boat. Logan handled the knife with mastery and the slices soon piled up on the meat platter. They both headed to the dining room, each carrying food and he the wine.

She was getting anxious to be sitting across from him. The table was set for an intimate dinner, with lit candles.

Logan poured the wine and lifted his glass.

"To my lovely bride-to-be who is an exceptional cook too."

Trina chuckled. "You haven't even tasted it yet. Aren't you leaping ahead with this bride-to-be, we were just supposed to really get to know each other first?" But she raised her glass with his and sipped looking over the rim at him with love in her eyes.

Logan was surprised at her look, she had been drawing away from him ever since she met him at the plane. He was now gratified and touched her glass saying, "to Us."

She responded with a radiant, "to Us."

They exchanged conversation on his convention activities and she on her family. After dinner, she had brought out a fruit and cheese tray to round off the meal, which she served in the living room with more wine.

They spent the evening talking while soft music played in the background. The conversation flowed between them like a happily married couple.

—

Over the next few days, Trina took Logan to several of her favorite places to view the scenery of her beloved Vancouver Island. They spent time walking on the beaches and seeing the grandeur of the mountains around them. She wanted him to know and feel her love for this place, she was finding so difficult to leave.

One day they were sitting beside Qualicum River. The sounds of rushing water stimulating to her thoughts. Dancing tiny cascades of water, spilling over rocks and boulders in its rush to the waterfall, waiting to hurl itself with a rushing force to the lower valley and the lower waterfalls waiting there. She realized that they both appreciated this moment with nature in its purest form.

He talked about spending time on Fraser Island and she remembered how happy she had been there. Realizing that she would miss her island life but could be content there too. She even thought about her time in Sydney and knew she would enjoy living there also.

Logan's promise of no pressure, was being jovial and friendly. Enjoying the pleasant walk through the forest.

—

Saturday they were meeting Amanda and Ted for drinks before dinner. When they arrived, David was there also. Trina was surprised but should have known as they had always been such good friends. After the introduction to Ted and Amanda Trina turned to David. "I would like you to meet David. David this is Logan."

"Hello nice to meet you Logan. It took you long enough to arrive to sweep this lovely girl off her feet. I tried but she had high hopes in your direction."

"Hello David. You had me worried that you could have succeeded. No offense but I'm glad she waited for me even though it took me so long." Logan laughed and the rest joined in. The awkwardness was behind them.

The time passed with jovial conversation and a bit of ribbing regarding their future and how they would miss Trina. Apparently, there was no doubt in their minds that she would be travelling to Australia. Logan was hopeful that would be the outcome of his visit. They eventually gaily said their goodbyes.

They went on to an intimate dinner, at the Castle Inn. Where thoughts of last New Year's Eve came into Trina's mind, so much had happened in her life since then. How little did she know what was to transpire in her life, and what the New Year would actually have in store for her? She was now faced with an important decision, because her destiny was waiting.

Over dessert Logan said, "we should arrange to meet Doris tomorrow. Can you phone them tonight and let them know to prepare her for our visit?"

"If we leave right now I could," Trina replied.

Logan asked for the check and arranged payment.

The dinner was wonderful and the setting romantic. Logan took her in his arms in the car in the seclusion of the parking lot, to give her a long breathless kiss. Letting her know that he was having difficulty keeping a space between them.

She responded openly and fully and it wasn't long before they wanted each other more intimately. He broke away saying with a waver in his voice.

"Let's go home. Doesn't that sound wonderful, home?"

"Logan you're reaching. You promised, giving me until the end of our week together."

"You can't blame a guy for trying, can you? I do feel we are well suited and I am finding it difficult to be in the next bedroom knowing how wonderful it would be to share the same bed. I think I deserve a medal for valor keeping to my room each night. Laying there thinking of you and not being able to touch you."

"I know."

"Trina, we have so little time together and I have to convince you that this can work. I cannot part from you this time as just a friend. I am afraid if we leave things until the end of the week, you will decide against marrying me. Then I won't have time left to change your mind before I have to leave," he said disheartened as he let go of her and started the car.

Logan drove home. On a lighter note he said, "this is a nice car, thank you for letting me drive."

"Your welcome, I thought you might like to try it."

After making the call to the Retirement home about their pending visit to Doris the next day, Logan again pulled her into his arms.

"When I am with you, I know this is so right. You are the one I want in my life." His lips met her lips with tender kisses that soon intensified and they were kissing each other deeply. Trina was returning all that Logan was offering and wanting more.

He took her hand and drew her towards the bedroom with its soft tones of pink, reaching down to put on the lamp giving the room a warm glow.

They were standing beside her bed but he didn't do more than kiss her intimately. He wanted to make sure she was ready by letting her make the move to end just being friends, opening the path to become true lovers.

She kept running her hands through his hair as she kissed him with the yearning he had been hoping for. Then she felt an urge. Her hand eased its way between their bodies to the buttons on his jacket wanting access to his chest.

He helped her by slipping off his jacket and she opened the buttons of his shirt, to gain contact with his masculine form. Her questing hands were quickly parting the buttons. She was almost frantic trying to remove his clothing but Logan knew that was mostly nervousness. He was trying not to rush her but this was not easy, he wanted to undress her too.

She ran her hands over his bare chest excitedly. This was the signal Logan had waited for. He pulled the zipper down on her blue silk dress giving admittance to the treasures hidden beneath. Her lacy bra barely covered her, only enough to enclose the tips of her budding breast, which were pushing outward wanting release from the filmy bra.

He released the bra and it fell away to reveal her fullness. He looked into her eyes. The look he hoped for was there. She craved this as much as he did. Her hands pushed his shirt off his shoulders dropping it to the floor. She was feeling a sensation of need.

Logan was not immune either, he wanted this treasure his loving eyes were beholding. He slipped her dress over her hips, to pool at her feet. Then he laid her gently on the bed, laying down beside her, taking in her beauty.

Logan's mouth went back to her lips to sip on their sweetness. Small sounds of pleasure slipped through her lips. He kissed her temple then her ear. He slowly made his way down to the pulse in her neck and his lips took in the fast beating pulsation there. Did Trina know the barriers between them were crumbling? He did; he felt them fall away as she quivered. He knew the precise moment her body yielded to her heart.

Kissing her mouth tenderly once more. She knew this time their love would be fulfilled. He was so gentle and it was driving her mad with desire.

His hand was moving in a loving motion, but his gentleness was about to run out. There was no stopping this time. He still had his clothes on, and Trina only had her lacy panties separating them.

He got up from the bed, removing his clothes, all the while holding her loving eyes. Then he gently slipped her panties off. Easing down beside her his lips joined with hers. He caressed her lips passionately.

He looked deeply into her eyes veiled with desire.

"Trina please make sure you know what you are asking for. If we do fulfill our love tonight, we are and will be as One. There will be no more just friends. I want more and I hope you do too. So, stop me now or we are going to become One for always."

Trina arched her body up towards him invitingly, letting him know she was ready to become One with him.

"Logan, I know I love you but I am afraid too. I feel like this is the first time. Please show me the way to really love you."

That was what Logan wanted to hear and he moaned.

The ultimate attainment of their love, was a pure love sonata of fulfillment for both of them.

After he recovered, Logan was so happy he wanted to express his feelings. "Trina, I love you. I want to be more than just a lover. I want to be your husband."

He placed a couple of light kisses on her lips then gave her time to respond.

"Logan, I do love you but I know deep down it will not be that easy."

He knew they were so right together, and that they both wanted the same loving gratification.

Slowly he got up from the bed. He reached for her clothes and gave them to her with a smile.

"We'll discuss this further when we are both dressed."

Picking up his clothes, Logan removed himself to the bathroom down the hall.

She sat there for a few moments clutching her clothes to her breasts. She was trying to gather her pride and her thoughts. She couldn't just abandon her family. He had to realize that she cared for them deeply. She did love him and would gladly move to Fraser Island or Sydney if it was only about her.

She slowly got up from the bed and went into the adjoining bathroom to wash away the tears that were running down her cheeks. She knew she was about to disappoint this love of hers, but she felt she had no choice despite the chance that he had given her, to stop their love fulfilment. She had secretly wanted this special memory of their perfect love, when Logan went back to Australia.

chapter
TWENTY-ONE

Trina stood in the living room doorway noticing Logan drumming his fingers on the sofa arm in an absent way. He glanced up as he felt her presence. He had made a fresh pot of tea which was waiting in the kitchen. Rising he moved towards her with a smile, picking up her hand, and proceeding into the kitchen.

They both sat down in the breakfast nook. Through the bay window darkness was shrouding the trees. Logan poured the tea before he reached across to pick up her hand. It warmed his heart to touch her.

"Trina, I gave you a chance to stop me. I told you if we completed our love making, there would be no more doubts that we would be together. For me that meant total commitment, and marriage was to be part of it. What happened?" he asked softly.

Trina shifted uneasily.

"I know that was what you had asked of me. I wanted you too much to stop. But I also knew I had to say no to the commitment of being your wife. I am yours and I will always be yours but not in marriage." Expelling a deep sigh.

"The distance I admit is a concern. But we can come to some practical solution over time. I know we can somehow. You are too loving a person to just walk away from your daughter and her family," he said to Trina beseechingly. "But just for now tell me this, if there wasn't the ocean between us, would you marry me?"

"Yes Logan, you know I would. I love you so much and I do want to marry you, but that doesn't resolve the fact the ocean is keeping us apart."

He brought her hand up to his lips, kissing the palm gently. Her hand tingled in response and he felt her quiver.

"See darling, you are moved by me as much as I am moved by you. Your body is telling you just how much. Please give us a chance?"

Trina wanted to say yes, she would give them a chance but stayed silent.

He raised his cup, took a drink and gave her a wink at the same time. She smiled and raised her cup sipping. But they each knew they wouldn't be sharing the same bedroom this night or maybe never.

———

When they got up the next morning, they had the appearance of being very happy, as today they were going to see Doris Reilly. Then after their afternoon visit, they were going to Briana's for dinner. Trina knew it was time for her family to meet Logan. She was surprised Briana hadn't forced the issue before now.

Neither made overtures to last evening's intimacies.

He made a big production of making breakfast for her. She sat there with a coffee and laughed at his antics. He was really showing off but she didn't care, she just enjoyed watching him. He looked so good in casual clothes. He was a well-groomed muscular man. His height added to his stature. She knew, she could easily spend her future with him and enjoy every minute, if only she didn't have to leave her family.

Logan was trying to keep things humorous rather than serious. Seeing her sitting there watching him, he knew that this woman was the one he wanted to wake up to each and every day, for the rest of his life.

He drew his attention back to the present by saying.

"Let's go see Doris at two. That way she will have had her lunch and we won't be interrupting any of her morning activities."

"I told the nursing home we would probably be there in the afternoon when I called last night. I am glad we have had this time together before we went to see her. You know we will have to explain our relationship to her."

"We can always just say we are just friends, if you prefer," he replied with some sadness.

"No, I want our relationship out in the open. No one is going to misunderstand how we feel about each other. They just have to look at us to know, we have something more than just friendship."

She reached up giving him a kiss on the lips as he bent over to place her plate before her. He hid his surprise but his heart leaped a bit. He sat down beside her at the table, their bodies touching, he needed this contact with her. It was important to him, too soon he would be leaving. They both ate with enthusiasm. Trina did give him a little razing about the large portion of scrambled eggs. He helpfully took more of the eggs on to his plate which was also filled with rashers of bacon.

The sun was shining in the window. In the rays falling on them, the eggs were a brilliant yellow. A robin in the tree just beyond the window called to his mate with his burnt red breast expanding demanding her response.

———

When they arrived at the Mountainview Retirement Home, they were met at the door by a girl with a winning smile.

"I am Karen. I am glad you came today instead of yesterday because I wanted to meet you."

"Karen, I am Trina Grant and this is Logan Hunter. Thank you for being so helpful when I called here."

Logan offered his hand to Karen and she took it with a welcoming smile.

"Doris is quite excited about your visit, particularly when I said that Mr. Hunter was from Australia."

"I hope we don't cause too much excitement for her, she may not be the one we are looking for," Trina said.

"Doris is easygoing and will regale you with her stories, if you will listen. If it works out that she isn't the one you are looking for, it may be someone else in one of the other nursing homes in the area," Karen said trying to be helpful and not to discourage them.

Karen led them down the long hall that branched off the main lobby. They passed a lounge with people sitting around talking. Some were family members that were visiting for the afternoon.

When they reached the last room, there was a lady with a light blue knitted sweater over her pale blue dress with pink flowers dancing around on it. She was sitting in a wheelchair by the window. The sun was beaming down on her. She looked like the sunrays blessed her because she had such a tranquil look of peace on her face.

When they glanced past her out the window, they could see her beloved mountain that Karen had mentioned. It was majestic, its lightly snow-capped peaks reaching to the sky. It was inspirational.

She turned her head towards them as Karen called gently to her, not wanting to startle her.

Her face turned into a wreath of beauty. A smile that was reflected in her eyes. She was indeed very frail, and Trina just wanted to put her arms around her.

"Come in," her voice was stronger than her frailness indicated. "I have been waiting for you both. I have had another visitor before you so I knew you were coming."

Trina stood just inside the door sort of hesitant. Logan went over to Doris and took her hands she held out to him. When she grasped his hands, she felt a slight jolt. He reacted by stiffening. It was a weird feeling but she took it in her stride.

"You are Logan," she said. "You look like your uncle. When you were a little boy, he liked to take you out, because he used to pretend you were the little boy we never had. Adam used to call me and tell me all about you. I never knew how much I would regret my final decision not to stay in Australia. When he begged me not to leave? He tried so hard to convince me but I wouldn't listen. Enough of me for now. Please introduce your lovely lady, and then both of you sit down near me."

Logan released her hands. Turning to Trina, reaching out his hand for her to come to him. "Doris, I may call you Doris?" with Doris' nod he continued. "This is Trina. She is the lady I am trying to persuade to come back to Australia with me," he said with a winning smile for Trina.

Trina stepped to the side of the wheelchair. She felt compelled to reach down and kiss Doris on the cheek. It was warm from the sunbeams that had caressed her face. Karen placed chairs near Doris, motioning to them to be seated.

Doris took Trina's hand and one of Logan's, as Karen slipped out of the room. She then reached for the door to shut it in privacy.

Doris wanted to feel really close to this loving couple. She had a tale to tell them, with hopes of touching their hearts. She started off by telling of her visit to Australia. "Adam and I bumped into each other the first day I arrived. I stepped back into his path while trying to take a picture. Adam grabbed me to keep me from falling. When we looked into each other eyes, we knew we were destined to be more than just strangers. We spent my two weeks together. Adam showing me around."

"The two weeks passed too quickly and he begged me not to leave." Doris went on to tell them of the number of times he begged her to stay with him but she wouldn't stay. Then after she came home the telephone pleas were many for her to return. Doris paused as if in regret, then continued.

"But that meant leaving my daughter and son who both had children. To this day I have regretted the decision to stay here." Doris' voice was sad.

She continued her story. "Adam kept up the calls for a few years but even they became a chore to maintain. When Adam kept phoning I kept saying, I would eventually come. When my daughter got over this situation, or my grandchildren had done that. Until he got weary of phoning and hearing the same but different excuses. But I made a more serious mistake in not releasing him. I just couldn't let him go, I kept saying one day I would return. I held on to my true love because I wanted to be with him. But I couldn't make the break from my family."

"Adam kept threatening to just come and get me but I would put him off, saying right after this situation or that. There always seemed to be another event on the horizon so it was never a right time to leave. Then it was too late. Adam finally stopped calling," Doris looked from Trina to Logan.

"My son eventually moved to Calgary and my daughter moved shortly after to Victoria but I chose to stay here." She glanced at Trina.

"Trina, you have a decision to make like I had. I can see the way you keep glancing at Logan, that you are in love with him. I made the wrong decision. I know that now. I want you to know how wrong I was, and how much I regretted it in the end." She glanced at Logan.

"You know Logan, you look so much like your Uncle Adam. I thought it was him standing there in the doorway, that he was finally coming for me. I would have gone with him this time, had it been him." Doris ended plaintively.

Karen interrupted her by bringing in a tea cart holding fine china and pastel colored little cakes on a china plate. She poured the tea, handing a delicate cup and saucer towards Doris, mentioning the fine china tea set belonged to Doris personally. Doris let go of their hands with great reluctance, taking the tea she was offered by Karen.

Logan shifted in his chair as though he was feeling something. He dipped his shoulder then straightened it. There was that feeling again the way his uncle used to place his hand on his shoulder when they walked together. He didn't let on to the others. He wasn't sure he could explain it to them.

For some reason Logan seemed to miss the connection to Doris too. He didn't know why he was feeling so strange, but it wasn't an unpleasant feeling. He didn't want it to fade away. He was really at a loss for words, this strange connection he felt to Doris and this room they were in.

Doris continued her perusal from one to the other as she lifted her cup to her dainty lips. The cup as fragile, as she was.

Karen served Trina and Logan tea and offered the cakes before excusing herself. They hardly noticed her leaving with their automatic thanks, as they were so engrossed in each other.

After a few sips Doris started again.

"You know Adam was a man who wanted the moon but settled for the sun and Australia without me. If only he ignored my request to wait. Adam may have given me the strength to leave if he had come. We would have been together. It wasn't his fault really. He would have come in a jiffy, but I kept putting him off saying that I was coming to him. It was entirely my fault, and I was so wrong to keep him tied to me with empty promises."

She put down her cup and reached for Logan and Trina's hands again. Linking to them as she continued her message. They both set their dainty cups back on the tray and turned their attention to Doris.

"This morning when I was getting ready to get out of bed, Adam came to me. He walked right through that door. There he was and he came to stand at the bottom of my bed."

"Adam said I was to convince you both to be together as One as Logan is encouraging. He wanted this for us too, but we never completed our oneness. He said, he wanted it for Logan who had been like a son, we had never had."

Logan felt that pressure on his shoulder again and he gave Doris a beatific smile and a wink exactly like Adam used to. Doris understood.

Trina knew something was happening because of the looks on their faces. She held still so as not to break the moment between them. They just sat there transfixed.

Doris broke the spell by turning to Trina.

"Don't make the same mistake I did. Your family will grow and they will have good lives, but you deserve happiness too. The loneliness as the years pass without your true love can never be made up by your family. Adam suggested buying them a video camera to make videos. Give them a carton full of blank ones before you leave. All their lives, you will view the videos, enjoying those special occasions along with their voice messages. You will still watch your grandchildren grow."

"Your love for each other, which I can see mirrored on your faces is too precious to ignore. Don't repeat the mistake that Adam and I made. Also, he said 'Trina that you are concerned about the age difference between you two. Age is only a state of mind, never important where love is concerned,' and Adam is right." Doris paused.

Logan looked at Trina to see her reaction to what Doris had just said. Did she believe now in the spirit world or would she think Doris was over imaginative because of her age and frailty.

"Love is what is important and I can see you both have that, as you sit here before me." She looked from one to the other and smiled. A warm feeling passed through their linked hands.

Trina smiled at Logan, and he gave a sigh of relief. Again, he felt that pressure on his shoulder. 'All is going to be okay' were the words that came into his head. It felt like his Uncle Adam was reassuring him.

Doris looked at Logan and she winked which surprised him totally, but he felt she knew what was happening to him. There was another presence in the room.

Now how to explain this to Trina logically. But not now, later before discussing the 'spiritual' with her. He wasn't sure he could say anything at the moment he was a bit stunned.

Doris was looking tired so Logan broke the link by removing his hand after giving her an added gentle squeeze. He stood up indicating it was time to leave. Trina stood too and moved away from the two of them. Logan bent down to kiss Doris' cheek and he whispered in her ear.

"He was here, wasn't he?" Doris whispered back, "yes". She turned and gave him a kiss on the mouth, and they both knew that was from Adam.

Trina watched what was playing out before her eyes. Again, she felt that these two were communicating on a spiritual level that didn't include her. She was happy for them both, because she knew Logan had a special place in his heart for his Uncle Adam. Maybe being with Doris had brought those feelings back to him.

He straightened then turned to Trina, placing his hand on hers drawing her towards him.

"Well my true love will you accept me now? Did Doris' mistake she admitted to convince you, for us to be together in love?" Logan paused awaiting her reply anxiously.

"Yes, I love you Logan, and I want to be with you forever. The children will get a camcorder and a carton of blank videos before I leave for Australia with you. When that carton runs out, we will send more."

Doris gave a little "Yip" and then she grabbed Trina's hand and pulled her down to kiss her in congratulations.

"Do this and love him forever, for Adam and me," Doris said wistfully.

They said their goodbyes and left the room.

As Logan and Trina paused at the door, they glanced back and there was Doris with the sun on her serene face. She was looking out at her majestic mountain.

———

On the return trip they were excitingly discussing the arrangements for her move to Australia. They had just one more hurdle ahead of them, Briana's dinner.

When they arrived home, they just had time to refresh themselves before it was time to leave.

Trina handed the keys to Logan saying, "Briana will not be receptive to my decision. We will have to convince her that I have met my destiny. Our love for each other is such, we don't want to be apart."

"Are you sure you want to say destiny?"

"Yes, I felt right from the beginning when I won the trip to Australia that destiny was to play a part in it. To me it was when I met you."

"Will you be able to convince Briana you really want this?"

"It won't be easy. Surely, she will know how much we are in love. Besides I do not intend to change my mind now."

Logan gave her a light kiss as he helped her into the car.

"You know, I feel confident that we will convince Briana because I was so lucky to meet you, my darling. Our future has to be together now." Logan started the car.

"I wish I was as confident as you. Videos will have to be the answer for Briana's comment on missing Scott and Kathie's growing up. Besides we will come and visit them. It isn't as if we intend on breaking contact with them completely."

Trina pointed out the house. "Well we are here so we will soon find out." Pulling up to the house.

Scott and Kathie came bounding out the door.

"Grandma you're here. We have been waiting all week," they said in unison.

Hugging her tightly as she got out of the car. Kissing each upturned smiling face, she said, "I want you to meet Logan Hunter. This is Scott and Kathie."

Logan on reaching the sidewalk gave them a big 'Hi' and a wave as they were still hugging Trina.

They both said. "Hi." They turned, running towards the house.

Ken was at the door. "Come in, dinner is almost ready. Hi I am Ken and you are Logan," reaching out to shake his hand. "Nice to meet you."

Shaking his hand firmly Logan said, "nice to meet you. I've heard all about you and your family from Trina."

"Hi Mom." Ken gave her a kiss on the cheek and a hug. "Briana is in the kitchen. She is trying to have everything ready so we can sit right down."

"I will go see if I can help her." Walking down the hall to the kitchen.

Scott and Kathie went into the dining room with their father and Logan.

"Dad can we eat fast as I want to watch the baseball game on TV."

"Scott you can do without TV for one night, we have company.

Besides you have been lamenting the fact that Grandma hasn't been here all week."

"Well she hasn't. I miss her and so does Kathie. She usually drops in a couple of times at least during the week." Scott was missing the visits.

"I am sorry, I guess I kept her pretty busy all week," Logan inserted.

"That's all right she mentioned you were coming for a week and spending it together." Scott sat down.

Briana and Trina arrived with the serving dishes placing them on the table.

Ken said, "Kathie you sit next to your brother so Grandma and Logan can sit together." Kathie scooted around the table dropping into the chair beside Scott.

Trina introduced Logan to Briana.

He came forward to grasp her hand firmly. "Hi nice to meet you."

"Logan I am pleased to meet you at last. I was beginning to think Mom was hiding you away from us." Laughing gayly Briana sat down.

"Not really, she was just busy showing me the sights."

The meal progressed to the usual chatter from the children and Logan's views on his visit to the island and their trip to Long Beach and Tofino ending with. "I have really enjoyed all our trips. It is quite the drive to Tofino."

Ken inserted, "yes and worse when the weather is bad."

The meal was almost over when Trina mentioned.

"This afternoon we met with a lady, Doris Reilly. She had met Logan's Uncle Adam years ago in Australia. She is staying at the Mountainview Retirement Lodge up near Arrowsmith Golf Course. Her stories were interesting. It was a similar situation to ours." Looking at Logan with a smile.

Briana quickly put in. "Did she move to Australia?"

Trina turning to her daughter replied, "no, she couldn't leave her family."

Briana grinned in relief.

Trina went on, "her message in telling her story was, don't make the same mistake she did."

"Oh." Briana's grin disappeared.

"Briana, Mom has a right to some happiness in her life. If it requires moving with Logan to Australia, then that is what she should do," Ken said gently.

"Thank you, Ken." Trina gave him a smile for his support.

Logan inserted, "Briana, I know you will miss your mother. I am sorry I am taking her away from you. If it wasn't for the fact that my father wants to retire, and I will be taking over the business for him, I would consider moving here." He watched Briana with interest.

"Logan, I understand why you have to live in Australia and I can see the way you and Mom look at each other you are in love. I will miss her, she is so much a part of our lives. She will miss the children as they grow up," Briana said plaintively.

Trina interjected, "Briana, we have a solution for that from Doris. She suggested we buy you a camcorder and lots and lots of videos. Then you can record all the events for me to see, throughout their lives."

Briana wasn't ready to give in. "But Mom it won't be the same."

Logan trying to ease the situation put in. "I will obtain a long-distance plan so your mother can call you frequently."

Ken interrupted, "Briana we could plan a trip there for our summer vacation."

"Yeah! Yeah!" squealed the kids.

"Okay I know when I am out numbered. I want what is best for you Mom always. You know that." Smiling at them both. "Besides I really like your choice in men." Everyone laughed.

"Dessert anyone?" Briana said cheerfully as she started cleaning the table with the children's help.

chapter

TWENTY-TWO

T rina and Logan were spending their evening, sitting close with Logan's arm around her. Viewing the latest videos from Briana. She always numbered them so they would view them in the proper order. They had just arrived that day from Canada.

The special occasions, parties, along with school accomplishments and Christmas plays were there for them to view.

On each video there was a message of love, for both of them from Trina's family. Scott and Kathie had added their unique message. "Grandma we are saving all our money, for the planned family visit to see you and Logan in the spring." Then the children were blowing kisses to them.

There was even one video with Doris sending them her message of love.

"Thank you for your messages. My wish is for your complete happiness that I am sure you both are already enjoying. When you were here visiting me, it was obvious you were meant for each other. I hope to see you again someday. I miss you both." Her face wore a special smile as though their past visit was still clear in her mind.

The screen switched to Briana. "I thought it would be nice for you both to have a video of Doris' reply message to you. In our last phone call, you had mentioned if I got the chance to drop in to see her, to pass on your messages from you and Logan. She was happy to see me and receive your messages."

The video ended with Briana wearing a huge grin. "I ran into Amanda in town and she asked if I had heard from you recently. I filled her in with the latest news of your phone calls. I mentioned I would be sending videos soon. She asked if she could borrow the camcorder as she wanted to make one for you too. I will delay sending these until she returns the camcorder and video. Good Night Mom and Logan. Love you both."

The last video was marked SURPRISE! Amanda said they were very happy in their marriage but really missed Trina. They were hoping to get over for a visit sometime next year. The next views were a dinner party taken at the Castle Inn Restaurant. They must have had the waiter doing the video as it was of Amanda, Ted, David and a lady that was introduced as Edith. They raised their glasses and yelled, "**Happy New Year Trina and Logan**." Then the video switched to Amanda and Ted's living room with a view of Amanda. "We know we are premature as it isn't New Year's Eve yet but we hoped you would share a glass with us on New Year's Eve while watching this video."

She continued. "David is recording this for us. We have saved the best for last. The special surprise message is that we will be bringing our baby with us, our unplanned miracle." Ted looking like the proud boasting father, while Amanda's hand had fluttered against her tummy in a caress.

Trina looked at Logan in amazement then giggled gleefully. He was wishing secretly that he could be a proud Dad too with his new ladylove as the mother.

Amanda's video ended with a tour around the Christmas decorated Qualicum. "A lot of memories for us Trina. Love You both." Ted and Amanda were blowing kisses to them.

Stacking the videos with a warm heart, a warm glow lighting up Trina's face. She loved these evenings when new videos arrived from Canada. It gave her such a tender feeling and a little yearning to be with them.

She went over to Logan where he was now sitting in his favorite chair beside the glowing flames of the fireplace. It was really too hot for a fire at this time of year in Australia but in Canada it would be perfect, so Logan insisted on the fire before viewing the videos. He eased her down on his lap. Trina's arms embraced his neck. She kissed him lovingly. Grinning she pulled back to look at him saying.

"Those were the nicest videos. It is like having the family here with us. I love you so much Logan and I want you to know Doris was right, you are my true love."

"And I agree wholeheartedly," answered Logan warmly embracing her.

ABOUT THE AUTHOR

Dorothy Collins is excited to connect with readers. She lives on Vancouver Island, British Columbia. Today the Waiting was her first novel, and No time for Daddy's Girl will be in print soon. Learn more at DorothyCollins.ca.